THE DOCTOR'S SECRET

A FORBIDDEN, MEDICAL ROMANCE

SOFIA T SUMMERS

DESCRIPTION

Keeping a secret for over a decade killed me inside... until a silver fox billionaire forced me to confront it.

I was made to give up my son for adoption when I was only 16.

Seeing him again in my office with his *dad* made me shiver to my core.

I loved my boy.

It was clear that Jace did too.

It broke my heart to see Christopher in pain and struggling with a medical condition that only I could help him with.

As his doctor, I had to maintain my boundaries.

And I certainly had to keep my distance from Jace.

But holding hands during those late nights at the hospital led to decisions that could ruin my medical career.

The excitement of being in Jace's arms would have to compete with the life I'd built for myself.

This new and shaky beginning rested on one secret I could tell no one.

Especially not Jace.

Christopher was my son.

He was *our* son.

But did that matter if we could *never*, in fact, be a real family?

PROLOGUE

Jace

Mindy was incredible. Her tits bounced and swayed between our bodies as I thrust into her. She convulsed and clawed at my sides as my body released all the pent-up lust from the entire night of talking and holding her. My balls drew up and I filled that condom until I thought it would burst open. And when we were both calm, I kissed her shoulder, then her jaw, then stole a breath right out of her mouth.

"You're amazing, Mindy," I whispered before I pulled out. She lay on the bed in ecstasy, sprawled out with her pussy gaping slightly from being played with so many times. Her skin dripped with sweat, her pussy with moisture made during our sex. She was gorgeous. I'd never been more in love, not even with Connie when she was here.

I pulled the condom off carefully and tied it shut, then dropped it into the trash bin with the others from earlier in the night. My dick went limp almost immediately this time, spent from all the action she'd been giving me. I hadn't done much more than self-pleasure a few times a week for the past two years, but Mindy and I'd had sex enough times to use up a box of condoms in three weeks.

Climbing back into bed, I tried to catch my breath. I didn't mind the workout at all. It made me feel like a teenager again, or maybe it was because Mindy was sixteen years younger than me. The age difference didn't bother me a bit either, because she was perfect for me in every way. Smart, funny, sexy as hell. Her thick curves and bright smile were beautiful in every way.

"So good," she sighed, smiling at me. Her hair clung to her face, dampened with sweat from the exertion. I'd never done anything like that before, experimenting with her. I enjoyed it a lot. In fact, I wanted to do it every day for the rest of my life. If Christopher, my twelve-year-old, wasn't still hurting so badly over missing his late mother, I'd ask this woman to marry me right now. But his reaction to Mindy being here earlier at the dinner table was enough to make me hold back a little.

"Yes, so frickin' good," I told her, peeling a sticky hair off her fore-head. I smoothed her chestnut hair back so I could see her emerald eyes better. With flecks of gold and chocolate in them, they were quite possibly the most incredible eyes I'd ever seen. Just another thing to add to her beauty.

"Jace, can I tell you something?" She looked serious suddenly, as if she needed to tell me some dire secret. I asked her earlier if she'd done any experimenting with other guys, and I wondered what she could need to tell me. It didn't matter what it was. I loved her so much, and nothing in her past could hurt our future.

"Yeah, of course." I held her, ready to listen to whatever it was she had to say.

"The day we met in the coffee house wasn't the first time I'd seen you." She watched my face carefully.

"It wasn't? You mean you really did see me around the hospital before?" I remembered the conversation we had when I thought I'd seen her before. It was like déjà vu at times. She was so familiar. I felt it was fate drawing us together. I felt so safe and so comfortable around her, and she was so good with my son as his doctor, I genuinely felt like she cared about him more than just this diagnosis.

"Not exactly. I was given a picture of you twelve years ago. The day I gave birth to a tiny, premature baby boy."

I watched the way her forehead crinkled and her eyes narrowed, but I shook my head. I was confused. She had a picture of me twelve years ago? But how? We had never met. We didn't know each other. When I met her in that coffee shop about a month ago was the first time I'd even heard the name Dr. Scriber. And twelve years ago? She had to be a child then? Like sixteen or something.

"What are you talking about?"

"Jace, I ran a DNA test on Christopher when we drew his blood for the Crohn's test." She sat up and curled in on herself. "I recognized you from the image the adoption agency gave me. You were older, but my gut said it was you. The man and woman who adopted my son were Jason and Constance. I never knew their last name, just had a photo. So when I saw you and I noticed Christopher looked a lot like my father, I ran DNA." She turned and looked into my eyes, and my heart went cold.

My body felt like it had seized up, my breathing shallow. My field of vision started to narrow and I thought I'd pass out. "What?" I sat up and stared at her, hurt and confused. I shook my head, unable to comprehend what was going on. I studied her face, searching for something that made sense, something to ground me in the present because my thoughts were reeling. I climbed out of bed, feeling all the sudden like I might get sick. I stared at her; I couldn't put words together.

"Say something?" she whispered, slipping off the bed on her side.

"I'm... You're..." My chest rose and fell in an accelerated breathing pattern and tears welled up in her eyes. I watched them pool above her lower eyelashes and linger there. I was afraid my reaction would scare her or hurt her. I loved her more than life itself but this was shocking. I expected her to say she'd tried a threesome, or that she once had an STD. Maybe that she liked women too. Not this. Not ever this. My mouth hung open in shock and I turned so she wouldn't be frightened by my facial expression.

"I'm Christopher's biological mother."

I dropped to the bed, completely speechless. My chest ached. My heartbeat hammered in my ears. All I could do was breathe—deep breaths in and slow breaths out.

"Jace..."

When the door clicked shut, I remained frozen. She was the biological mother of my adopted son? How the hell does that even work? Was this some trick? Or did fate really tie the red string to our pinkies?

1

Jace

It was a normal exam room, just like the five previous ones we'd been to in the past several months. Christopher sat on the table swinging his legs like any normal, healthy eleven-year-old, but after the fresh round of severe symptoms over the past week, I knew he was anything but. I wrung my hands in my lap, trying to keep a straight face. A father's greatest fear is losing one of his children prematurely. And since I had only one, it seemed even worse than what other parents might go through, especially after losing Connie two years ago.

"When is the doctor coming? I want to go home." Christopher— "Topper" to his friends— was impatient. As many tests as he'd had and I would be just as impatient. No one seemed to be able to tell us what was wrong with him, and each time he got sick he had differing symptoms. I just wanted answers.

"Not long, bud. Dr. Scriber was really kind to squeeze us into her schedule. Just be patient, okay?" I sucked in a deep breath and tried to relax my shoulders. I couldn't lose my boy. My heart was still a wreck after losing my wife of thirteen years. She was my everything, but when cancer strikes sometimes there is nothing you can do.

"I wish Mom was here." Christopher didn't seem upset about the appointment, not in terms of fearing what was wrong with him. His childlike innocence protected him from the fear of things like cancer. He knew his mother was gone and that's it. One day he'd understand, but for now I wanted to protect his little mind from all the anxieties we as adults had to bear.

"I wish she was too, Top." I glanced at the clock. We'd been waiting twenty minutes already, a normal delay for a doctor I supposed, but to a worried patient it was eternity. I distracted myself by studying the images plastered on the walls—pictures of the human body complete with internal organs labeled and diagrams of the cellular construction of tissues. Three pediatricians and two general practitioners we'd been to, but not one of them recommended a specialist or doctor of internal medicine. Only by chance had I run into Dr. Scriber at a coffee shop, and I believed fate had intervened.

"Can we get ice cream when we leave?" he asked and I chuckled. There wasn't any situation where this child could be patient without a bribe, so I nodded.

"Sure, kiddo. We'll get whatever you want. You're doing a great job being patient." I made a mental note to have a talk with him about not using food as a reward for behavior. It sets a bad habit up for his life later on.

The door pushed open and I looked up to see Dr. Scriber walk in, staring down at a tablet in her hands. Things sure had changed since I was a kid, when doctors wrote everything on paper with a pen and carried the patient's chart with them in the room. Dr. Scriber was clearly up to date with the latest technology, which hopefully meant she was up to date with any new illnesses or diseases. I sat a bit straighter as her chin rose and she looked up at Topper.

"Well, who do we have here?" she asked warmly. Her smile stretched to her eyes which sparkled. I immediately felt at ease in her presence.

"Dr. Scriber, we met at the coffee shop." I stood and shook her hand. She looked at me briefly but turned back to my son with intrigue. Why would she look at me? I wasn't her patient. I sank back onto the chair as she laid her tablet on the countertop next to the sink and snagged two latex gloves out of the box.

"I'm Christopher. My friends call me Top... sometimes Topper." He didn't look enthused as he spoke.

"Any latex allergies, Dad?" she asked, still not looking at me.

"None." I shook my head, watching her don the gloves.

"So, Top, I guess we're friends now." Her smile brightened and Topper nodded. "What is going wrong?" Dr. Scriber took the stethoscope from around her neck and put it to her ears, holding the bell in hand and pressing it to his chest. She looked down at the ground as she listened and Chris spoke.

"My belly hurts a lot. Sometimes I throw up; sometimes I get diarrhea." He cringes as he speaks, probably embarrassed. I nod at him, encouraging him to keep going. It's best if she hears the symptoms straight from him. I couldn't begin to remember everything he'd been through for the past few months.

"I see... Any food allergies, Dad?" She placed the tool in another location on his chest and listened again.

"None that we know of, but Christopher is adopted, like I told you, so I'm not sure if they ever ran tests on him before he was brought to us at the age of a few weeks old." Her hand moved across his chest as I spoke, finding another place to listen. Then she straightened.

"Well, they don't usually run food intolerance or allergy tests on infants. They do run what's called a PKU test. It tests for high protein levels in the blood which would indicate a genetic condition that may damage the brain, but you'd have seen that years ago." Dr. Scriber stepped back and put her stethoscope back around her neck. "Are you pretty active, Topper? Do you like to play sports?"

"Yeah, they're okay I guess. I really like video games too."

She chuckled. "So you exercise a lot? Do you eat a lot too?" She sat on the stool and made some notes on the tablet then focused back on him as he answered.

"Uh, yeah, I guess. I like pizza and chicken nuggets."

"Anything that you notice makes his symptoms worse?" She turned to me for the first time, tablet in hand.

"I can't really make sense of it. One day he's fine, the next day he has a fever or headache. Sometimes he gets sores in his mouth." I felt at a loss for so long, I just wanted her to fix this.

"Well, we're going to figure out what is going on. Do you mind if I listen to your belly?" she asked him, and he shrugged.

"Fine, but can I still eat ice cream?" Topper lifted his shirt up and she laughed at him.

"You like ice cream?" she asked standing. She gestured for him to scoot back, patting the table behind where he sat.

"I love ice cream."

"Go ahead and lay down here," she instructed, and he followed her direction. She took her stethoscope and listened again to several places on his stomach. While she did so, she didn't talk. Not one single doctor we'd been to had taken so much time to speak with Chris and make him feel at home. Most of them wanted to talk over his head at me. I was smitten by her bedside manner, not to mention that Dr. Scriber was a gorgeous woman, and I didn't see a ring on her finger.

At that thought, I felt guilt creeping into my conscience. Connie was my heartbeat, not any other woman. I'd been told by friends I could move on now, but despite being desperately in need of sexual release, and highly attracted to other women at times, I couldn't allow myself to feel something like that again. Not yet anyway. I scolded myself for noticing how pretty she was and watched her work.

"Does ice cream hurt your belly?" she asked him, finding another spot to listen.

"Nah, I don't think so."

She eyed me and I shook my head. "He hasn't had ice cream before an episode. I don't think it's lactose." I heard that one before too, that it was just lactose intolerance and he should avoid dairy. He was miserable for those six months while we tried that. "Look, other doctors told us it was just in his head because of his mother's death.

She held a hand out to him and he took it, and she helped him sit up. "You miss your momma?" Her expression turned to one of compassion as she stood by him. I truly hoped that she wouldn't just give up at the thought that grief made his belly ache.

Christopher's shoulders fell the way they did every time someone asked him about his mom. They were close, and his grieving was hard. No matter how much time passed, he still hurt, and I'd hear him crying in his room some nights.

"Yeah..." he mumbled.

Dr. Scriber placed a caring hand on his knee. "I know just how it feels to lose someone, buddy." His chin turned up and they looked into each other's eyes. "It's really difficult, and I totally understand. It's okay to be sad and miss them."

"Yeah..." he mumbled again and she patted his knee.

"Why don't you go out to the waiting room and get one of those suckers from the nurse. I will talk to Dad a bit and we'll sort this out." Her smile returned and he looked at me seeking permission.

"Go ahead," I told him, anxious to hear what she thought.

She walked over to her stool as Chris slid off the table and walked past me out the door. It slammed shut and she chuckled. "He's a sweet boy."

"You're really good with him." I felt my heart swelling. There was so much hanging on this appointment, and all my hope was in her now. I felt like we would end up giving up and I didn't know what would happen.

"Kindness is essential for medical practice," she recited, but I got the feeling there was something more there.

"Thank you for being so kind with him. He's had it rough." I felt comfortable with her, like I could open up a bit and maybe it would help her understand Top better. "When his mom died he stopped eating for a while. I thought maybe his issues were because he got malnourished. I fed him supplements and vitamins, but he never improved. He kept having these episodes of diarrhea and vomiting, headaches, achy body, fever. This last one, I'm pretty sure there was blood in his stool." I would never forget that night when I was terrified. I had no clue what to do, so I called and set up this appointment.

"Grief can definitely hit us in different ways, but this doesn't sound like grief, and I don't think his lack of eating for a while did this." She looked down at his chart. "It appears to me that you've had several tests done. Have you tested for celiac or Crohn's?" Her eyes met mine and she searched me, but she looked more concerned than curious. For a moment we gazed into each other's eyes and I swore I'd met her somewhere. Like, I'd seen her face in another life or maybe a vision, as if fate really did ordain us to meet.

"Uh... I... Uh, no, those two tests were never done." I swallowed hard, my chest pounding. The unexplainable connection between us seemed to be felt by her too. Her cheeks flushed and she looked down.

"I think we need to see each other again." Her hand shook as she typed into her tablet. "I mean, I need to see Christopher again," she clarified, and looked up at me. I wasn't sure if she had misspoken or if she felt the same way I did, attracted and interested to get to know her more.

"Of course."

"We'll run some blood work. I have a hunch and I think just a simple blood test can determine if the disease is what I think. You can schedule an appointment with my receptionist. In the meantime—" she reached into her pocket and pulled out a card and handed it to me "—our emergency line is listed there. You can call and leave a message or talk to a nurse on call. Then if it's something we can address, one of the doctors on call will call you back." She stood. "It was really nice meeting you, Mr. Turner." She held out her hand and I stood and took it.

"Please, call me Jace."

"So nice to meet you, Jace. Let's get that appointment set up and get Chris back in to see me."

When I pulled my hand away from hers I realized my palm was sweating. I hadn't done that in years—gotten nervous over speaking to a woman. There was so much going on inside my head I felt like my brain was scrambled as I made the appointment for next week. A really sexy, curvaceous woman just entered my life and I was totally smitten, but I had to take this seriously. My son was everything to me, and Dr. Scriber was a pathway to understanding how to better care for him. I couldn't let my feelings get in the way, which only paved a way for guilt to climb on my back and weigh on me the entire drive home.

I couldn't do this to Connie. She deserved better. What was wrong with me?

2

Mindy

When Jace and Christopher were down the hallway and out the door, I locked myself into my office and hid behind my desk, reeling over the interaction. Mr. Turner was exactly how I imagined the man who adopted my son, polite, kind, respectful. And I knew his face matched the image shown to me eleven years ago when I handed my newborn over to the nurses. I was never given a copy of that picture, but my mind played the faces of Constance and Jason Turner over and over in my dreams for years. No one had to remind me.

Still, with eleven years came aging, and I doubted how good my memory was. It had been so long and I was so young when it happened—just sixteen years old. I had no proof that Christopher was the boy I was forced to give up for adoption. I just had a gut feeling backed up by far too many coincidences, chiefly how much Christopher looked like my father.

I scrolled his chart again, looking for anything that may indicate a family heritage. Adopted children often had little or no medical record unless the agency the mother used had been very thorough. In this case, I was silently hating myself that we didn't find a better agency. His medical records were so limited, not even his blood type was on this chart.

The best way to diagnose him was with bloodwork, though, and that meant a chance at a DNA test. I would have to keep those separate from the other tests, but with the help of a friend down in the lab, I believed I could pull it off. Everything about this screamed at my sense of moral obligation to disclose my relationship—or potential relationship—with the boy to my boss. It was an ethical nightmare, but I knew if I handed this over to another doctor, even with my suspicions about his true condition, I'd lose the chance at finding out for certain if he was my son.

My heart ached. I closed my eyes, unable to look at the chart any longer. Tears wanted to well up but I pinched the bridge of my nose and forced them away. The whole situation had brought up so many hard feelings toward my family. I was just a kid; I was experimenting. I never intended to get pregnant, but my parents' response to that unplanned event felt like being cast into Hades to be tormented. They had no idea the pain it caused me.

They should have known, but they refused to listen to me. My father didn't speak to me for nine months—until the baby was born. And I only got to hold his tiny body for a few hours before they ripped him from my arms at the command of my mother to be handed off to social services and delivered to his new family. My father came to drive me home, and then it was my turn to not speak —not for seven weeks, when I finally decided to apply for college.

Dread washed over me as I realized lunch with my parents today would be next to agonizing. Carrying this hurt in my heart had been a burden for years anyway, forced visits where I had to play nice and respect people who didn't deserve my respect at times. But now, with this fresh wound opening up all the pain of years ago, how would I even sit across the table from them?

I shut. the tablet off and plugged it in to charge for my afternoon appointments, then rose and picked up my purse and coat. I felt my cheeks burning, both from unspoken emotion over meeting Christopher face to face and the anger burning in me about meeting my parents for lunch. As I stepped into the hall and locked my office door, Dr. Andrews rounded the corner. Our eyes met briefly and he looked at me with intrigue.

"You seem a bit flustered, Dr. Scriber." His eyebrows rose and he snickered. "Finally meet someone?"

The standing office joke got old at times, but I was glad my nervous energy was read as me being flustered over a hot date and not the truth. If Andrews knew about Christopher and my suspicions, he'd force me off the case. I couldn't have that, so I played into the good humor of the day. Everyone always picked on me for being almost thirty and never having had a serious boyfriend. That died too, the day I told my son's real dad that I was pregnant. He ran like a wild mustang.

"Uh, maybe." I forced a smile and shoved my key into my pocket, then draped the coat around my shoulders and shoved my arms down the sleeves. "We'll see."

"I'm just picking on you. I have no room to talk honestly." He winked at me, but I knew it was only a professional thing, besides I had no interest in him. My only thought was of my career—and now, my son.

"I gotta run. Meeting my parents for lunch." I jerked a thumb over my shoulder and he nodded.

Enjoy the weather. I hear it's warming up out there."

"Thanks," I muttered as I escaped, strangely glad to get away from him even though it meant I was going closer to my worst nightmare.

I stewed over the appointment and how desperately I wanted to know if Christopher was my son the entire drive across town to my parents' house. It was agonizing. I should have just done the blood draw myself today, which would have lessened my torture by a few days at least. As it was, I'd have to wait for the appointment next week, depending on when they scheduled him, and then another week at least for test results.

My phone rang and I used the hands-free button on the steering wheel to answer it. As the call connected I breathed a silent prayer it wasn't my parents calling to nag me about being late. I was pleasantly surprised when I heard Georgia's voice come through.

"Hey, girl, what are you up to today? Want to meet for coffee at our usual spot?" Her chipper attitude always lifted me up. It was a far cry from the nervous anxious woman I met last summer.

"Oh, I'm so sorry, Geo. I have to have lunch at my parents' house today. Rain check?" I would have much rather had coffee with her than sit across from my parents and listen to their nagging.

"Bummer. Charlie and I were excited about the new shamrock latte they have for St. Patrick's Day. I wanted to try it with you."

"Yeah, I'm sorry." It was hard to not allow the disappointment to filter into my tone. This whole day was weighing on me more than I planned. I never expected Jace to make his son's appointment for the same day I had to meet my parents.

"Is everything okay?" Georgia was so astute. She understood me better than anyone in my life. At times I wished she didn't though, like now. I knew I needed to speak to her about this, friend to friend, but not yet. I wasn't ready yet.

"Yeah, I'm fine. Just don't want to face my parents today. Look, I'll call you later?"

"Sure, babe. I'm here if you need to talk."

Georgia hung up and I finished the short drive. When I stalked into my parents foyer, I was in a sour mood to say the least. I hung my coat on the coat tree and left my purse on the coffee table and made my way through the house to the kitchen. Mom had the windows open, letting the breeze blow in through the back and carry the scent of lilacs indoors. It was a heavenly scent, reminding me of childhood and cutting a fresh twig of the potent scented flowers to take to school to my teacher. I'd wrap them in a moist paper towel followed by plastic wrap and they would make the classroom smell like my back-yard for a few days.

"Hello, dear," Mom said, bustling around the kitchen. She acted like she herself had made the meal, but I knew better. Her maid did all the cooking. She had for years now. Still, Mom wore an apron and carried a towel in hand, playing the part.

"Hey, Mom," I mumbled, dropping onto a bar stool. I tapped my fingernails on the marble counter, remembering a time before we had so much money that the counter was just Formica. Everything changed when Dad's job took off.

"Don't look so sour, Mindy. Life is good." She draped the towel over her shoulder and gestured toward the sliding glass patio door. "Dad is outside waiting. We should join him."

I glanced out the back window and noticed Dad seated at the white wicker table. He smoked his pipe as if he'd already eaten and was enjoying an after-dinner habit. The breeze thankfully did not carry his smoke indoors, or I knew Mom would have lectured him. Reluctantly I rose and followed her outside. The maid had already set out everything with table settings for only three.

"Isn't Vi coming?"

Mom winced at the use of Violet's nickname. "Your sister will not be here today."

Even better, no one to shield me from their incessant nagging that I'm not giving them grandchildren yet. I didn't know how many times I'd had to bite my tongue when having that conversation. I sat and prepared myself for misery for the next thirty minutes at least. My heart pounded in my chest; I needed to calm down before I gave myself a heart attack. I of all people knew that. My blood pressure was probably already high just from the anxiety of the day.

"How are you feeling, dear? You don't look well." Dad's question took me off guard. I shook my head and tried to clear my mind.

"I'm okay, Dad. Stressful day at work so far." I wasn't lying. I was majorly stressed out.

"Well eat," he said, lifting the lid off the serving dish. Some sort of pasta salad filled the dish, whetting my appetite. My stomach grumbled, and he spooned a bit onto the plate in front of me. "You look pekid."

I hated that he pretended to care when I knew he hadn't cared since the day I told him I was pregnant. Staring into my plate was more difficult today than it had been in years. I'd done these family lunches every week since the dawn of time, but never had I been so emotional. I wanted to tell them about what I'd discovered, how I may have found the boy I lost, but I knew what their response would be—anger not happiness.

"Dear, I'm so excited. I talked to Ms. Garret and she said her son is visiting for Pesach." Mom spoke as she dished food onto her plate, heaping it high with salad and bread. "His name is Fletcher. He is a doctor also, and he's single." Her eyes sparkled as she smiled at me, probably hoping for a pleasant response. I had no response. I was sick of them setting me up with men I had no interest in, or men in general. I could find my own life partner, and he probably would not meet any of my parents' expectations.

"Mom, I really am not interested in Ms. Garret's son. I told you I'd rather not date anyone right now." I stabbed some noodles and pushed them around my dish, not even interested in eating despite my hungry belly.

"Well how are you going to give us grandchildren before we die if you don't even date?" Her snarky tone did something inside of me that I was shocked by. Something rose up in me that I had suppressed for years, something angry and bitter. And I couldn't restrain it when it burst out of my mouth.

"You have a grandchild and you sent him away. Now you want more? Why? To force me to send them away too?" I felt instant guilt when both Mom and Dad looked at me with ice in their gaze. My stomach sank, and I watched Dad place his cloth napkin on the table and stand.

"Please excuse me," he said in a firm tone, then walked out of the room.

I felt my cheeks warm and shame filled me. "I'm going to go." I stood and laid the fork down, walking back through the house to collect my purse and coat. No one followed. They didn't try to stop me. I was alone, the way I had been in my mind for years. This pain would drive me to do and say ridiculous things sometimes.

I just wanted it to end. Maybe Christopher Turner was the end of this.

3

Jace

I walked down the hallway with a bit of skip in my step this morning. Even now, finishing a meeting with my partner Howard and discussing one of the most important strategic moves our company can make in the near future, I felt on top of the world. For two days I'd had hope that I thought would never return. Finding Dr. Scriber was an answer to my prayers, and I already felt like we would learn what was wrong with Christopher and be able to help him feel better. I'd slept better and even had a few dreams instead of nightmares.

"What's up?" Howard asked. He grinned and shook his head, eyebrows furrowed as he chuckled. "You seem distracted. I mean, we got the important stuff out of the way but we only have a few minutes left here and there are a few things we still need to discuss." He leaned forward and tapped the tip of his pen on his notepad. Jenny eyed me cautiously. My secretary, she always sat in on these meetings to take notes of everything for me, so I could look over them later on when I needed a refresher. Howard opted to do it all himself.

"Nothing, I'm not distracted." I straightened, realizing I was in fact a bit distracted, but only because I was thinking how happy I was to finally have a doctor who could help us move forward and help Chris heal.

"No, you were definitely distracted." Howard looked to Jenny, who shrugged and grimaced as if she agreed with him. Her brown hair fell across her eyes and she swished it away, though I got the feeling she'd have rather hidden behind it for a moment.

Howard—with his three-piece suits and coiffed silver hair—knew I wasn't one to share personal details in the workplace. There was no space for that. We catered to very important businesses and being distracted or unfocused was the easiest and fastest way to screw things up. I inwardly scolded myself for allowing my mind to wander and cleared my throat.

"Okay, so we have a new doctor for Christopher. I told you last month at the company mixer that he has been ill for quite some time, almost since Connie died."

"Yeah, I remember that." Howard capped his pen and laid it on the mahogany conference table then sat back in his leather armchair and folded his hands in his lap. "How's that going?"

I felt a smile creep onto my face as joy welled up. "Well, we're making strides now. We've found a doctor to really look into things. Her name is Mindy Scriber; she's a doc of internal medicine. She's going to run more tests. She already seems to be on top of things and she's just fantastic. Brilliant, driven, really good head on her shoulders." Not to mention the way she seemed to take her patients very personally—at least Christopher. I left that part out because Howard didn't need to know I found her attractive.

"Ah, well that's fantastic news." He studied my face with narrowed eyes as I continued.

"Yeah, I was just at a coffee shop when I bumped into this woman and her son who reminded me of Chris. We chatted a bit and I was pleasantly surprised to be introduced to the doctor. The two ladies are friends and they were just having coffee. It was purely a coincidence, or maybe fate. If you believe that sort of thing that is. She just walked in and listened to me and that was that. I made an appointment and here we are."

I knew I was smiling a lot, but how could I contain what I was feeling? After losing my wife I had been so scared that I'd lose my son too. Mindy's manifestation in my life was nothing less than a miracle. I had no idea where to turn. Connie always took care of these types of things. I didn't even know doctors of internal medicine existed, and our family doctor wasn't helpful at all.

"I know how difficult it was losing Constance. Christopher was so down. I really thought what the doctors thought, that it was all in his head. I'm really glad you're getting help for him now. But..."

Howard's lip curled up on one side into a smirk. I didn't mind that he pried a little, though I'd rather have left my home life at home. Still, it was work, and he was right. I needed to be focused.

"What?" I asked, and I watched Jenny squirm in the corner near the Ficus. She had no reason to be here if we were just casually talking about our families. She probably felt like she was eavesdropping but felt too awkward to excuse herself.

"Seems like there's a bit more going on though. You're too happy for this to be just about your kid. Seems more like you've met someone and you're in love." Howard burst out laughing and I felt a twinge of guilt. Was that what was happening? I was falling in love again?

I shook my head sternly and scowled. "Nonsense. My wife's been dead for only two years. I just found a great doctor for my son. I'm thrilled we'll get help for him now." I fought my own racing heart because with every word of protest that crossed my lips, I was losing the battle. My cheeks burned, humiliating me.

"Ah, that's it. You have it bad for the doctor. That's alright, buddy. I bet she's a firecracker. If she's single, nail her." Howard stood and straightened his tie, buttoning his suit coat. Then winked at me. "I want all the details—after my meeting with the Jones account."

And with that he was out of the conference room and I watched him walk past the windows as he shot finger guns at me. I stared at the window long after he was gone, trying to formulate a coherent thought. Howard's teasing threw me off guard, mostly because even though I knew I wasn't falling in love with Mindy, I did really have a fondness for her. And I also had a massive amount of guilt inside my heart. Connie was my soulmate. I couldn't replace her.

"Sir?" Jenny asked, and I blinked slowly, raising my eyes to meet her gaze. She stood in front of me clutching the notepad and pen.

"What is it?" I asked, not even knowing how long I had sat there staring after Howard, lost in thought.

"If it's any comfort, I think it's wonderful that you're at the part of your grieving process where you feel open to new love, even if this woman isn't the right one for you." She smiled and nodded then backed toward the door.

"Thanks, Jenny," I mumbled, ashamed that people in my life could read me like a book. I didn't need their permission to move on or open my horizons, but Jenny's words were encouraging to me. I lingered on them the rest of my workday, even as I skipped out of the office to avoid Howard after his meeting.

Christopher was the first kid out the school door, and he raced down the sidewalk to my car. Breathless, he grinned at me as he buckled his seatbelt. I knew he was happy for not having school tomorrow, but I also knew he was a bit nervous about his tests. I pulled out into traffic and forced the thought of Mindy out of my head for the moment to focus on my son.

"How was school, Top?"

"Eh, it was okay. Crystal stole my lunch box again so Mr. Stein sent her to the principal. That was funny. And I got an A on my math test." He pushed his hair out of his eyes and his chest heaved as he caught his breath. "How was work?"

"It was alright." My shoulders tightened as he asked the question. It was pretty routine for our ride home from school, but I just wanted to forget work today and be grateful I had the day off tomorrow too so I didn't have to hear more of Howard's infantile teasing. "What do you think about tomorrow?" I opened the door to the topic of Christopher's tests, and as I pulled up to the red light I realized just how nervous he was. I looked over at him and his head was down, his hands in his lap.

"Hey, bud, it's okay. I promise. The tests won't hurt except a pinch of a needle for drawing blood. And we can go to the waterpark afterward to celebrate having it over." I reached over and patted his shoulder.

"Yeah, okay," he mumbled and I had to pay attention and drive again. It took him a few minutes to speak again; we were pulling into the driveway as he said, "I like Dr. Scriber though. She's really nice."

"Yeah?" I asked, my heart soaring again at the mention of her name. So Christopher had the same feelings that I did. That proved that Mindy was a sensational doctor, not that I was falling in love with her. Howard was completely wrong.

"Yeah. She's really pretty too. She reminds me of Mom." He didn't even wait until I had the car shut off. He was out the door and racing toward the house as soon as I put it in park and the doors unlocked. I chuckled and climbed out, feeling messed up inside.

Kids are so honest. They just tell it like it is. But there I was, wrestling with the whole thing because my heart wouldn't let me have that same freedom. I could admit to Howard that Mindy was gorgeous without it being anything more than a man paying a compliment to a woman in a professional way.

I followed Christopher into the house and we had dinner. He shut himself into his room to play video games with his friends online and I retreated to my bedroom like normal, but my body was agitated. After being so worked up emotionally with the way Howard teased me like we were in high school again, I felt tense. And given the fact that we would do testing for Chris tomorrow to find out what was wrong with him, I felt a bit of nervous energy too. A hot shower seemed like a good remedy.

Before I turned on the water I stripped off and tossed my dirty clothes into the hamper. The water steamed up the bathroom quickly, and I stepped beneath the flow. Mindy was the last thing on my mind until I started replaying the conversation with Christopher in the car in my head. He had mentioned how pretty Dr. Scriber was, and now that was all I could think about. Her curvy figure, the way her lips turned into a full pout when she smiled. I found myself being aroused by thoughts of her, thoughts like, I wondered what she'd look like in a nice dress instead of scrubs or a lab coat. And I wondered if she'd be interested in an old man like me. But why would she? She was probably dating someone her age, and I was almost old enough to be her father, but that didn't stop my dick from swelling.

The water rushed over it, teasing me, and when I washed myself, it made the problem even worse. Mindy Scriber had gotten in my head, or maybe Howard's words had just planted an idea there. Either way, I just wasn't a strong enough man to resist. I found myself touching more, and I started to stroke my dick as it swelled further.

I tried to think of my late wife, the way her lips felt on mine. The way she smiled in the morning when she kissed me goodbye, but it was no use. Mindy's face invaded my imagination, seductively taunting its way into every memory I had of Connie and replacing her. Soon, it was Mindy on her knees with her ruby-red lips wrapped around my throbbing cock and god was she good at it. I imagined her smiling up at me as she slid her lips back and forth, teasing me, making me want more.

"Oh god, Mindy," I gasped quietly, and my hand sped up. Hearing her name out loud only made things more real. I pictured her perfect tits, perky nipples pointing at me as she slid her fingers into her own moisture and swirled them. I saw her beautiful face, flushed with lust and grinning at me as I approached climax. I saw her perfect ass tensing and relaxing as she fingered herself. Mindy Scriber was in my head, and she was going to stay there forever.

Soon I was on the edge, getting closer and closer with every stroke. My balls tightened up as I imagined myself pressing into her from behind, her breasts bouncing with every hard thrust of my hips. I pictured her looking over her shoulder at me with those big, beautiful brown eyes.

I could feel the cum rising, and I knew I was ready to blow my load. Small grunts crept up and out of my mouth as I felt release come. My cum sprayed out in thick, white strands, landing on the shower wall. I imagined that it was Mindy's fingers, her mouth, her perfect pussy that had made me cum, and the thought itself was enough to make me cum harder, longer. I loved it. I loved the idea of Mindy Scriber, and I loved what fantasizing about her had made me do. I wanted more.

As I splashed water on the shower wall, Christopher knocked on the door. "Dad! I gotta pee. Hurry up!"

Shame weighed me down. What was I doing? Mindy was my son's doctor, not my fantasy, not even if she was the most beautiful woman I'd met in fifteen years. Quite possibly more radiant than Connie was, rest her soul. I couldn't think like this. I couldn't be this man. I was grieving and my son needed me. No, Mindy had to get out of my head. I had to be stronger. "Just a minute, kiddo."

Now how would I look her in the eye tomorrow and not feel guilty?

4

Mindy

As the lab tech placed the cotton swab and bandage on the crook of Christopher's elbow following his blood draw, I picked up one of the vials and slid it into my pocket. No one saw me, and that was exactly how I planned it. I busily wrote out the paperwork for his testing as the lab tech labeled the other vials; there were five there—six if you count the one in my pocket. When she looked up at me confused, I asked, "What's wrong?"

"We had six vials here," she said, pointing at the tray.

I handed her the paperwork for the tests and shrugged. Guilt gnawed at my conscience and I thought my hand shaking while holding the papers out to her would give me away but I pushed a lock of my chestnut-colored hair out of my eyes and shook my head. "Nope, just five. These orders are all you need." I felt like a criminal, a liar. My face burned and I had to look down at the tablet on the countertop to keep a straight face. I was lying. I was horribly guilty and I deserved to be fired.

"I am losing my mind. I tell ya," the lab tech said, chuckling. She put the paperwork on her cart next to the caddy with the vials of

Christopher's blood and rolled it toward the door. "Tammy will be in to get him in a sec."

I nodded at her as she pushed the door open and tugged her cart behind her through the door. Jace was calm, Christopher grimacing. "I'm sorry if that was a little painful, Topper." I'd already grown comfortable using his nickname, which he seemed to prefer over his given name. I remembered thinking how strange it felt when my son was hours old and was taken from my arms without a name. I never got to choose what he would be called because I gave up that right when I signed the adoption papers.

State law allowed me ten days to change my mind, but no matter how I protested or how upset I got, my parents were in charge of me. It was their decision because I was a minor.

"Everything okay, doc?" Jace asked, snapping me out of my painful memories. I smiled at him and moved away from the blue Formica countertop.

"Yes, sorry, I was lost in thought."

"Will it hurt?" Christopher asked, forehead drawn in fear.

"The CT scan?" I leaned toward him, cocking my head.

"Yeah."

"Oh," I chuckled, patting his knee. "No, it won't hurt a bit. You drank all the juice?" I asked and he nodded. "Good boy. That stuff is already working down in your belly. It's going to help highlight anything going on in there. You'll climb up on a big table and lie down. They will put a belt on you so you don't roll off, and then they'll push some buttons. The table will slide into a giant tube. Do you like the tube slides at the park?"

He shrugged one shoulder and said, "They're okay."

"Well this should be no problem then. You just lie really still for a few minutes. They take some pictures, and then the table moves back out of the tube and you're done. That simple." I clapped my hands and watched his body visibly relax as he breathed a sigh of relief.

"I've tried telling him a few times, but he's just nervous." Jace stood and put a hand on Christopher's shoulder.

"Nothing to worry about. You can actually go with him if you want." As I spoke the door opened and Tammy came in with a wheel-chair to transport Christopher to radiology.

"No, I actually want to talk to you about a few things." He looked down at his son. "That okay?"

"Yeah, I'm fine." Christopher hopped off the table and sat in the wheelchair. "Just remember we're going to the waterpark." His expression made me chuckle as Tammy checked his wristband against her tablet readout.

"Off to radiology. Back soon," she said as she backed out of the room into the hallway and the door swung shut behind her.

"What do you need to talk about?" I asked Jace as I pulled up my stool and sat down. I felt really uncomfortable being alone with him since I was lying to him. The vial in my pocket was only part of the lie —sneaking his kid's blood to test against my own, which I'd already drawn and stored in my locker. The fact that I believed myself to be his birth mother and hid that from everyone made me guilty of so many ethics violations I'd be fired for sure.

"Well," he started sitting down. He scooted his chair closer to me and I swallowed hard, forcing my nervous energy down. "I just wanted to tell you that I'm so grateful that you've come into our lives. It feels like you actually care about what happens to Chris."

"He's a great kid. You know I've been meaning to ask how he's been eating the last few days. He seems to have more color now." I tried to direct the conversation toward only his medical condition to alleviate some of my guilty feelings, but Jace wasn't having it.

"Like that. You pay attention to the small details like that. Most doctors don't even care." Jace folded his hands in his lap and stared at me. Everything out of his mouth about how amazing I was just made me feel worse. Shame dripped from me. "And I know this is strange but I feel like fate destined us to meet."

"Well, I'm not sure about that, but I do believe that sometimes things line up a certain way at a certain time to work things out in a better way." Rabbi Benjamin always said, "Everything happens for a reason." It was one lesson I never understood, especially after the pain I went through when I was younger. The reason that happened was because my parents were cruel and heartless. I felt pain contorting my face and tried to relax.

"No, I mean, I feel like we've met before. I like I know you from somewhere..."

My heart felt like it literally stopped in my chest. I abruptly looked down at my hands so I didn't give Jace a deer in the headlights look. I knew where I'd seen him before, that photo they gave me of my son's adoptive parents. I only saw it briefly but I knew Jason Turner was this man, Jace Turner, sitting in front of me. I knew it because how many Jason Turners could there be who adopted kids my son's age. This DNA in my pocket would prove that. I was certain. I just didn't know how I was going to bring it to light.

"Uh, I'm sure we just saw each other in passing. You said you've seen other doctors for this condition. Maybe we saw each other in passing." I looked up at him and our eyes met. My chest pounded. I knew if he looked at my chest instead of my face, he'd see how panicked I was. My hands were sweaty, my mouth dry.

"I don't know..." He seemed to be disappointed.

"I'm glad we met too. I'm glad to be able to help Christopher start to feel better. I'm sure after these tests, we will have a diagnosis and we can take strides to better health." The only thing I could do was keep pointing back to Christopher's ailment. If Jace remembered seeing my photo—had they given him a photo of me back then too? —this would all get very complicated.

"Are you seeing someone?" he blurted out and I felt pain in my chest. Like the gun went off at the starting line of a hundred-meter dash and I was supposed to run, only I froze.

"What?" My thoughts did a complete one-eighty, ricocheting around inside my brain like a loose bullet. Was he hitting on me?

"I asked if you're seeing someone." Jace wrung his hands. He looked like a schoolboy with a crush, licking his lips, blinking furiously. "Because I was thinking we could get coffee sometime. Maybe at the coffee shop where we first met."

Relief flooded me at the same time more guilt bubbled up. He wasn't prying because he'd figured out who I really was. He liked me.

He was hitting on me. A man nearly old enough to be my father, from whom I harbored a dark secret was asking me out. I stared into his eyes shocked. Standard procedure was to tell him I could not date him because I was his son's doctor. But doing that might just make him take Chris to another doctor, just so he could ask me out. And just thinking that made my conscience feel like it was on fire, burning in the pit of Hades where liars and cheats go.

"Mr. Turner, I..."

"Please, call me Jace." His eyes pleaded with me, though I could see him trying to mask his disappointment. I couldn't date him, not in a million years. Yes, he was hot. Yes, he was an amazing man so far as I could tell, and a great father. But things were already so complicated and tricky, I had no desire to make it worse by getting romantically involved with him.

"Jace, I just..." I watched his face fall and my heart felt crushed. I was already breaking the rules and I just knew when he found out he would hate me. I didn't want to start the animosity already.

"I just thought we could get to know each other out of the hospital. Christopher even seemed favorable. He said he likes you." Jace grinned and looked down. "He said you're pretty, and I agree."

When his chin rose and he looked at me I felt my cheeks warm again. His smile put me at ease, comforted a part of my heart that longed for fulfillment after years of neglecting it. Friendship outside of the hospital would be okay. And if the DNA test came back positive like I assumed, I could refer him to Dr. Wilks in pediatrics. Besides, I really wanted to get to know Christopher outside of doctors' appointments, and this might be a great segue into a relationship where I could make that happen.

I found a plan formulating in my mind. Get to know Jace as a friend, then when his—my—son was off seeing another doctor, I could open up about my "suspicions" and find out if he'd be open to testing again. No one would ever know, and I'd be in the clear.

"Okay," I said, and it brought an immediate smile. "We can meet at the coffee shop to discuss his results. I'd like that."

"Oh," Jace said, his smile fading again. "Yeah, okay. We'll discuss the results." He spoke as if trying to adjust to the idea that I wasn't going to date him but just continue our professional relationship in a different, less clinical setting. "I think that will work."

"Look, I have to run down to the lab. You tell Christopher we'll have coffee to talk about his tests. I'll have my office set it up as soon as the labs come back." I stood and thrust my hand out, and he took it. This time, however, when he shook my hand it was not a firm grip of a man shaking the hand of a doctor. His grasp was soft, tender even. His eyes lingered on my face.

"I really look forward to it."

I walked out of the room with my tablet in hand feeling like a horrible person. I was lying. I had stolen DNA. I held secrets that were eating me alive, and now I was leading him on. My self-loathing carried me all the way to my locker where I retrieved the vial of my own blood, and labeled it as patient X. Then I headed down to the lab. My friend Evelyn would do favors for me from time to time, and the only way I was getting this done under the radar was to call in one of those favors.

Now if my conscience didn't eat me alive, I could move forward with my newfound plan. Befriend the man I believed to be my son's adoptive father and convince him I have suspicions about my relationship to Christopher, all while keeping my cool and not allowing either of them to know I have been lying this whole time, or anyone else for that matter. Especially my boss.

5

Jace

The first drop of hot coffee hit my tongue and I closed my eyes to savor the flavor of it. Waking up in the morning used to mean coffee with Connie at the breakfast nook while Christopher got ready for school, and on the weekends we'd have alone time while he slept in. Now it was lonely, sitting at the bar listening to the analog clock tick the seconds by while I waited for my son to join me. It took a while to adjust to the new routine, and it was harder on Christopher than it was on me, but we managed. Life had changed, and I felt like it was changing again. I wasn't even sure how to feel about this change though.

Mindy Scriber—just her name made my heart feel full. I was inexplicably drawn to her caring nature and compassion. She was a beautiful woman in her own right but her personality made her magnetic. I had never wanted to get to know someone this desperately, and each time I interacted with her that feeling grew more intense. I found myself smiling into my coffee mug as I took a sip, just thinking of our next appointment. Yes, it was to discuss Christopher's test results but it would be in a casual setting, which would allow me to be more personal.

I sipped my coffee and thought of Chris, how he'd react to me wanting to date someone new. I knew he still mourned Connie so much. I wouldn't want to upset him; God knows I already struggled with guilt of moving on, though I felt like I had mostly handled that now. Connie wouldn't want me to feel lonely and leave our son without a feminine influence in his life. At least, I believed she wouldn't. We had never discussed how we would react in the event that one of us passed early in life.

"Dad...?" Christopher wobbled out of the bathroom holding his stomach. His face was scrunched up, lips slightly parted.

"Hey, Top, what's wrong." Setting my coffee on the bar, I turned on my stool to face him as he walked in. "Belly hurts?"

"Yeah... really bad." He leaned against me and I put my arms around him. I hated that this happened to him. I would do anything in the world to take this pain and make sure he never felt it again. I kissed his forehead and pushed his mop of hair back. He didn't feel warm; instead, his forehead was slick with perspiration.

"You drank plenty of water last night?"

He grunted and doubled over, laying his head on my lap and nodded. "Yes... Dad, I think I'm going to have diarrhea."

I patted his back. We had been through this so many times, I felt at a loss. I lifted him up until he stood on his own again and pulled his chin up so I could speak to him. "Go lie down on the couch, bud."

Christopher whimpered and shuffled over to the couch. The t-shirt he wore was his favorite one, a little too small because he'd grown in the past three years since his mother gave it to him. It stretched tightly over his swollen belly, while his gym shorts sagged a little, leaving a bit of skin exposed. I stood and left my coffee, heading to the sink for a glass of water. In the back of my mind I thought of calling Mindy, but I didn't know if there was anything she could even suggest either. So maybe I just wanted the moral support. I just didn't have her number. All I had was the emergency line for the doctor's office and that would just be a nurse.

"Dad, please... my belly."

I glanced at my boy, who now lay on the couch with a pillow tucked under his stomach. It looked very uncomfortable to me, but if it helped him he could lie that way. The only thing besides pressure on his belly that ever worked was a warm compress, so I got out the hot water bottle from under the sink and ran the tap as hot as I could get it to fill it up. With the full bottle and the glass of water, I headed into the living room to sit next to him. He took the water bottle greedily and lifted his torso up to shove it between his body and the pillow.

"It hurts pretty bad this time?" I asked, setting the water down. He was white as a sheet. From personal experience, I could see that maybe he was going to throw up too, though that symptom was usually rare.

"Yeah... I wish Mom was here. She always knows what to do." His sad little voice broke my heart. Constance really did know what to do. She was a people person; I was a technology person. I rubbed his back in a small circle and acknowledged his need.

"Yeah, Mom was pretty good at all this sort of stuff, wasn't she?" Talking about her was never easy. They say it helps, but with Christopher I felt like it only brought up more pain.

"She was the best...."

"Yes, she was. But there are other people who can help too."

He turned his head and looked up at me out of the corner of his eye. "You mean the doctors?"

"Yeah, like Dr. Scriber." I raised my eyebrows and smiled softly. "She's trying to help a lot, you know?" The pain in his eyes wasn't just from mourning his mother. I could see the ache from his physical condition and also a look of concern.

"Yeah, but she's just a doctor." He buried his face in the pillow again and all I could think was that Mindy could be more than just a doctor to him. For a kid who had been through so much in his short life, having a mom who was also a doctor might actually be exactly what he needed.

"She's a nice lady though." I didn't want to push the idea of me and Mindy onto him right now. He was in a lot of pain, so I decided to back off of the conversation. "Would you like a drink?"

"No," he said, but it was muffled. I watched his shoulders rise and fall. He was breathing too deeply, trying to suck fresh air through the pillow. I patted his back.

"Hey, bud, what's wrong. Talk to me."

Christopher turned his head and I saw tears in his eyes. "You like her?" he asked, an accusation in his tone. "Like you don't care that Mom is dead?"

"Oh, Topper, we don't have to talk about this right now. Your stomach hurts too much. Okay? Let's just try to get you feeling better."

He pushed himself up to a sitting position and held the hot water bottle on his belly. A few tears streamed down his cheeks and he looked upset, frowning at me. "Mom is dead."

"Chris, Mom died two years ago. It's okay if we remember her and let go a little. We don't have to live alone the rest of our lives." I reached out and squeezed his knee and picked up the water and tried to hand it to him but he just scowled at it, crying harder.

"I don't want to let her go. I want her back. I want my mom here, not someone else."

My heart felt like it was being torn out of my chest. Two years was a long time to be alone. Seven hundred thirty-plus days of sleeping alone. Meals alone. Vacations alone. Raising a child alone. I missed Connie more than I could even articulate, but my need for companionship was greater than it had ever been. I just couldn't explain that to a twelve-year-old who was suffering physical and emotional pain.

"Okay, bud, you're right. I would love for her to be back too, but that's not how life and earth work. Okay? We'll just take it slow."

"Ow..." he yelped, bending over. "Dad..."

I could tell the pain was worse this time than previous events, but I knew the emergency room would only send us home and tell us to see our regular doctor. So I helped him lie back down. "Look, kiddo, you lay here for a minute. I'm going to get the emergency contact number for Dr. Scriber's office and call them, okay?"

He nodded his head and cried harder. I couldn't help but feel like talking about Mindy had upset him more and made his stomach hurt worse. I knew stressful events tended to make any physical ailment worse, so as I walked toward my home office, my mind was filled with guilt. I sorted through my wallet, which I had left lying on the corner of my desk, and made my way to the bedroom to retrieve my cell phone from the nightstand.

By the time I returned to the living room, Christopher had calmed a little, but I knew the pain would come in waves. I sat back down on the edge of the couch next to him and rubbed his back again as I dialed the number. It was an automated system I had to enter my phone number into, and I got put in a queue for a call back.

"They'll call soon, okay?" I rubbed his back a little more firmly, which seemed to help. Talking about Connie sometimes caused flare ups in his emotions like this, but I'd never seen it make his physical condition worse. If the doctors who originally told me his ailment was all in his head could see him now, they'd think I was crazy for pursuing something other than counseling. But I knew my son, and he needed help.

After a few minutes, my phone rang with an unknown number. I picked it up and answered right away. "Hello? Jace Turner here."

"Hey, Jace. How's our little patient?" I was surprised to hear Mindy's sweet voice, not a nurse.

"Hey, Dr. Scriber. Uh, well Christopher is having some belly pains."

"Topper," he hissed, scolding me for not using his nickname. He scowled at me and I almost chuckled.

"Alright, let's see. Where is the pain exactly?" she asked and I hadn't even thought to ask him.

"Uh, let me ask..." I held the phone away from my mouth and spoke to Christopher.

"Show me right where your belly hurts."

Christopher turned over to lie on his back and pointed to his stomach right below his ribcage, mostly on the left side. I didn't know much but I knew lower right abdomen pain could be his appendix, so it was good that his pain wasn't there.

"He showed me near his pancreas." I gestured for him to lie down again and waited for Mindy's response.

"And is it sharp pain, burning pain? A dull ache?"

"Chris, does it feel hot or like a knife?" I pushed a few strands of hair out of his eyes and he looked up at me.

"Like I'm going to have diarrhea, I don't know." He grimaced and curled up into a ball again and I sighed.

"Did you hear that?" I asked Mindy.

"Yes, I did. Now look, I don't have the test results back yet, but given my experience, I strongly suggest you get some warm compresses for his belly. You can try a warm bath to soak. Make sure he's drinking water. Slippery elm bark tea is good for tummy pain too, though I don't know where you'd get that this early in the morning and it takes a few hours to really start working."

"Wow, how do you know all this?" I asked her, amazed that she had an answer immediately. I expected her to tell me to take him to the hospital or something.

"Just part of being a doctor." I could tell she was smiling just by the sound of her voice. "You can always take him to the ER if you're really worried, but I think given his history and the things we are testing for right now, he isn't in any immediate danger and they would likely just observe him until his pain went away. You can give him children's painkillers too, but make sure you follow the label. Don't do that for more than a day or so, because it's hard on his kidneys."

The suggestions she offered made sense to me and I was thankful she had taken time to personally call me this morning. I didn't think a nurse would have understood the situation as well as she did.

"Hey, Dr. Scriber, thank you so much for personally calling me back."

"No problem, Jace. I was just the doctor on call for today, but hey, you have my personal number now. Save that in your phone. I'll trust that you respect my personal life, but if you need anything at all, any time of the day or night, you can text me or call me."

My chest tightened and I looked down at my son. I had her personal number now. I could call or text her any time I wanted, but now there was an added layer of guilt. Christopher needed me to be a father first and foremost, and that meant protecting his heart from being hurt again. I knew I was healing faster than him, and I should wait on his timing to move on, but my heart wanted what it wanted. I had to find a way to help him through this or I'd watch the most amazing woman I'd ever met slip right through my fingers.

6

Mindy

I sat in my little silver sedan just down the street from the school Christopher attended. There were only a few schools in Hudson, so when I saw his address on his chart, I knew which one was his. Kids milled about outside the tall brick building tucked in the heart of downtown Hudson. A group of teens kicked a hacky sack around, laughing and joking, and a few girls sat on a bench out front with textbooks on their laps. I scanned the faces for a familiar one, and noticed Christopher standing against the building. He wore jeans and a light blue windbreaker, his hair hanging in his eyes.

My heart felt warm and full watching him, though I realized this would probably be considered stalking or something. I didn't want him or his father being creeped out, but the closer I got to this case, the more I wanted answers. I knew the results were in; I'd gotten a call from Evelyn this morning to let me know they'd be on my desk. I just hadn't seen them yet. I was a walking bundle of nerves. This young man could very well be my son, and my gut told me he was.

My only problem was that I didn't know how to tell Jace what was going on even after I had proof. If someone approached me and told me they'd been sneaking around with my DNA and knew I was his mother, I'd have been very upset. I'd feel violated. The thought made me look away. I stared at my radio dial, trying not to cry. If I'd have had the sense to be truthful about things from the beginning, none of this would be happening right now. Jace might have taken Christopher away though—afraid he'd lose his son to me, but I'd never have done that to him. I just wanted to be a part of his life.

When I looked back up to where the children were, Christopher was gone. A steady stream of bodies funneled through the double doors on the front of the building and a bell sounded. It was time for the school day to start, which meant it was time for me to head to the hospital and get the results of the DNA test. I sat there for a few more minutes, frozen to the seat. I was terrified that I was right, that Christopher was mine. And I was also terrified that I was wrong; that I'd never see my son again. Either way, this situation wasn't going to resolve itself.

I drove across town feeling my stomach tie itself into a knot. My whole world was changing around me whether or not this little boy was mine. The feelings it dredged up had already opened the wound of the past and I couldn't sit through another Saturday lunch with my parents until it was resolved. Being forced to give away your baby is a horrible pain no one but a suffering mother would understand. I thought it was in the past, but I'd been irritable and moody for weeks now.

At the office, I tried to hide from everyone, taking the long way around through the cafeteria. When a few nurses smiled and waved, I scowled and looked away. I didn't have the emotional energy to interact with people, let alone have boring small talk about someone's date or how their pet chewed something up again. So I scurried to my office and sat behind my desk. The manilla envelope lying on my otherwise empty desk had the answer inside, and my hands trembled as I picked it up.

The white sticker in the corner of the envelope had Christopher's name on it, along with his patient number and the list of results detailed on the paperwork inside. My body flushed when I saw the

DNA results were listed alongside the blood work for his complete blood count and vitamin panel as well as the tests for Crohn's and a few other things. It meant someone had put them all together in the lab, which meant someone knew my blood sample was tested against his. I felt the hair on the back of my neck stand up before I even heard the knock on my door. I looked up to see Evelyn walk in.

"Hey." I laid the envelope down and tried to stay calm. My heart raced, panic urging my body into fight or flight mode, but if I acted guilty, she'd know I was guilty. She wouldn't even have to ask a single question. "What's up?"

"I see you got the test results..." Evelyn walked in and shut the door, then stood with her arms crossed over her chest.

"Uh, yeah, thanks. Normally someone just delivers them. No need to discuss things. It should all be here." I pushed the envelope a few centimeters away from me nervously, then licked my lips. It was bad enough that I had to deal with the reality of what was actually happening. Now my guilt and shame were intensified because I knew Evelyn knew. The look on her face left no room for doubt.

"What's going on, Mindy? That was your blood on that sample. And you ordered those tests against a patient?"

I felt the color drain from my cheeks. I also felt a little dizzy so I didn't try to stand up. "I, uh... Yes, the patient needed to be tested for a few conditions. I ordered the tests." Chewing on the inside of my cheek had become a bad habit, but right now it was the only thing grounding me to the present so I didn't fall into complete panic.

"Be straight with me, Mindy. We're friends, but I can't put my job on the line. The ethics of this are a nightmare. You think you're his mother? Why do you think that?"

I looked up at her face—the face of a friend who really cared about me. We weren't extremely close, not like my friendship with Georgia, but Evelyn was always there for me when I needed to talk. We'd had coffee a few times. I knew, however, that she had a very strong code of ethics. I did too, until now.

"It's hard to explain." I looked down at the envelope and knew what the DNA test said before I even opened it. My gut had been right all along. Evelyn wouldn't be here warning me how bad I screwed up if it wasn't a positive result.

"You know I have to report this, right? I can't just not do my job. You can't treat your own child for anything. Only if it's an emergency and—"

"I know," I snapped, not able to hold back my emotion. "I know," I said more calmly, then stood. "Please, Eve." I looked her in the eye pleadingly. "I can't explain everything right now; you just have to trust me."

"Mindy, you are risking everything for this? Your entire career? They can yank your license to practice medicine. You know that, right?" Evelyn's face softened to a look of compassion and I sank back into my chair and let the tears flow. God did I ever know that was a risk I was taking.

I was stupid, throwing my life away for this. Or was I? Wasn't my son worth it? I'd have given my life for him years ago, to keep him. But I was a child myself, and I had no rights. I didn't want to lose my career, but I needed this more than I'd ever needed anything my whole life. Christopher was mine. I had the proof in front of me now, and I didn't even know what to do with that information yet. So I sat there and sobbed, falling apart in front of someone who had the evidence to destroy my professional life.

I heard her sigh loudly and I wiped my eyes and looked up at her. "Just make it right, okay? Refer him or something. I can't have this over my head. I have bills to pay. If they find out I knew about this and didn't report it, I could get fired." Evelyn shook her head. I could tell she was upset, and she had every right to be.

"I'm so sorry I dragged you into this. Please, just give me some time. I swear I'll make it right."

"I know you will. I have to get back to work now, okay?" She didn't wait for me to acknowledge her goodbye. She just walked out and left the door open when she did.

I was too overwhelmed with so many feelings to work today, so I scrawled a note on a sheet of paper and took the envelope and note to Dr. Andrews's office, placing it on his desk. I let him know I had to take a personal day and that I'd be back tomorrow. Hopefully that would give me plenty of time to calm down before my lunch appointment with Jace to discuss the results.

I headed to my car, hands still trembling and tears still flowing, and sat behind the wheel again. I was in no shape to drive, so I sat there for a while just letting the emotion out. When my phone buzzed inside my purse, I pulled it out to see what it was. I thought maybe Dr. Andrews had texted me, but it was from Jace. He'd sent me several messages over the weekend about Christopher and how he was improving. I swiped right to read the new one.

Jace 8:29 AM: Can we meet at my house instead of the coffee shop? After Chris had a bad weekend, I took a personal day to work from home. I'm only a few blocks from school if he needs me instead of a 20-minute drive.

I stared at that message so numb that I didn't know how to respond. As if a coffee shop wasn't personal enough, he wanted me to come to his house now? I knew Jace liked me, and this was his way of trying to help me feel more comfortable with the idea of dating him, but I had no intention of dating him. Yes, he was hot, but this thing was way too messy. I didn't want to respond. I wanted to travel back in time and change my choices.

Still, part of me was curious how Christopher was being raised, how they lived, what his house looked like. And if I had the courage to tell Jace the truth, it would be better for him to receive that information in a private place, not a coffee shop or hospital exam room. My hands shook as I typed in a long response, and then I deleted the whole thing and sent a single word.

Mindy 8:38 AM: Yes.

7

Jace

When Mindy pulled up, I was nervous. Not over the test results—I knew we'd figure out what was wrong with Christopher and help him feel better. I was more nervous about being alone with her. I woke up this morning to a very erotic dream about finding her in my shower and her asking me to have sex with her, which of course I did in the dream. My cock was so hard I wanted to touch myself, but I didn't have time because I had to get my son off to school.

I stayed home today after the difficult weekend for Christopher. If I needed to get to him quickly, this was the closest place I could be and still get work done. So I was thankful that Mindy graciously agreed to meet here at my house instead of across town at the coffee shop. It just set me up for sweaty palms and butterflies in my stomach because I was so attracted to her.

"Thanks so much for agreeing to meet here," I told her as she walked in. I gestured to the left, toward the kitchen. My home being an open concept, there wasn't much of a mystery as to where I planned to sit and chat. I had a pitcher of lemonade, two glasses, and a plate of cookies sitting on the patio table just outside the back door. She glanced at it and then back at me as I shut the door.

"Outside?" she asked, and I smiled.

"Yeah, it's a gorgeous day. Thought we could enjoy the fresh spring air."

I followed behind her as her eyes took everything in. She studied my home as if she'd never seen something so exquisite. To me it was normal, boring even. Constance had picked white leather for our kitchen chairs, to go with a thick mahogany table nestled beneath a plain chandelier. The marble bar top and stools coordinated in more rich browns and whites, with gold laced into the smooth stone. I'd seen it a billion times, day after day, but to Mindy it was new. Her hand smoothed across the surface as she walked past it.

"Fancy," she whispered beneath her breath, but I got the feeling she felt out of her league. I thought doctors made a lot of money, but maybe she was still repaying student loans, or maybe she was just a fan of tastefully decorated kitchens.

"My late wife picked it..." I felt stupid saying that. Here I was hoping to let her know how interested I was in her and I brought up my dead wife. I wanted to smack myself in the forehead but I pushed away the embarrassment and joined her as she headed for the patio table.

There was a nice breeze and we sat in the shade, but today would be the warmest day of the year so far. Soon we'd open the pool and Christopher and I would spend Saturdays splashing and getting our vitamin D. Mindy scanned the small backyard before sitting down.

"I bet Christopher loves to swim." She set a manilla envelope on the white, wrought iron table and pushed a strand of her chestnut hair out of her eyes. God, her eyes were gorgeous, hazel with flecks of emerald in them.

I sat across from her and couldn't help but grin at how beautiful she was. "Yeah, he loves swimming." For a moment I forgot the reason we were even sitting here. I got lost in memorizing every single millimeter of her face, her dimples, the way her eyebrows were slightly uneven, her full pouty lips. Until she cleared her throat and batted her eyelashes nervously.

"So, the test results...." She pushed the folder toward me and I opened it, but I couldn't make sense of the words on the page, probably because my mind was only on her. "Christopher has the blood markers of a condition called Crohn's disease. It's not a conclusive test, but I believe we are looking at a solid diagnosis. We'll want to do a few more tests, but if this is what he really has, then we have a path forward."

My eyes pored over the words, but they were all Greek to me. "What does this mean? I mean, for his treatment?" I looked up at her, suddenly brought back to Earth with her. I hadn't ever heard of Crohn's disease, so I didn't know what it meant.

"Well, it's an inflammatory bowel disease. It causes inflammation in the bowels and colon. It's quite painful..." When her words caught in her throat, I knew something was wrong. She blinked rapidly, her mouth hanging open. Then I realized that she looked a bit tired, maybe like she'd been crying. Her makeup was smudged a bit, smoky eyes indicating she'd rubbed them recently. "Um, can you excuse me? Where is your bathroom?"

"Uh..." I stood as she did, feeling like something was wrong and I had been too swept away with the idea of her being in my home to notice. How selfish was I? I pointed to the door. "Down the hall, first room on the right."

And Mindy was off, leaving her envelope on the table. She rushed to the bathroom and I stared at the table of lemonade and cookies. I didn't know what was wrong, but my heart went out to her whatever it was. I paced nervously, finding myself inside next to the bar waiting as the lock on the bathroom clicked and the door opened. She slunk out, dabbing her eyes, and when our eyes met, she looked ashamed.

"Hey, is everything okay?" I asked her as she approached, weaving her way around the couch and dining room table to stand next to me.

"I uh..." She fumbled with her words, looking down at her feet. I could tell something was weighing on her heavily but we hardly knew each other. I didn't actually expect her to open up and talk to me, though I'd have been there to listen if she did. Her chin turned up and her eyes met mine. "I just have Crohn's disease too, so I know how Christopher feels. I just…" She blinked and tears cascaded down her cheeks. "I'm sorry."

My heart swelled with compassion. The level of empathy of this beautiful woman was astounding. I didn't even think. I pulled her into my arms and held her there tightly as she cried. She felt rigid in my embrace for a few seconds but her arms went around my body and she relaxed.

"Listen, it's okay. I am so glad Chris has you. I know you're going to do everything you can to help him." I pushed some hair out of her face and kissed her forehead and she looked up at me.

"Mr. Turner, I …"

Before she could protest, I kissed her. My emotions got the better of me, not to mention my attraction to her. She was perfect in every way. Gorgeous to look at, empathetic, compassionate, smart, funny, and I wanted to learn everything there was to know about her.

Mindy protested, pressing against my chest lightly, but I didn't let up. I kissed her harder until she forced me to pull back. Our eyes met in a heated gaze. Her lipstick was smeared, likely onto my face. There was confusion in her eyes, and pain. Her eyes darted back and forth, but she didn't step away. The atmosphere was so charged I found it impossible to restrain myself again. I cupped both of her cheeks and kept my eyes open, locked on hers, as I moved in for another kiss. This time, she didn't protest at all.

As we kissed, I felt Mindy's body melt into mine. Her hands found their way to my hair, pulling me closer to her. I ran my hands down her back, feeling the smoothness of her skin beneath her shirt. Our breathing became ragged as we continued to kiss, lost in the moment.

Suddenly, Mindy pulled away from me, her eyes filled with fear and uncertainty.

"What's wrong?" I asked, concerned.

"I can't do this," she said, her voice shaking. "I'm sorry, Mr. Turner. I can't be with you like this."

I felt a pang of disappointment in my chest, but I understood. We were in the middle of the kitchen, and it wasn't exactly the most romantic setting. However, the heat between us was undeniable, and I didn't want to let it go.

"Tell me you don't feel it too..."

She looked at me hesitantly, still unsure. But then, she leaned in and kissed me again. This time, it was softer and more tender. I ran my hands down to her waist, pulling her closer to me. I could feel her curves against my body, and it was intoxicating.

Without a word, I lifted her up onto the counter, and her legs wrapped around my waist. We continued to kiss, our bodies pressed together. I could feel her heat through her clothes, and it made me ache with desire.

I began to kiss down her neck, and I could feel her breathing quicken. I made my way across her collarbone, and she let out little gasps of pleasure.

As I moved my hand up her shirt, she shuddered. I broke the kiss and looked up at her. Her eyes were shut, and she looked so vulnerable. "Is this okay?" I whispered. She nodded.

Slowly, I moved my hand up higher. When my hand cupped her breast, Mindy let out a small sigh of pleasure. I could feel her nipple stiffen underneath her bra. A wave of desire washed over me.

I pulled back from her and took off my shirt. She looked at me in surprise, but she didn't stop me. I pulled her back into a kiss, and began to undo her buttons. After a moment, I pulled her shirt open, exposing her bra. I kissed down her neck again and began to pull her bra down. I felt as if I were about to explode. We continued to kiss for several more minutes, our hands exploring each other's bodies.

When Mindy's hands began to move lower, I stepped back and tugged my fly open. She frantically unbuttoned her slacks and pushed at the waistband. From her seated position on the counter, it was impossible to remove her pants on her own, so I leaned into her and grabbed her pants and panties at the same time. With her arms draped around my shoulders, she lifted herself slightly and I pulled her pants off, hearing her shoes drop to the floor one at a time.

"I don't have a condom," she hissed when my fingers found her tender nub.

I buried my face in her cleavage, raking my teeth across her creamy mounds. This wasn't like my shower dream—it was better. She was here, letting me touch her. I could smell her arousal wafting up between us and knew she wanted me too.

"Don't worry about it... I'll protect you," I told her, and I pushed a finger into her. She hissed and sucked in a breath, arching her back and thrusting her tits out. I bit down on one again, her shirt parting so wide it began to slide down her arms.

"Jace... I..." Mindy's hands clawed at my shoulders as I sucked the side of her tit, then pulled the bra lower to take her nipple into my mouth.

"I want to taste you," I told her, and moved my lips lower. She gasped as I took the nipple into my mouth and swirled my tongue around it. She was so incredibly wet. I could feel her juices on her thighs as I slid another finger between her folds. I needed to feel her insides.

"Jace, please," she begged, and I couldn't resist her. I thrust my fingers into her, and she moaned my name.

Mindy arched her hips, grinding herself against my hand. I pulled my fingers out, then pushed them back in. I pulled her nipple into my mouth, sucking on it deeply. I couldn't get enough of her. She was so perfect.

I kissed down her chest and over her belly button and she sat up, her hands finding my hair as I kissed down her soft creamy skin. I could feel her quivering with every touch. Her hands pulled at my hair, obviously eager for me to move lower. So, I pushed her back gently. She scooted back, her knees on the counter. I could see how wet she was, her lips swollen and glistening with her juices. Her cheeks were flushed pink with desire. I kissed her right above her mound. She leaned back, her hands sliding from my shoulders, holding her heavy breasts. She pinched her own nipples as she watched me kneel between her knees.

When I felt her shudder with pleasure, I moved my lips lower, kissing her thigh, reveling in her taste. I pushed her legs wider apart, my hands cupping her ass, squeezing it as I kissed her. I looked up at her.

Her eyes were half-lidded, her lips parted, her cheeks flushed. "Jace..." She moaned my name as I licked her. The first time my tongue touched her, her eyes widened. Her moan was louder. The second time I licked her, she groaned, her head fell back. Her fingers threaded through my hair. The third time I licked her, she whimpered and bit her lip. I slid my tongue over her clit slowly, and she moaned again. When I sucked on it, she moaned louder.

I thrusted two fingers into her, and kept working them in and out, while I sucked on her clit. She tightened around me, her thighs quivering, her back arching. "Oh god, that's amazing." Hearing her confess to the pleasure she was feeling encouraged me. I sucked her clit into my mouth and she let out a muffled scream, her hands tugging at my hair. I felt her insides begin to clench around my fingers. "Jace!" she whimpered as her orgasm intensified, but the sound was muffled by her thighs closing around my head.

Mindy writhed so much I thought she'd squirm off the counter, and when she calmed down, she pulled my hair upward forcing me to stand. "Oh wow," she breathed, but the words were short-lived. I covered her mouth with mine again. letting her taste herself on my lips. She kissed me hard, using her hands to pull my hips deep into her valley where my cock—poking out of my boxers—dipped into her moisture. God I wanted to be in her so badly.

"I'm gonna..." I said, grinding against her. The tip of my dick barely pushed into her and she moaned.

"God, yes... now," she panted, pulling me against her.

I quickly pushed my boxers and slacks down. they fell down to my calves and I didn't even take time to kick them off. She was so eager to have me and my dick so swollen it hurt. I pushed into her with force, sinking my entire length into her in one thrust.

She moaned loudly, her head falling back. Her legs wrapped around my waist, and she threw her arms around me and held me tight.

"Oh Jace," she sighed, her hips bucking against mine. I thrusted into her again, her body lifting off the counter a little bit. "Mmm, yes," she moaned.

"You're so tight," I said, nipping at her neck.

"You're so huge," she gasped, her breathing heavy.

"You like that?"

"Yes," she whimpered. I licked her neck, sucking on it, before returning my lips to her mouth. I kept kissing her as I thrust into her. I was so lost in the moment that I almost forgot about her orgasm.

"Jace," she moaned. I kissed her lips, and she tilted her head back and moaned again. I pulled back and looked into her eyes.

"Come for me," I ordered.

"Jace," she moaned, her hands grabbing my hips. My thrusts began to speed up.

"Come for me," I ordered again. Her eyes fluttered shut and she moaned louder, her insides spasming around me. Her warmth was intoxicating, strong muscles milking me with each spasm of her body. She didn't need to tell me; I knew she was in the throes of climax again.

"Jace, I'm coming!" she moaned. Her orgasm made her writhe against me, her body shaking.

I picked up the pace, fucking her harder and harder. I felt the tingle in my spine, and I felt the warmth in my stomach. I thrust once more, my balls tightening, and I pulled out. A thick, milky stream of cum shot from my cock, splashing onto the cupboard door and running down it. Mindy kept spasming, touching herself to continue her orgasm.

I continued to stroke myself, covering the cupboard with my release. With each stroke, more semen landed on it. She finished her orgasm and leaned against the backsplash behind her, breathing heavily. I stopped stroking myself and took a step back, looking down at her. Her pussy was red from the orgasm and covered with her juices. I wanted to lick her clean.

"My god, you're beautiful," I said.

She avoided eye contact, catching her breath. One tit hung out of her bra, her shirt lying on the counter behind her. I glanced down at the pile of clothing on the floor, thankful I'd been able to direct my release away from it. Then I looked back up at her. She ran a hand through her hair, cheeks flushed with embarrassment. Her eyes were still moist from crying, and I felt a bit confused, elated, and massively drawn to her.

"Look... I ..." I didn't know what to even say to her.

She smiled softly and nodded. "I, uh..." Her face contorted. She was confused too.

"Yeah..."

It was really awkward. Neither of us knew what to say or do. I pulled up my pants and tucked my still-hard dick back inside my boxers and buttoned my fly, and Mindy slid off the counter.

"We should maybe talk about—"

"Yeah—" She cut me off, pulling her shirt back on and starting to button it.

And then I heard the front door jiggle. I glanced at it terrified. Christopher sometimes came home for lunch. "Crap!" I hissed, picking up her pants quickly. She looked at me frantically.

"Expecting someone?" she asked, jumping on one leg while she tried to balance and put the other one into her pants.

"Sometimes Top comes home for lunch. The school has open campus. He knows I'm working from home." I grabbed a hand towel and started wiping the cum from the cupboard door while Mindy wrestled her clothing on.

"Oh god, I'm so sorry, I..."

I wiped up the last of the mess that I could see and tossed the towel into the sink, then turned to her and without warning I grabbed her and pulled her in for a kiss. "Do not be sorry." I stared into her eyes as I heard the keys in the lock, then quickly bent and snatched my shirt. We had seconds to make ourselves look presentable, but that's all it took. I buttoned the last button on my shirt the same time she buttoned her pants and Christopher pushed the door open.

"Home for lunch, Dad!" he called and Mindy turned her back to him.

"So I'll ... uh, I'll see you later? We can talk about the tests..."

"Of course," I said, watching her scurry to the door. I wished we had more time to talk, to discuss what happened. But she was gone faster than she had come—literally. God that was amazing. I had to have her again. Soon. If only I knew what she was thinking.

8

Mindy

I barely made it to the car. Not only were my knees knocking from how amazing that felt, but now my nerves were even worse. I was not a weak, waffling woman who needed a man to take charge, but God did that feel amazing, letting Jace just consume me. I backed out of the driveway with nervous jitters still making my fingers tremble, and it took every bit of focus I had to drive straight. When I stopped at the stop sign at the end of the street I was thankful there was no traffic and no one around to see me. I kept my foot on the break and covered my face.

"What did I just do?" I breathed aloud, feeling regret sink into every cell in my being. I had gone to the Turner home to tell Jace the truth, share the test results, and discuss a path forward. After the lecture I got from Evelyn this morning, I knew I had to do the right thing, but now the right thing was even more complicated.

A horn honked and I looked in my rearview mirror. There was a car behind me I hadn't seen. The driver of the red sedan looked irritated, so I double checked the crossroad and pulled forward. I couldn't go back to work today even if Andrews demanded it. I was a mess, both emotionally and physically. I needed to have a shower and wash the sex off me because I felt so guilty for allowing him to be so amazing to me when I was such trash to him. All I knew is if I didn't talk to someone about this, the guilt would eat me alive, so I used my hands free unit to dial Georgia's number. She picked up as cheery as ever.

"Oh, hey, girl. I was going to call you tonight. Charlie has a base-ball game and Ben can't be there because he has surgery. Want to come? It's Saturday at nine a.m."

"God, Georgia, I'm so screwed." I felt like a horrible friend for ignoring her question but I needed her.

"Oh no, what's wrong?" Her tone immediately changed. I knew I could count on her to comfort me and kick my butt if needed. And I probably needed it.

"I had sex with him," I whined, though she didn't know a single thing about Jace Turner or his son. I hadn't told her anything yet because I felt so ashamed. Now that shame was eating me alive and I needed my best friend to help me find my way out of this jungle of deceit I'd gotten lost in.

"Ummmm, wait. This is news. Had sex with who? What's going on? Aren't you at work?"

I took a deep breath and let it all out. "Okay, so it's a very long story. I'm driving. I don't have emotional energy to go into all the details, but basically, I found my son. The man from the coffee shop with the sick kid... he adopted my baby. I'm treating the kid, and I snuck some blood samples and did a DNA test because I had suspi-cions. And I'm so ridiculously unethical, and I need my best friend to help me so badly. Georgia, I talked to him today about test results and I broke down crying, and he kissed me and we had sex right on his kitchen counter."

"Oh wow..." Based on the tone of voice she used, I could picture her sitting down to take the news in. I knew it was heavy, but she only had half the story. She didn't know I was swimming in guilt and frus-tration over my own stupidity.

"Say something. God, I'm so screwed." I turned to head across town, careful to watch for traffic. This wasn't the sort of conversation I should be having while I drove but I wasn't great at making good decisions recently anyway.

"Okay, so he knows you're the mother? And he had sex with you. That's not so bad..."

Her logic would have made sense if he knew, but he didn't know. "No, I haven't told him. I—"

"Oh god, Mindy." I heard the disappointment in her voice and shrank into myself. "You need to tell him, and you need to do it very soon."

I bit my lip, knowing she was right. I did need to tell him, if for no other reason than to clear my conscience because this was starting to affect my mental health more than I wanted to admit. I wasn't sleeping well. I wasn't eating right, and people at work thought I was being snappy with them.

"God, what am I going to do?" I turned again, a little closer to home and my shower and a bit of relief. At least I could curl up in bed and pretend the world didn't exist for a while.

"You are going to call him and tell him. Own up to it, Mindy." Georgia used a firm tone with me and I knew it was because she really cared. "Take it from me. Keeping a secret is a torture all its own. Unburden yourself and maybe it won't be as bad as you think."

"As bad as I think?" I groaned. "I could lose my job."

She sighed and said, "Yeah, that's pretty bad."

Just a few blocks left and I didn't really feel any better. "Okay, I'm almost home. I just need time to think about things I guess. Call me later, okay?"

"Yeah, sure. I care about you, girl."

"Love you too, Geo..." I reached out to touch the end call button but she ended it first. And as I glanced at my phone I saw Evelyn's caller ID image flash on my screen before the car's radio speakers started chiming with my ringtone. I scowled at it. I didn't need another lecture right now. Not after what just happened. I pressed the decline call button and put my hand back on the wheel. She could leave her disappointment with me in a voicemail.

I turned into my apartment complex and found a parking spot, and as I shut the car off my phone chimed with Evelyn's message. I shoved it into my pocket and collected my things. I just wanted to get inside and hide from my guilt even though I knew there was no hiding from it. Beating myself up wasn't making me feel better either. I knew the only way to feel better was to do exactly what Georgia told me to do—fess up, but fear of losing Christopher again after I'd just found him paralyzed me.

I let myself into my apartment and dumped my things on the table, locking the door behind me. I went straight for a bag of chips and a soda, my go-to snack when I felt miserable, and sat down on the couch. The message left on my voicemail by Evelyn haunted me though, needling at my conscience until I couldn't take it. I crunched some chips in my mouth while I pulled my phone out and opened the voice mail to listen.

"Hey, Min, it's Eve. Look, I'm really sorry if I upset you this morning. I wasn't trying to. You know I really care about you. I didn't mean to go off like that. I'm worried, girl. You could lose everything over this. And I'm worried I'll take a hit too. I'm trying to be a good friend here. You need to refer that kid to someone else and tell Andrews what you did before that dad files a lawsuit. Okay? Look, if you need to talk I'm here."

The line beeped and the voicemail started to play over again. My heart sank. Evelyn was such an amazing friend, and she was only looking out for me. She just didn't understand how complicated this all was and how afraid I was. So afraid I almost called my mother to talk to her about it, but I knew better than that. So I called Violet instead. My younger sister might have been only twenty-one, but she knew our family dynamic better than anyone else. And my heart as well.

"Hey, Min! What's up?" Violet's sweet voice was instant comfort.

"I'm not feeling so hot." I munched on chips as I talked, a bad habit of mine, but I knew Violet would understand something was wrong immediately. How many times had I called her to vent, or sat on the foot of her bed to unload my emotions? We were inseparable.

"Oooof," she said, her trademark expression of sympathy. "Tell me everything. What has you emotional eating?"

I felt tears welling up as I chewed. My mouth was so dry the chips stuck to my tongue. I slurped a drink of soda and sniffled, clearing my throat before speaking. I poured out my heart, telling her everything —the chance meeting with Christopher and Jace, how I snapped at Mom and Dad at lunch that day, the DNA test, the sex. When I got done with my emotional purge I was drained. I had nothing left in me. I set the chips on the coffee table and lay down on the couch.

"That's heavy, hun."

"I know," I moaned. My entire body felt exhausted, like I'd just run a marathon.

"What do you want to happen?" Her question struck me. Unlike Georgia and Evelyn, Violet watched me walk through the pain of losing my baby. She was there when I didn't eat for weeks on end, when I didn't get out of bed for a month, when I didn't shower for days. She knew how much I wanted to keep my baby despite the social pressure and the fact that his father left and refused to submit to a DNA test. She wanted me to have peace. I knew that.

"I want him, Vi. I want my little boy, but I don't want to take him from his dad. He already lost his adoptive mother." Saying the words out loud made it feel more real, so I continued. "I want to not lose my job. I want to not feel afraid or sad. I want to not be angry with Mom and Dad anymore."

"Then what do you think you should do to make that happen?" She was calm, attentive, patient even. Her sweet demeanor calmed me, and even though I knew the answer was the same now as when Evelyn and Georgia had both told me, somehow I felt different saying it out loud to her.

"I need to tell him. It's the only way forward." Swiping at some fresh tears, I sniffled and closed my eyes.

"Yeah...." She sighed and said, "Mom and Dad are pretty worked up over your comment. I know there is some animosity there still, but the only way to find the healing you need is to do as Hashem instructs us. I know you're not really active in the synagogue or anything, I'm not really either. I just think you should apply that wisdom. Forgiveness opens doors to your heart that you keep locked and guarded by anger."

I rolled my eyes and shook my head. Violet was the last person I thought would ever bring religion into this situation. I expected that from my parents who served at the synagogue regularly, but not my sister. I wanted to protest, but I knew she was right. Even if I wasn't a hardcore zealot, I knew Torah instructed people to offer mercy and forgiveness, and that it was a means to healing. I had harbored this resentment for far too long. I wanted freedom from my own bitterness.

"Come to lunch next week?" she asked, and I heard the hope in her voice. "It will go a long way toward getting things back on track. Maybe with Papa's help you can work this out with Christopher's dad and be a part of his life."

"I doubt it," I grunted, turning onto my back. I knew my cynicism probably upset her and it came from a place of bitterness, but I also knew my father. He would never support me in this.

"Just come. Please. They're miserable to be around right now."

I almost growled in frustration. This was my fault and she was suffering because of me. "Fine. If they ask, I'll come. But only because I don't want you to have to bear the brunt of my mistakes again."

"I love you, Min."

"Love you too, Vi."

I hung up and dropped my phone on the floor. Sometimes doing the right thing means doing the hard thing. I hated my life right now and it was only going to get worse before it got better. The only thing I could do is wade through the storm and pray Hashem offered me the same forgiveness he expected me to offer my parents.

9

Jace

I pulled up to the school and put the car in park. Christopher was eager to jump out of the car and get into the building to be with his friends for the school day. He planned to sleep over with a friend tonight, and I had given him a cell phone that I kept for just such an occasion. He was excited to show his friends and also for the sleepover.

"Remember not to take that out in class. Your teacher will give you a detention if she sees that."

"Dad, I know the rules. I'll just show them in the hallway and I'll keep it in my backpack in my locker the rest of the day."

I tousled his hair and smiled at him. He was growing up so quickly and I was so glad that we finally had an end in sight to all of this pain that he had been going through. After the nurses called me earlier this week to schedule an appointment with Dr. Scriber to start the capsule endoscopy, I had wrestled with feelings of rejection and mild insecurity. Mindy and I having sex on my kitchen counter wasn't something that I had planned, and it happened so quickly neither one of us had a moment to react. We hadn't spoken since the event, and I had no idea what she was thinking.

"Remember to call me once you're at Danny's house, okay? And I want you to have a good weekend."

He sat with his hand on the door handle ready to open it, but I saw some hesitancy in his eyes. "Dad?"

"Yeah, Top?"

"What's that test supposed to be like on Monday?" His eyes searched me for a moment. I could see he was nervous.

"Well, it's super simple. You're just going to swallow a tiny pill that has a camera in it and we monitor the little recording machine to make sure it's working and come back in a few days." He still looked concerned so I continued. "I mean, Sunday you'll have to drink some gross stuff and you probably won't like it. And you can't really eat anything until Monday night, but we can get whatever you want to eat."

His head dropped and so did his hand. I saw him wilt like a neglected plant. "What is it looking for?"

It was difficult for me to explain it to him because I didn't really know. I wished Mindy was here because she'd know exactly what to say. In fact, she'd even know how to comfort his emotions better than me. She had a maternal side even Connie didn't have. It was a shame that she had no children yet. If she did, they'd have the most amazing mother on the planet.

"Well, the doctors will use it to look for clues of what's wrong. And with those clues, just like a detective hunts a criminal, they'll find out what's wrong. Then we'll know if you need medicine, or just to change your diet."

"Surgery?" he asked, looking up at me in fear again.

Mindy never expressed a potential for surgery so I didn't know what to tell him. I did the only thing I could do. "I hope not, and I don't think so, but if so, I'll be right by your side. Okay, bud?"

"Yeah, Dad." He reached for the door again and opened it. "See you tomorrow."

"See ya, kiddo."

He popped out of the car and slammed the door, then raced toward the school where his friends were waiting for him with smiles. I watched for a second before pulling away and got lost in thought as I headed for the office. I found it strange how even in mundane conversations I now thought of Mindy. It had been this way all week long, me being so distracted by thoughts of her that I was less productive at work, less attentive in conversations and always checking my phone to see if she responded to any of my myriad messages I'd left her, both voicemail and text.

When Wednesday rolled around and she hadn't responded, I gave her space. What happened did so very suddenly and it took us both by surprise. If Christopher hadn't come home I wasn't sure what I would have even said to her, or her to me for that matter. And if my guilt about being a good father to Christopher in his grieving process wasn't bad enough, I had buried myself now. He was too young to know the details of how this relationship might or might not be developing, but I knew how he felt about it. He wasn't ready for a new Mom, but I was.

At the office, I hid myself away behind a locked door, hoping Howard left me alone to brood over the apparent rejection. The more time that passed without speaking to her directly, the more I became convinced that she thought it was a mistake and wanted distance. And that thought made me regret having even made the first move. Not only had I done something I knew would likely upset my son, but it had meant nothing, or at least it seemed that way. It made me feel guilty again, that I had tarnished Connie's memory by having a fling, when she had been such a treasure to me. Now I felt like I cheated on her and broke my son's heart in the process.

I spent the majority of the day agonizing over fine details in our new contracts but I was still unable to focus. I read part of the twenty-page agreement at least ten times before I realized I was probably making mistakes. I yoyoed between knowing I should give Mindy space and having strong urges to just show up at the office. I needed to know what was going on because not knowing was killing me. If she was actually rejecting me and putting space between us, at least

I'd know. But maybe she was just under the weather too. She said she had the same thing she thought Christopher had, and what If she was sick? What if I could be nursing her and helping her feel better the way I did him?

I couldn't stand it anymore. I glanced at the clock and decided I had to have an answer. If she wanted space I'd give it, but she had to tell me that, not just ghost me. I stood and picked up my keys, wallet, and cell and headed out to my car. I got a few confused looks from staffers, and when I walked past Howard's office he gestured wildly for me to come to him, but he was on a call so I pretended to not see him. If I was going to make it to Mindy's office before she left— assuming she was there—I had to hurry.

Traffic was light and I was thankful. I made it with ten minutes to spare, so I got out of my car and leaned against the back end, one leg crossed over the other, hands folded in front of myself. I watched a few patients leave; the parking lot on this side of the hospital grew emptier by the second. A few nurses walked out chatting with each other and my anticipation swelled. There were three cars left, mine and two others. A stout woman with an arm full of files waddled past me, nodding as she did, and then it was just my car and one more.

The probability that it was Mindy's car was both very high and sort of low. If she had come to work today, it was definitely her car. She hadn't left yet and there were no cars left to drive away. But if she was sick, then I had no clue how to find her. I didn't know where she lived. I waited with bated breath, my eyes glued to the door. After another fifteen minutes of standing there I almost gave up and went home, thinking the car was abandoned by someone else for the night, but movement in the entryway sparked my pulse to race.

Mindy walked out with her purse and keys in hand, and turned her back on me as she locked the office door. My entire body was on fire. I wanted to run over to her and bombard her with questions, but I restrained myself. I didn't want to seem too eager or come across as desperate. But I was desperate—to know how she felt, to find out if I had a chance with her. And there was a war going on inside my mind, because it had been so long since I wanted someone like this, wanted something for myself, but I felt what I was doing was wrong maybe, or at the very least hurtful to people around me. People I loved.

"Jace?" she asked as she turned around. She glanced around the empty parking lot intended for staff of the internal medicine office and patients who came from outside the hospital. "What are you doing here?" She looked stunning even in her blue scrubs and lab coat.

I shrugged and offered a calm expression, though I felt so much emotion roiling through my body. "I called and texted, but you didn't answer."

She moved toward me, studying me carefully. Her expression fell a little; she looked worried or scared, sad maybe. I couldn't read her. "I'm sorry, the week has been so hectic..." I wished to god I was better at reading people because I couldn't tell if that was an excuse or a brush off, or if she had really been under stress.

"Would you like to have dinner with me? My treat." I offered that last tidbit because these days women liked to do things themselves. I wanted her to know I was old fashioned in that regard.

She glanced at her car and sighed, her shoulders dropping. "I'm really not in the mood for being in public tonight."

Rejection—I knew it. My heart sank. "I totally understand. Would you like me to walk you to your car?"

Mindy raked a hand through her chestnut waves and nodded. "Yeah, that would be nice."

We walked slowly. Her car was parked at the back of the lot, so we had a minute or two. She was quiet and I let her have space to process whatever it was she was thinking. When she spoke up I listened.

"So I don't really get along with my parents very well and I have to have dinner with them and my sister tomorrow. It's just put me in a mood. I hope you understand." Mindy squeezed the strap of her purse and watched the ground in front of her while she walked.

"Yeah, no, I totally get it." So there was a valid reason for her turning me down. I could physically feel the emotion she was carrying like sharp pain in my chest. Only one other woman had ever done that to me—moved my heart like that. "Is everything okay?"

We stopped by her car and she stopped and faced me. "You know, I don't know. It's just messy and confusing." Her head dropped as she pushed the key fob unlock button. "Honestly, I could use a good friend to talk to, someone who is objective." Her chin rose and she looked at me through veiled lashes. When she blinked slowly, I got the feeling she was inviting me to be that friend, and friendzone is closer than flat-out rejection.

"Do you need to talk?" I asked, hesitantly. I didn't want to pressure her.

"Yeah. Want to follow me to my place?"

My heart thumped hard, palpitating in my chest. I thought I'd choke on my own words as I said, "Uh, yeah, sure." She was inviting me to her place, and now I had to figure out if that meant more than friendship or if I'd end up drying the tears of a woman I'd never get to enjoy again.

God, I prayed it was the former. And I hoped I had a condom in my wallet if it was.

10

Mindy

I waited at the door to the building while Jace parked and made his way toward me. I thought I'd done a decent job all week of avoiding a conversation with him. I never expected him to show up at the office and surprise me. My ethical dilemma had become nothing but a fight to keep my raging hormones in check when he kissed me—a fight I clearly lost. A fight that started immediately the instant I saw him waiting by his car. He was so hot, I didn't think I could control myself at all anymore.

"This is a nice little complex," he said as he walked up to me.

"Yeah, it's new, just opened last year. I was on the waitlist as they were building it." I used my key to let us in and led him to my place, 1A. Having a first-floor place had its perks though security wasn't as great. But the rent was low and I didn't have to bother with maintenance and repairs like a homeowner.

I let us into my little two-bedroom unit and left my purse and keys on the table. I was tired and I felt awkward wearing my scrubs with Jace here, but I didn't want to leave him waiting while I changed. He shut the door behind us and I gestured at the kitchen.

"Want a drink?" I asked, nervous. I had some milk, a few diet sodas and a bottle of wine. My fridge was practically bare. I never spent enough time here to use the stove really, since I mostly ate hospital food.

"Have any beer?" he asked, setting his own keys next to mine. He glanced around the small space but I didn't detect any hint of discomfort. My standard of living was way below his, but not for lack of money. I just liked to live frugally. Why spend a heap on a giant apartment when I could bank that money and save for a future?

"Wine?" I said, turning to the cupboard where I kept my stemware.

"Sounds perfect." He rubbed his palms together while I collected the wine and glasses, then we headed for the couch to sit. He took the wine bottle from me and opened it and poured some in each glass. When he handed me one, I nodded and sat. He sat too, facing me with one arm stretched over the back of the couch. He was close enough his fingers could brush my shoulder if he wanted, but he didn't. "So tell me what's going on."

He took a sip and I did too. Talking to Jace about my family troubles felt too intimate. True, we'd had sex which was way more intimate, but other than Christopher's medical issues and the fact that Jace was a widower, I knew practically nothing about him. I started to regret telling him I needed to talk, because I wasn't thinking of talking to him at all right now. I was thinking about how incredible his dick felt when he pushed into me. It had been so long since I'd had sex, I forgot how amazing it felt.

"Well, it's just that, when I was a kid, my parents hurt me pretty badly." I sipped again, trying to hide the blush on my cheeks. I could feel it, but I hoped he didn't see it.

Somehow I had to segue into telling him about my pregnancy, the forced adoption and then Christopher. It was my chance to—as Violet said—unburden myself. I had to take it. Especially if I had any chance of being in Christopher's life from now on. Even if it meant this strange thing with Jace was over. I tried to rationalize that he was way older than me and that it would never work out anyway, but I just felt so attracted to him.

"Go on..." He was so patient. He set his glass on the coffee table and scooted closer, as if he wanted to hear me better. His knee touched mine and a sizzle of electricity shot through my body. I was being aroused by him, which was not a good thing at all. The sex was amazing but I needed to get this off my chest.

"So I just don't have a good time at family dinners. I have so much anger and resentment built up. Seeing Christopher just brought it all up again." My throat constricted. I could just tell him and it would be over. I had to tell him.

"Was it about your condition? The one you think Chris has? Did something happen?"

"No." I shook my head. He was getting the wrong idea. "Because Chris is adopted." I took a deep breath and braced myself as I continued. "I was sixteen years old and I made a poor choice to do some experimenting with my boyfriend at the time. I got pregnant." Tears welled up. I couldn't finish. The pain felt as fresh now as it was then. I started crying so hard I almost spilled my wine.

Jace took the glass out of my hand and set it on the table, then pulled me into his arms. "I get it, Mindy. They made you give your baby away. What an awful thing to do to someone." He pulled so hard I had no choice but to sit on his lap wrapped in his strong arms. His hands smoothed down my back, but even through the scrubs and the lab coat, I felt how hot they were. I wanted that heat on my skin the way it was earlier this week. "Everyone looks at their parents and thinks how things could have been different or better. You're not a bad person for being upset. Okay? It was probably a horrible situation for everyone."

I sniffled and blubbed a bit and then looked up at him. I knew he was trying to comfort me, but all I wanted was for him to read my thoughts so I didn't have to confess the real truth of why I was crying. But instead of him reading my mind, his eyes darted to my lips, then my eyes again. I swallowed hard as my body responded to the look.

He wanted to kiss me and he was asking for permission. God, I was so confused. I wanted that too, but I needed him to know the truth.

"Jace, I..." I looked at his lips too, lost in the moment as a surge of hormones took over.

He kissed me softly at first, then more deeply. I didn't initiate this but I sure as heck wasn't telling him no, not after the way he made me feel before.

As his lips moved over mine, my hands tangled in his hair, pulling him closer. He deepened the kiss, and I felt his tongue brush against my lips, asking for entrance. I opened my mouth, and he explored every inch of it with his tongue, eliciting a moan from deep within my throat. He pulled away for a moment, panting. "God, I've wanted to do that all week," he whispered, his breath hot against my face.

I smiled, my heart racing. "Me too."

He pulled me in for another kiss, this one more urgent than the last. His hands roamed over my body, pulling at my clothes until they were nothing but a pile on the floor. I straddled him, naked and vulnerable but also completely at ease. The only thing separating us was his clothing and the massive secret I harbored which I tried to push to the back of my mind.

Jace's hands roamed all over my body, eliciting shivers of pleasure with every touch. I pressed my body closer to him, wanting to feel every inch of him against me. His lips trailed down to my neck, nipping and sucking at the sensitive skin there. I moaned, arching my back as his hands slipped between my thighs.

He teased me with his fingers, circling my clit before dipping them inside me. I gasped, my head falling back as he worked me with his skilled fingers. I wanted him so badly, but I couldn't forget the secret that weighed heavily on my mind. It tried to act like a barrier to my satisfaction, but he pushed a few fingers into me and I forgot about anything except the sensations in my groin.

I gasped, my hips bucking against his fingers. I wanted more, and I wanted it now. I slipped him out and slid down his body until I was on my knees and he rose to his feet. I took his pants off, dropping them to the floor. He stood before me, hard and ready. I stroked him slowly, letting my fingers run up and down his length until he was covered with a thin film of pre-cum. I licked my lips, my mouth watering. I had been craving him for days.

I opened my mouth and took him inside, sucking him off while his hands wound their way into my hair. He moaned softly, thrusting gently into my mouth. I couldn't believe I was doing this, but I didn't want to stop. I stroked his shaft with one hand while I sucked him with the other. He groaned, thrusting harder as I took him deeper into my mouth.

When he pulled me up and kissed me hard, I whimpered with desire. "Lie down," he ordered and I was his slave to do whatever he wanted. I lay down on the couch, and let my knees fall wide as he stripped his shoes, pants, and boxers off. My fingers found my soft folds while he pulled his shirt over his head, and when he knelt on the floor and lowered his face to my mound, I shuddered.

My eyes rolled into the back of my head as he licked my pussy, tasting me. I whimpered and arched my back as his lips moved to my clit. He sucked it into his mouth, and swirled his tongue around it. So, I made a soft sound of pleasure, and bucked my hips against his mouth. He sucked and licked at my clit, his tongue darting in and out of my slit. I moaned, and tangled my hands in his hair as he licked and sucked at me.

I cried out when he slid a finger into me, my hips arching as he stroked me. He added another finger, curling them inside me. I gasped and writhed as he worked me with his fingers; his tongue circled my clit while he did.

He sucked at my clit, stroking me with his fingers until I was shaking and moaning, my hips bucking against his face.

"Oh, oh, oh," I moaned. "Oh!"

"Come for me," he moaned, flicking his tongue against my clit. "Come for me."

"I'm coming," I whimpered, my hips grinding against his hand. My whole body shook and spasmed, and I clenched around his fingers hard. "Oh god, Jace..."

"That's it," he groaned, and as my orgasm subsided he crawled over me, settling his body between my thighs. He leaned down and captured my lips with his, kissing me hard. He reached down between us, and I whimpered as I felt the tip of his cock press against me. His cock slid inside me slowly, and I moaned into his mouth as he stretched me around him. I arched my hips, pressing against him, and he slid all the way inside me.

"Oh god," I moaned, and he kissed me again. He held still, letting me get used to his cock inside me. My hips rose up to meet him, and I moaned softly as I started rocking against him. He slid his hands under my ass, and lifted me off the couch slightly, thrusting into me.

We rocked together, grinding against each other. He groaned as he slid in and out of me then back in, filling me up. I came again, hard and fast, and I cried out as he thrust into me. I felt his cock pulse and twitch inside me, and he groaned my name. He thrust into me harder, and I knew he was close.

I had just the smallest presence of mind to whisper, "Condom."

"Oh god," he growled, and I knew he didn't want to stop. I'd already had my fill, two orgasms and a very tired vagina. I pushed on his shoulders.

"I'll suck you." I tapped his chest and he got the point, pulling out. He stood quickly and I took him in.

Jace's explosion in my mouth was salty and hot. I swallowed and swallowed, gulping down his cum, and he groaned. His fingers wound through my hair and I felt his cock relax, the pulsing in it slowly dying down. When I backed away and licked the tip of it, he jolted and pushed my head gently, then grinned.

"That was intense."

"Yes," I snickered. "It was." I looked up at him and felt so ashamed that I'd let my urges get the better of me again. I was supposed to be confessing to the lie, not having incredible, pussy-melting sex. He had to stay here until I built up the courage to tell him. "Stay the night?" I asked, and stood to my feet next to him.

"Only if we can do that again like twelve times.... Do you have condoms?" He kissed me and I tasted myself on his lips. I was in so much trouble.

"A few," I mumbled. This was going to be a long night.

11

Jace

The sun was beating down on my back when I woke up. The sheer curtains did nothing to block the heat either, so I lay here sweating slightly. It wasn't just from the sunrise either. Mindy wrapped in my arms was just about the most amazing feeling I'd had in decades. I kissed the back of her shoulder and felt my own hot breath ripple between our bodies. She had totally shocked me by inviting me to her house, and even more so when she allowed me to kiss her.

Our post-sex conversation about her parents' refusal to let her keep her child turned into a near therapy session as she unloaded a decade's worth of pain and depression. I poured her more wine, and when she exhausted herself, I held her until we both fell asleep. To my knowledge I hadn't even turned over once. I held her the entire night.

I missed the feeling of a woman in my arms, especially in bed waking up to one. Constance wasn't as much of a cuddler as I was, but she enjoyed being held until she fell asleep each night. Her death was so sudden and it tore my heart out. We had spent so many years together, planned our future, the fact that we wanted to grow old together. I wondered if she would be upset by how quickly I was moving on, or if she would move on at the same pace.

Mindy stirred, mumbling something. Her arm pushed mine away and she whimpered, then I heard her say, "No, please. You don un... stand." The words were slurred and mumbled, but I knew she was upset. She was likely having a nightmare or bad dream. I wanted to wake her and get her out of the pain, but I heard it's not smart to wake someone when their brain is processing a bad dream like that, so I gave her a little space, though I did keep holding her.

She rolled to her back, and I saw tears trickle out of the corner of her eye. I kissed her forehead gently. My heart ached for her, as she mumbled more words, this time completely unintelligible. In fact, I'd have done anything in that moment to make her pain stop, even if it became my pain and I had to carry it the rest of my life. I used the tip of my pinky finger to push some hair off her face and watched her face contort. I was falling hard for her.

Mindy turned to face me, and her eyes slowly blinked open. She looked dazed for a moment, but when I pulled her against my body she relaxed and offered a half smile. "Good morning," she mumbled as I kissed Mindy's forehead.

"Morning..." I woke up with morning wood, but hearing her sweet voice made it a true erection. I felt it swelling and stretching, and it was squeezed between our bodies, resting on her thigh.

"Sleep well, Jace?" she asked, readjusting herself in bed, which left a small amount of space for her to squeeze her hand between us. She gripped my cock and squeezed it, slowly stroking.

"Yeah," I said, smirking. "Had a good dream too."

"Want to tell me about it?" Her eyes blinked slowly; she was still tired, but I liked that she was being playful.

"Sure I do. I dreamt there was the most amazing, incredible, beautiful woman in my bed and we screwed like horny teenagers. And then I made her breakfast in bed."

Her eyebrows rose and she stroked me more firmly. "You did, huh? Well this isn't your bed."

"Guess you're cooking breakfast then," I joked, leaning down to kiss her. "But the horny teenager part... We're doing that. Right?"

"Obviously," she said, kissing me back. She nipped at my lower lip and grinned against my mouth, and I rolled on top of her. She wrapped her arms and legs around me, and I was suddenly thankful that it was a Saturday. I kissed her hard and deep, pressing myself against her, and I felt her respond, arching her hips to meet me.

Her breasts were full and high – not too big, but not too small. I worshiped them with my eyes, and then with my lips, and she sighed happily at the attention. I licked and sucked on each nipple, teasing and pinching them. She panted, breathing harder, and she ran her fingers through my hair. "You're so good at this," she whispered, her voice tight with pleasure. She reached down to stroke me again, and I groaned, pressing myself against her hand. I was throbbing, hard and huge, and I was ready to slide up her body and enter her, but she pushed me away slightly.

"Condom?" she asked, breathlessly. Before we fell asleep, she found a few she had lying around stashed in her medicine cabinet and put them on the nightstand.

"I'll get it when I'm ready. I have a few things to do first." I winked at her as I backed away, pulling my cock out of her grip. I kissed down her torso, nipping at ner skin as my mouth left a wet trail of kisses across her tummy.

"Oh, God," she moaned, and I grinned to myself. I kissed down her thigh, nipping and sucking as I went, and she shivered. "What are you doing?" she asked, her voice slightly shaky.

"Oh, you know. I'm just seeing how long it takes for you to scream when I give you what you want," I teased.

"Jace!" Mindy stroked my hair, and I gave her thigh a playful slap as I returned to my fun. I teased her inner thighs gently, and then I nipped at her outer lips, and she shivered and arched her hips up to meet me. I took my time, kissing her gently, but her legs were shaking, and I could tell she wanted me to eat her so badly. I slipped a finger inside her, and she moaned, "Oh, Jace."

She was so wet, and it was so easy to slide my fingers in and out of her. I put my head between her legs, and licked her gently, and she shivered. "Jace."

"You like that?" I asked, and she groaned in response. I licked and sucked on her gently, but it wasn't enough. I needed to really taste her —to make her come.

"Jace," she moaned, and I slid my fingers inside her again, stroking her hard and fast. I could feel her body tensing, and I knew she was close. I reached up, and pinched her nipples, and she moaned. "Oh, God, Jace," she said loudly, and I felt her body clench around my fingers. I removed them, and she moaned again, louder, as her body shuddered. I slipped my fingers into my mouth, tasting her, and she moaned, watching me. I licked her juices off my fingers, and she shuddered again before her orgasm subsided.

"God, Jace, you're so hot," she said, her voice trembling. I smiled, and she shuddered again. "You have to get in me now."

"Oh, really?" I asked, again my voice filled with mock disbelief. "You're going to make me?"

"You know what I mean," she said, her voice breathy. "Please."

I smirked at her as I crawled up over her and reached for a condom. Mindy kissed my chest and ran her hands across my skin and around my sides. She whimpered when I straightened and pulled away from her so I could tear the condom open and roll it on. Her eyes took in every single inch of me and she licked her lips.

"Please, Jace," she said again. "I need you."

I positioned myself between her legs and slid my hands under her backside so I could pull her closer to me. She moaned, looking up at me as I held her and slowly entered her. "Mindy," I gasped as I felt her around me. "You're so tight."

She moaned, and I lowered my head to kiss her, and as I did, I thrust into her completely. She gasped into my mouth, and I grunted as I held her tightly and pushed into her again. "Oh," she gasped, and her eyes widened. I could tell she was unused to the feeling of being filled so completely.

I slid my hands up her back and into her hair, pulling her head back slightly to expose the column of her throat as I thrust into her again. I licked and sucked on her neck as I did, and her body shuddered. "Oh, God," she moaned.

"Do you like that?" I asked, my voice deep. "Do you like it when I move inside you?"

"Jesus," she moaned, and her eyes rolled back in her head. I could tell she was close again, so I moved my hands from her hair to her breasts, and I pinched her nipples.

"Jace," she moaned, her voice rising higher. "Oh, please."

I increased the speed of my thrusts as I continued to pinch and roll her nipples. "Oh my pussy, Jace," she cried out, and then she was crying out my name as she came. I let go of her breasts and wrapped my arms around her, thrusting into her with enough force that she was lifted off the bed a little with each stroke. I groaned as I felt the muscles of her pussy contracting around me, and I reached between us to rub my thumb across her clit. Her orgasm intensified, and her nails dug into my back.

"Jace," she cried out, her voice high-pitched. "Oh, God, Jace."

My orgasm hit me hard, and I thrust into her one more time as I held her close. It went on forever, and I closed my eyes and groaned as I felt her body racked with the aftershocks of her climax. I felt her melt into the bed, limp and completely unable to move. I could feel her heart pounding against my chest, and her breath was coming in fast pants against my skin. "Jesus," she groaned. "That was incredible."

I chuckled, and I pulled out of her slowly, rolled us over and pulled the condom off. I tossed it toward a trash can by the bed and nearly missed, then turned back to hold her again. She snuggled into my chest.

Mindy sighed, then kissed my skin softly. "What is actually going on here? I mean, what is this?"

I pulled her tighter against me and kissed her sweat-slicked forehead. "What do you mean?"

"I mean, is this just sex or do you like me? Because this took me completely by surprise, and honestly I'm in the middle of a huge ethics violation and—"

"Woah... I can appreciate that you were surprised. I was shocked that I felt so drawn to you too. My wife only died two years ago. Topper is pretty hesitant to move on and see me dating. I just know when I'm around you I feel happy. I feel better. And I am really certain that I like you a lot."

Mindy looked up at me and I saw the hesitation in her eyes again. It was like she was holding something back from me, something she wanted to tell me but she was afraid. She licked her lip and said, "You aren't telling me something."

My chest tightened. She was right. I wasn't, but I knew she wasn't either. I took a deep cleansing breath and decided if this was the beginning of a relationship, I had to be the leader in being honest and transparent. Maybe if I opened up to her, she'd open up to me because she'd feel safe.

"I feel like a criminal caught red handed. Guilt is eating away at me because I'm afraid maybe I'm moving on too quickly and that my wife would be hurt by this." I kissed her again, then asked, "Is there something you're not telling me?"

Her countenance fell, her eyebrows drawing in, and she opened her mouth to speak when I heard my phone going off. I listened carefully for a split second and knew it was the ringtone I had set up for the phone Christopher carried. "One sec," I told her, throwing the covers back. The phone was still in my pants pocket on the floor by the couch. I barely heard the thing chirp.

I raced out to the living room and dug into my pocket and answered it after the fifth ring. "Hey, bud, what's up?"

"Mr. Turner, this is Marie Gregor. Christopher isn't feeling well this morning. He asked me to call you and see if you can pick him up. He said he's not contagious but—"

"Hey, Marie, no he's not contagious at all. It's a condition we believe is called Crohn's disease. He's being tested for it right now. Do me a favor. Get a hot water bottle or a heating pad and have him put it on his belly. I'll be there as fast as I can. I'm about a twenty-minute drive away, okay?"

"Of course. I'll take care of him."

I hung up the call and picked up my boxers and climbed into them as quickly as I could. Seconds later, Mindy emerged from the bedroom tying the belt of her robe around her waist. She looked concerned.

"It's Christopher. He's sick again. I have to go get him." I jammed my feet into the pant legs of the slacks I wore last night and then crammed them into my shoes, sockless.

"Oh gosh, did you get that slippery elm like I told you?" she asked, moving closer. I could see the pain in her eyes.

"I did, but he didn't like it." My shirt was wrinkled so badly, but I had nothing else to wear. I slid my arms in and fumbled with the buttons but she was there, pushing my fingers away. She deftly buttoned the shirt while I raked a hand through my hair. "I'm so sorry."

"No, he needs you. You go be a dad, okay? Just add some honey and lemon to the tea. He'll love it. Make him drink it even if he doesn't. It will calm the flare up." Her hand smoothed down the front of my chest and I kissed her forehead.

"Alright. I'll call you later. I love you," I told her, as I turned and bounded toward the door. I didn't even realize what I was saying until I was out and the door was shut. I told her I loved her? But it wasn't wrong.

I paused in the hallway for a second and felt a stupid grin starting on my face, then realized that was something I'd have done with Connie before she died. Just that fast, guilt squashed my joy again, and I didn't even have time to psychoanalyze my thoughts. I was all the way to the car before I realized I left my keys on her table and felt dread at the thought of returning after my Freudian slip.

When I looked up at the building, she stood in the doorway dangling the key from her finger. I felt my cheeks flush and I dashed up to collect them. "We need to talk. But you need to take care of your boy.... Have a good day. Call me if you need me."

"Thank you," I pecked her on the lips and raced to my car.

What had I gotten myself into?

12

Mindy

The hot water had already steamed up the entire bathroom and I hadn't even finished washing my hair. After Jace left I sulked around the house wishing I'd have had the nerve to tell him everything. I thought we were headed toward that discussion following sex this morning, but when Christopher called I knew that was more important, so yet again, we were interrupted. Now I just wanted to wash the sex off my body so I didn't reek of it when I sat across the table from my parents.

Jace had been so comforting to me, talking me through some of the pains of my past, and he didn't even realize how connected we were. That connection grew stronger in me every time we talked, and I didn't know if I wanted it, or if it was right. I felt like my life was a soap opera just waiting to be written and cast. To find my son after twelve years of separation, only to have a fling with his adoptive father and make things messier—definitely TV drama material.

I rinsed off and shut off the water, climbing out of the shower to dry off. At least Violet would be at Mom and Dad's house today to help keep the tensions low. I didn't feel like I needed to apologize for what I said, but maybe perhaps for the way I had said it. I heard once that ninety percent of arguments are caused not by what someone says, but by the way they say it. Of that I was guilty, my snarky, sassy tone.

I piddled around the house a bit getting ready, wasting time. I wanted Vi to be there before me, so I got ready as slowly as I could and left when I knew I had exactly the right amount of time to drive across town to their house. I even took the long way and hoped for traffic, but for a Saturday at lunch, it was fairly calm. When I pulled up out front, I noticed Violet walking into the house, so at least my objective to arrive after she was already here worked out.

I slunk into the house, this time leaving everything but my keys in the car. These things were always tense. If I felt emotionally over-whelmed and decided I needed to leave quickly, having fewer things to carry would be better.

Mom welcomed me at the front door and kissed my cheek like normal, but she didn't say much. I followed her into the dining room. The table was already set with a nice floral cloth and the good China, like always. The only thing that changed was the color of the table-cloth. Dad sat at the head of the table in his spot, a stern expression on his face. He barely acknowledged my appearance.

"Hey, Dad." I wiggled my fingers and sat down next to Violet who was busy on her phone. She glanced up at me as Dad nodded curtly and then looked to my mother, who bustled around the table filling plates with a half smile on her face. I could tell things were tense between them; maybe they'd argued before I came. Violet wasn't kidding when she said things were challenging.

"Look, Mom. I'm sorry I snapped at you before. I should have handled myself better. I know you both only want what's best for me." I wished the chair would open its jowls and swallow me whole. If anyone deserved an apology it was me, for putting up with them and the way they controlled my life.

"Water under a bridge, dear." Mom, finished with serving, sat at her spot and smiled at me, this time a genuine show of happiness. "Let's eat."

Dad grunted then glanced at the table. Next to Violet sat a box of cupcakes, still sealed. He raised his chin and asked her, "Are those Kosher?"

Violet put her phone down and nodded. "Yes, Papa. I made sure they are. I got them at the little bakery on tenth street. They have a Kosher kitchen to serve Hudson's Jewish community."

While most of the halakhic tradition had gone out the window during our family meals—since Violet and I didn't really practice it anymore—Dad was still a staunch believer in certain things. He'd never eat anything that wasn't Kosher, and he still followed every one of his traditions at every other meal he ate, even if it was just him. I had to hand it to him, his dedication to his faith was a beautiful thing. I just wished he was as dedicated to me.

"Dad, I have been there. They have amazing cannoli." I smiled at him as I picked up my fork and plunged it into the salad Mom prepared.

Mom whimpered and smiled, turning her face down as she, too, took a bite. Dad said nothing, instead choosing to fill his mouth with food. He was still upset and I didn't understand why. Unless maybe he felt upset with himself for the way he treated me years ago and that guilt had him so ashamed he couldn't speak, but I hardly believed that was the case.

Dinner was tense. Not a whole lot of conversation was had except between Violet and Mom. They were planning the family Pesach meal with my aunts and uncles and cousins. It was a huge event and a major tradition. I loved the rituals of Seder and seeing my family, even though kids in school would get to celebrate Easter and have chocolate bunnies while I fasted and waited until midnight to eat. This year, however, seemed it would be more difficult than others. The longer they talked about it the more depressed I got. Even family dinners and parties sucked. I wanted a family where I could look forward to holidays, even ones I didn't really celebrate.

When we finished eating, Dad helped Mom clear the dishes. Violet and I retreated to the patio where the cloudy sky gave us refuge from the hot sun and the spring flowers surrounded us with their rich scent. Violet sneezed as she sat down, her allergies playing up a little.

"We can sit inside," I told her, sitting next to her.

"Nah, I can tell you need to vent a little, so I chose out here."

I sighed. "Thanks. Yeah, that was tough. Dad will get over it eventually. He's always a little moody and stern. It's just his personality."

Mom appeared in the doorway with a pitcher of lemonade and two glasses. She set them on the table and nodded at us. "You girls chat a bit. I will rinse the dishes and join you."

"Thanks, Mom." Violet picked up the pitcher and filled the glasses as Mom headed back to her chores. The lemonade looked fresh, like Mom had just made it this morning. It never ceased to amaze me how she cared for us even into adulthood. It made me think of what being a mother truly meant. That long after a child turns eighteen, they need their parents.

"So what's going on?"

"I slept with him again," I told her, to my own shame. "And I didn't have the guts to tell him yet."

"Oh, Min," Violet cooed. "Girl, I know this is impossible for you but you have to do the right thing." She reached out and touched my hand. I wanted to shrink back, but she wouldn't let me. "You know that right?"

"You don't understand what's at risk. If he gets upset, I'll lose everything. I feel so ashamed." I sat back in the chair and stared out over the backyard feeling despondent.

"So if he got upset, would you challenge him for custody?" Violet's question forced me to turn and face her.

"What?"

"Would you fight for him, legally I mean." She sipped her lemonade and waited for me to respond but I didn't think I'd give her the answer she wanted.

"No. Chris is better with his dad. He has a better job, nicer home. They can afford his medical care. He's better off there." The realization made me sad. It felt a little too much like I was agreeing with my parents' sentiment that I couldn't' raise a baby myself.

"What if he was better off with both of you?"

My throat started to constrict. The idea of Chris having both of us in his life was one I'd thought about tirelessly for hours every day, especially after Jace's slip of the tongue saying he loved me. I didn't believe that was true—yet—but I wondered. I initially just wanted it to be visitation or something, but when Jace kissed me, then we had sex, I started to let the stupid idea into my head that he could want me. The stupidest part of all of it was that if I told him nothing and just fell in love with him, I could have the family I wanted, and no one would be the wiser. I just didn't see that working out, not with how much older than me Jace was, not to mention Christopher's reluctance to move on—or that's what Jace told me. And I was no good at relationships anyway. This was bound to end badly no matter what.

"Look, you just do it for him. He's your son. You do what you have to do to love your son." Violet touched my hand again and I shrugged.

"What?" I whipped around to see Mom standing there with a tray of cupcakes, taken out of the box and neatly organized on little napkins of coordinating colors. "What son?" She looked at me with horror on her face and Violet wilted like a desert flower. "You contacted your son?" she asked harshly and set the tray on the table between us.

"I... uh—" I stood, suddenly feeling like a deer in headlights.

"Mom, it's not what you think." Violet came to my rescue but the lioness was already on the hunt.

"Explain then. I'll wait." Mom glared at me and planted her hands on her hips. I'd seen that look before, just last week.

"Mom, can we talk about this rationally?" I felt my tongue swelling. I was supposed to be calming things down today, not making them worse.

"Why are you digging up ghosts? Why do you want to punish your family?" Her eyes pleaded with me to tell her this wasn't happening, that it was all a lie.

"I'm not digging up ghosts, Mom. And my child was never a

punishment for this family. Maybe the reason you feel like Christopher is a punishment is because you feel guilty for what you did." I glanced at Violet, thankful I had left everything in the car. "I'm leaving. I'll call you later, Vi." With the moves of a gazelle evading its attacker, I sidestepped Mom and headed through the house.

I just needed some place to be at peace now, even if it was ripped away the instant I told him the truth.

13

Jace

The entire appointment, Mindy had been so professional and tactful, I wondered if my slip of the tongue had frightened her. I hadn't meant to say that, though saying it made me wonder if it was true, if I really was falling in love with her. But she didn't act cold toward me, so that was comforting. It was likely that she was being hypervigilant. She had expressed a concern about how unethical the relationship would be if we dated because of her being Christopher's doctor. I tried to not let my emotions get in the way of the appointment, which went very well.

"Alright, Topper, you just keep track of this little device like we talked about, and let me know when it stops lighting up blue. That's all." Mindy ruffled his hair and grinned at him. At times I felt like Christopher's smile resembled hers, though it had been so long since I'd seen him smile my mind had to be playing tricks on me. Seeing him happy with Mindy warmed my heart. I knew if he could just let go of his mother for a moment, he'd see how amazing Mindy was too. "Want to wait in the waiting room while I give Dad some final instructions?" she asked.

"Sure," Christopher said, hopping off the exam table.

"Actually, Mindy, I have a few questions. Is it alright if I take him down to the cafeteria to get him set up for lunch and we can have a short meeting?" I asked her, hopeful she had the time. She glanced at her watch and then looked back up at me.

"Sure. I have lunch next, so I'll just run to my office and grab my lunch box and meet you there?"

"Sounds perfect." I guided a complaining Christopher toward the elevator and down a few floors to the cafeteria.

"I don't want hospital food."

"You can buy the pizza or the chocolate cake. Now that you've got the little capsule swimming around in your belly, you're allowed a small snack."

He complained more when I told him he could only have one slice of pizza, but I finally got him situated at the table with a few quarters to buy a soda when he finished the snack. "Dad, are you going to talk to Dr. Scriber about me?"

I felt guilt wash over me. "Yeah, bud. I am." I wasn't. I didn't have any questions about the procedure or the results. I wanted to talk to her about my mistake and make sure we were okay, that I hadn't ruined my chance with her.

"Not flirt with her?" It was like his little twelve-year-old mind could see my guilty red hands.

"No flirting," I told him, holding my hand up. "Scouts honor."

He scowled at me as if he didn't believe me, but I made a mental note to have zero flirting in this conversation so I could be honest and not be a liar in my son's eyes. I walked back to the elevators and went up to Mindy's office. She was seated behind her desk chewing a bite of what looked like a ham and cheese sub. It made my mouth water, but not as much as the thought of kissing her did.

"Hey," I said, shutting the door behind me. I sat across from her and waited for her to swallow her bite. She laid the food down on the wax wrapper it came in and used a paper napkin to wipe her mouth.

"What did you need to speak with me about? Do you have questions about Christopher's care?" There was that darn professional tone again. I knew in my gut I had pushed her too far.

"No, it's not that." I held her gaze as the words sank in. She looked worried, fearful maybe. "I wanted to say I'm sorry. I was in a rush the other day and just let it slip. I used to never leave a room or a conversation without telling my wife I loved her. I'm sure you understand."

She took a deep breath and looked down at the half-eaten sandwich. "Jace, we can't do this. If I am going to continue to treat Christopher, I can't date you." When she looked back up at me I saw the pain in her eyes. I wondered if it was because she really wanted to date me but knew she couldn't. I'd transfer Chris to another doctor if that was the case.

"No, Mindy. We're good together. You'll see."

"I am so sorry, Jace." She stood and shook her head. I was certain the look on her face was shame or guilt now, not pain. But why? "And there's more. There is something I have to tell you."

I didn't know what could be so important that she needed to tell me right after she broke up with me. I stood and turned toward the door, resting my hand on the handle. She wasn't even giving us a fighting chance. It didn't matter to me which doctor treated my son, just that he got medical care. And the idea that she would so easily dismiss me hurt too. But there was the guilt in her eyes. She didn't want to hurt me.

I locked the door and turned back toward her. She looked confused. "I want you to listen to me first, and then you can tell me whatever else you need to tell me. Alright?"

Mindy's face pinched, a look of weariness washing over her expression. "Okay," she sighed and I moved toward her, taking her hand in mine.

"I did mean it."

"What?" she asked, shaking her head.

"I meant it. I do love you."

"But it's unethical."

I reached for her, pulling her against my body. "I don't care. Let them talk. We'll get a different doctor. I need you, Mindy. When

Connie died I didn't think I'd ever love again. But lightning struck, and when that happens, you don't ignore it. Please, tell me you feel the same way. That you believe fate, or the gods, or whatever has destined this to happen. Me and you to meet."

"Jace, I..."

She protested but I kissed her, not letting her speak. My heart wouldn't bear it if she broke up with me. I just couldn't. I pulled away and said, "Tell me you feel it too."

She nodded, and slowly draped her arms around my shoulders.

"I am so scared. I could lose everything." She kissed me, pecking first, then feverishly deepening the kiss. Her lips parted and I felt her tongue push into my mouth. I pulled away to breathe and spoke again.

"You will never lose me. Okay?" Mindy held my gaze and nodded. I knew it was going to be a tough road ahead, but I was ready to take it. I had fallen in love with her, and nothing was going to change that.

My body felt super charged, like I could run a marathon. I wanted her—now. I couldn't wait any longer. I needed her so badly. I lifted her up, her legs wrapping around my waist as I turned her toward the desk. My hands roamed over her body as I kissed her hungrily. Mindy moaned as I unbuttoned her blouse and unhooked her bra, baring her breasts to me. I took one nipple in my mouth, sucking on it hard as she gasped. My hand slipped between her legs, pushing her skirt up, finding her already wet and ready for me.

I nudged her panties to the side with my fingers, making eye contact with her as I slid them into her moist slit. "I want to do this to you every day for the rest of my life." I thrust in, finding that the more I did, the wetter she got.

Mindy's head fell back as I rocked my hips, rubbing my erection against her knee with each thrust. Her fingers searched for the button on my fly as I fingered her. "I want you inside of me," she whimpered.

"Do you feel okay? In here, I mean? At work..." I didn't stop my pursuit of her pussy, massaging her g-spot and smearing the moisture around her labia.

"Just make me come. We'll talk about that later," she said as my mouth covered hers again. I continued my ministrations, rubbing her clit with my thumb, and it took a coordinated effort, but she freed my cock from my pants and stroked it as I rubbed her off.

"Oh god, deeper!" she pleaded, and I complied. Her hips began to meet my fingers in a frenzy of passion, and I knew she was close.

"I'm going to come," she groaned. I continued to finger her, and after a few more thrusts, her body tensed. I felt her pulling at my shirt, so I leaned forward and she reached for my back, scratching as she came. Her pussy squeezed my fingers as she moaned, and I felt her body tremble.

I pulled out of her and took her hand and helped her stand. She did up her bra and blouse, and I slipped my pants down around my knees. "Bend over the desk," I ordered, stroking myself. Mindy snickered and winked at me. She turned around and hiked her skirt up again, this time slipping her panties down until they dropped to the floor. When she glanced over her shoulder I felt my body surge with a need to be in her.

I watched as she spread her legs, leaned over, and waited. Since the last few surprising moments of wild sex, I stocked up on condoms. I reached into my wallet and pulled one out that I had stashed there, then I put it on and stroked myself as I admired her ass. My balls began to ache. I felt her wetness on my fingertips, and I rubbed it against her pussy. I teased her, rubbing her clit in small circles and dipping my fingers back into her entrance.

"In me, Jace. Please..." she whined, moving her hips back and forth a bit. I slid inside of her, and she groaned loudly. "Oh god, you're so big," she moaned.

I grabbed her hips and picked up an easy rhythm. Her pussy was wet and warm, and I could feel my cock sliding easily in and out of her. She began to moan loudly, and I watched as her pussy lips stretched around my shaft. "Mindy, you're so beautiful," I said, feeling her body begin to squeeze my cock. Her pussy contracted, and I groaned. I felt her body begin to shudder, and she pushed back harder against me.

"Jace, I'm going to come again," she purred, and I felt her body tense. I pulled my cock out and rubbed her clit with my fingers. She moaned loudly again, and I felt her juices against my fingers. I continued to rub her clit and slide my fingers inside of her, and after a few more moments, her body began to relax.

It was my turn. Time to let all the stress of that conversation dump out of me and relax. I pushed back into her, spreading her wide so I could go deep. She whimpered and held onto her desk and I watched as the whole thing shook as I pounded her. Her sandwich fell to the floor, and her pen cup, but I didn't back down. I needed her.

My cock was throbbing, and I could feel her pussy tightening around me. I picked up my pace and watched as my cock slid in and out of her. Her swollen lips spread wide with each thrust. I felt her pussy begin to throb around me, and she moaned loudly. I felt her body begin to shake, and she clawed at her desk. I was close as well.

My balls grew tight, and the familiar feeling began to spread through my body. I grunted, and I felt my cock begin to twitch. I erupted inside of her, my cock throbbing inside her. Her pussy clamped down on me, squeezing every last drop out of me. I groaned, my cock jerking and twitching.

"Oh, god," I gasped, feeling my knees begin to shake. I held her tightly, her pussy milking every last drop out of me until I was empty.

I pulled out and she stood, fixing her skirt. She pulled her panties up and I disposed of the condom. It was a bit awkward, but I pulled her into my arms and kissed her forehead. "I have to go get Christopher. Why don't you come for dinner tonight? We'll work everything out then."

"Okay," she said, nodding as if she had to convince herself it was okay. There was something she wasn't telling me, and I didn't know what it was, but I didn't care.

"I love you, Mindy. And it's okay if you can't say that yet. You will hopefully one day." I left her office feeling lighter than air.

Now I just had to convince Christopher it was okay too. That would be a tough sell.

14

Mindy

Jace walked out and I sat behind my desk feeling ashamed and overwhelmed. I was speechless. After the disagreement with my mother on Saturday, I resolved to tell Jace everything, to come clean and do the right thing by Christopher. My mother knew something was going on, which meant she would tell my father. If they suspected I already had contact with my son, god only knows to what lengths they would go to stop me or get in the way.

My phone buzzed and I pulled it from my pocket and looked at it. Georgia had messaged me. I swiped right to see what she had to say and like salt in a wound, her message hurt.

Georgia 11:39 AM: So did you tell him? How did it go?

"My god," I whined, laying my head on my desk. I had to ignore that message for a moment because I was so confused and I didn't know how to answer. How did I tell my best friend that the man I've been lying to about everything now told me he loves me?

My body still felt warm and tingly from the sex, and my heart was already feeling despair. I lay draped over the desk crying quietly for the rest of my lunch break. My sandwich was ruined anyway, and I had no motivation to go to the cafeteria to buy a new one—no appetite either.

"Knock knock," I heard and before I even looked up, I knew it was Evelyn. My head rose slowly but my stomach sank. I didn't even bother to hide the fact that I had been crying. "Got a sec?" she asked and I shrugged. It didn't matter if I had a second or not; she had already shut the door behind her and was sitting across from me. I sat up and swiped at my eyes and hoped my office didn't smell like sex.

"What is it?" I rolled my head around and rubbed my shoulder. All this stress was starting to give me a kink in the neck. I didn't want that turning into a stress headache.

"Well I was going over the tests for Christopher Turner and I noticed that you ran only a few select ones." She sat straight in the chair with shoulders squared. Her lab coat parted in front, revealing her floral top, one that I'd complimented her on dozens of times.

"You snooped around behind my back?" Mildly irritated, I shook my head. "Evelyn, I asked you to not press this."

"You're lucky I did, Mindy." She sighed hard. Her eyebrows drew together and she pursed her lips. "When you have a patient with no medical history to offer, you do a full panel, not selective testing." The way she sat with her hands folded in her lap politely made me feel like she was acting better than me. Sure I had screwed up, but she didn't have to make me feel like less of a person.

"But I know his heredity... Why are you doing this?"

"But you didn't know his heredity when you ordered the tests. It was only after you did the DNA test that you knew. What if you missed something because you didn't test for other things and this kid was suffering needlessly? Your judgment is impaired." Evelyn scooted to the edge of her seat and reached out and took my hand. I wanted to flinch away but I knew she was only doing the right thing. It made me cry again.

"Eve... I knew it in my gut—that he was my son. And look, it's working out. We have a near positive diagnosis. We're just doing one follow up test and we'll know the best course of treatment. Can't you just cut me some slack? I'm going to make it right." I squeezed her hand hard and pleaded with her but she shook her head.

"It's actually out of my hands now." Evelyn sat back and rubbed her own forehead.

"What do you mean?" My heart started to beat faster, threatening to pound its way right out of my chest.

"I mean, the lab tech who helped draw the blood reported to Andrews a missing vial. That missing vial was the one you used for the DNA sample. When he came to me as head of the lab that day, and asked me what went wrong, I told him I'd look into it. I cannot lie for you about this. I have to give my full report, Mindy. I'm really sorry." I heard the emotion creeping into her voice as she confessed to me what had to happen.

Fear loomed over me. "You didn't do anything wrong. It was me. You don't have to be sorry. I'm so sorry I dragged you into this. You do what you have to do so Andrews will stay off your back. I'll figure it out." My head dropped but from the corner of my eye I saw her stand.

"I'm here if you need to talk, okay?"

"Yeah," I mumbled, letting more tears fall.

She left me alone to sulk in my frustration and obsess about things. Andrews would certainly have to report this to the ethics committee and then I'd be under review. That meant termination and possible revocation of my license to practice medicine, all to have my son back. Only, with the way things had developed with Jace, it also meant possibly losing an incredible man, quite possibly the best thing that had ever happened to me. All because I wasn't honest from the beginning.

I fumbled through the rest of my day in a mix of emotion, making little mistakes my nurses corrected me on. Dr. Andrews approached me close to quitting time and asked me if I was okay, but after trying to reassure him that I was fine, he asked me to go home and rest. I was upset that he didn't trust my judgment, but I knew I had no place caring for others when I didn't have my head on straight. I was also just thankful that he hadn't brought up the tests or what he asked Evelyn to do. I wasn't ready for that yet.

Parked in front of Jace's house, I sat for at least forty minutes feeling numb and paralyzed. I knew I needed to tell him everything, but the only thing I could think was how badly I wanted to feel his arms holding me. I never expected him to take interest in me. I thought he was really attractive, but my interest had been in Christopher from the very beginning. His desire for me blindsided me, but now that I saw it, I wanted it. I wanted him to love me—and to love me so much that he wouldn't see my flaws, or the way I messed up so badly.

When the front porch light went on, I realized it was getting late. I glanced at my clock and it said eight p.m. Almost an hour after I pulled up and parked. I climbed out and locked my car, wandering up toward his front door. I rang the bell and he met me with a smile and a hug and I hadn't felt so comforted all day.

"You look down. Is everything okay?" he asked, ushering me into the dark entryway. He locked up behind us and led me to the kitchen. The sight of the kitchen counter where Jace first had sex with me keeps my eyes glued to it for a while as I walk past and sit on a bar stool next to him. My stomach rumbles and tenses. If Jace really loves me, then when I tell him the truth, he will forgive me? Right?

I ignore his question and instead I see a bottle of aloe vera juice on the counter. It's the same brand I buy. "How's Christopher doing? I see you got the juice." I nod at the counter and Jace looks concerned but shrugs at me and answers.

"He's doing well with it. I think it's really helping... Now tell me what's wrong." His steadfast gaze refused to turn away from me. He wasn't giving up until I told him something, but this wasn't the way I wanted it to happen.

"The stress of all this." I dropped my chin to my chest. "I think my tummy issue is flaring up too. I mean, with everything going on with my parents that's enough stress to cause an episode, but today my friend Evelyn told me I need to come clean and tell you I can't treat Christopher anymore."

His hand shot out and he rubbed my back. "You mean she found out?"

I chewed the inside of my cheek and traced a pattern outlined in the marble countertop. It wasn't a lie to say she found out; he'd never know what she found out. I nodded but didn't say a word. The stress was the same no matter what she knew.

Jace stood without asking and got a glass out of the cupboard and filled it with juice from the fridge. He set it in front of me then stood behind me. "You're really tense, Mindy. Let me rub some of the tension out of your shoulders."

I couldn't believe the compassion of this man. My heart swelled and felt guilty at the same time. He was so amazing and I felt like a bunch of garbage. I didn't want to lie to him. I wanted to have all the secrets out so we could feel this way without pretense. I really liked him—a lot. Like, I could see myself being really happy with him. This had never happened to me with any other man.

"Wow, you have some knots in these muscles."

I reached up and rested my hand on his hand as he rubbed. "Thanks for listening. You know," I said, turning on the stool to face him, "you are such an amazing man." I didn't know how this would ever work out but suddenly I really wanted it to.

"I think you're an incredibly amazing woman, Mindy, so if it means transferring Christopher to another doctor, I fully trust your judgment. I don't want you to be in trouble at work, but I do want to see where this goes." He cupped my cheeks and kissed my forehead.

I knew the damage at work was already done, and coming clean would only bring a hurricane of chaos into my life. Still, knowing Jace felt this way about me made me hopeful. If I could get things with Andrews straightened out, maybe Jace would never have to know. Maybe it would be okay and he would still want me in his life. Being Christopher's mom was so important to me, but now being Jace's partner meant something too. I didn't want to lie to him, and starting a relationship with a lie was a horrible idea. I just didn't know how to turn it around.

"Where is Christopher?" I asked, resting my hands on his wrists as he cupped my cheeks and looked into my eyes.

"Already in bed," he said, "why?"

"Can you help me forget the stress of this day?" I took his hand and pulled it from my cheek, guiding it to my chest. He wrapped it around my breast and squeezed softly.

"I think I can manage that..." Jace leaned down to kiss me softly on the lips, and I all but melted into him. We knew almost nothing about each other, but I knew enough to know I wanted to know more. Everything actually.

He took my hand and pulled me off the bar stool, backing toward a hallway. I followed, nervously keeping eye contact. As we walked down the dimly lit hallway, my heart raced with anticipation. Jace had a confident swagger in his step that made me feel safe and secure. I knew I was in good hands. We entered a small bedroom, and Jace turned to face me and gently pushed me against the door, his lips crashing into mine with a hunger that left me breathless.

He pulled away, his eyes dark with desire. "I want you, right here, right now," he growled in my ear. I shivered with excitement as he lifted me up and carried me to the bed. The floodlight out back cast a few fingers of light in the room illuminating it enough to see him as he stripped his clothing off. I lay on the bed waiting, watching.

I hadn't even noticed how trim he was, our first encounters too fast and furious to really enjoy him. This time, I memorized every detail of his body, the curve of his hips, the way his abs funneled down into a deep V just above his hairline where his cock was already mostly hard. He reached up and unbuttoned my pants, shimmying them down over my hips and taking my panties with them.

I let him pull them off, along with my shoes. One by one he took my socks and kissed my feet. When he pulled the second one off, he kissed up my calf to my knee, then my inner thigh. "Do you forget yet? The stress of the day?" he asked, nipping at the soft skin of my thigh just above my knee.

"Not yet," I whispered, slowly unbuttoning my shirt.

"Okay," he whispered. He undid the clasp of his watch, and pulled it off. He laid it on the nightstand, then touched my cheek, looking into my eyes. "I guess I have to keep going."

His lips were soft, his tongue warm and gentle. He left a trail of kisses up my inner thigh, then gently pushed my knees apart with his hands and settled between them. I felt the warmth of his breath on my clit, and my breath quickened. I quivered with anticipation as he leaned in and kissed the skin near my clit without touching it. He was teasing me. I loved it.

"I think I'm starting to forget." I unhooked my bra and squeezed my breasts, pinching my nipples until they were hard, while Jace continued to tease me with light flicks of his tongue near my sensitive nub. "Make me forget, Jace."

My pussy ached for more, my body tensed. "Put your fingers inside me," I whispered, my voice shaking. Jace rose up and gently took a handful of my ass in each hand, squeezing gently. He lowered his mouth to my mound again, and this time, when he brushed his tongue near it I felt it flicker against my clit. I jolted in a sharp, hard spasm. My hands shot to his hair, and I took handfuls of it.

"Oh god," I moaned. He was driving me mad with desire. "Oh god, don't tease me."

"Come on, Mindy. I'm making you forget," he said, grinning up at me from between my thighs.

He teased me, tracing the outline of my clit again, then flicking it with his tongue again and again. I gripped his hair tightly, moaning and arching my back. I was already so close, so ready. I tugged at his hair, trying to pull him closer, to force his tongue inside me, but he pulled away. I think I whimpered a little.

"Stress is a trick thing," he said, using a finger to outline my soft folds, teasing my hole. I wanted him inside me so badly. "It might take some extreme measures to make sure you really relax and let that all go."

"Yeah?" I moaned, clenching, wishing he would just finger me already. "Like what?"

"Well, for starters, at least three orgasms, maybe more. And after that, maybe wine, a bath, more orgasms, more wine. More orgasms..."

He lowered his face again, and this time, he simultaneously sucked my clit while pushing two fingers into me. Like magic, his fingers found my g-spot and stroked it methodically.

"Oh god... Yes, I'm going to come!" I moaned loudly, clawing at his hair and shoulders.

Jace kissed my mound, his tongue flicking my clit, his fingers pressing into me as he made my pussy throb and clench.

"Don't stop! Don't stop!" I panted, my legs shaking.

"Come for me," he said in a husky, sexy voice, using the hand from my ass to pull me in close to his face. He sucked hard on my nub, making his fingers slide deep inside me.

"I'm coming! I'm coming!" I shrieked in pleasure. I came hard, my body shaking, my pussy clenching and releasing Jace's fingers. He sucked and pulled at my pulsing nub, and he thrust faster with his fingers, my orgasm rocking through me.

"Oh god!" I groaned, my eyes rolling back in my head. Jace's mouth stayed locked on my clit, sucking gently at it, as my pussy continued to shake and release for what felt like a long time.

When I finally released his hair and slumped back into the bed, my body was covered in a thin layer of sweat. My pussy ached, my clit throbbed, and all I wanted was more. I looked up at Jace, who smiled at me. "Better?" he asked with a devilish grin.

"M-maybe," I slurred, lust drunk and wanting so much more.

"That's just one. Two more to go." He smirked at me and rubbed my pussy, smearing my juices around. Oh god, I never wanted this to end...

15

Jace

I licked my fingers clean, tasting Mindy's moisture on them, and looked down at her as I massaged her pussy in a circular motion, rubbing down over her hole and back over her clit. She was gorgeous splayed out on my bed like this, shirt open, tits nearly glowing in the faint light from outside. If there had been any doubt about whether she wanted me before, it was gone now. The way she initiated sex was so sexy, I didn't think I could recreate that moment if I tried.

But I'd try.

I wanted all the moments with her, every single one.

I reached for her hand and guided her to take my dick into it. She gripped me and stroked as I rubbed her. Her body jolted each time I touched her sensitive clit, one orgasm never enough. I wanted to bring her to that point again and again, as long as I could hold out, because I wanted her to remember that feeling good, while being intimate with someone you care about, is about the best thing in the world.

"You like this?" I asked her, wondering if her stress was really starting to fade away.

She bit her lip and nodded, brushing her thumb over the bead of precum on the end of my dick. "Do it harder," she asked, bucking her hips against my hand.

I pressed my palm against her pussy and stroked harder, adding a little bit of pressure, and her hips rose up against me. I slid two fingers inside her pussy. She was hot and slippery and soft, and I wanted to sink my cock in her right now. I wanted to feel her wrap around me, her insides squeezing me tight, the way she had before.

I pulled out my fingers and brought them to my mouth, sucking on them.

"Do you like the way I taste?" she asked, slowly shifting the way she gripped me, using only her finger tips to tease my shaft.

"God yes... Do you like the way I eat you?" I growled, sliding my fingers back into her. The heel of my palm rubbed her sensitive nub and she jolted again and hissed. She bit her bottom lip, hooded eyes glued to my mouth. I leaned back down to kiss her, and her lips parted willingly as our mouths met.

"I love it," she said, playing with the head of my cock while I thrust against her hand.

"I like tasting you," I told her, rubbing my thumb over her clit.

"You want me to taste you?" she asked, raising an eyebrow.

"I want to taste you too," I said, and she smiled, as if she liked the sound of that."I want to come for you," she said, her voice low and raspy with desire. "I want to come for you again."

She didn't have to ask me twice. I lay down on the bed next to her and patted my chest, ready to enjoy that sweet pussy of hers. Mindy rose up and straddled my chest, backing toward the headboard until her pussy pressed down on my face. I licked her juicy slit, using a hand on each side to pull her open. She leaned forward and took my cock in her hand; then I felt her lips lock around it.

Mindy bobbed her head up and down on my cock, sucking and licking and stroking as she did. I wanted to fuck her mouth hard and fast, but I kept my grip on her hips loose, allowing her to control the pace. Her pussy was right over my face, dripping juices down my chin. I licked that too, making her gush more. Then I sucked her clit into my mouth and held it there, tonguing it gently while she ground against my face. I could feel her start to tremble, and I knew she was getting close. I wanted to watch her come, so I pulled her hips back away from my head, and she groaned in protest. But I held her thighs apart and continued to suck on her clit, flicking it with my tongue.

"Oh, oh my god... Don't stop.. Don't stop!" Her mouth pulled away from my dick, but that was okay. I wanted her to enjoy every second of this, and I knew how difficult it was to give and receive at the same time.

I held her there, licking her clit and sucking it into my mouth as she gushed down my chin. Her body shook as she came, and I licked her pussy as if it were a cupcake, drinking every drop of her sweet juices. When she finally calmed down, she looked back at me with half-lidded eyes and a faint smile, and I licked her again, watching her holes tighten then expand.

Each flick of my tongue across her nub made her clench and release. She clawed at the sheets, head arched back, moaning softly. "I need you now," I said.

"Yes," she said, softly.

Mindy's hand gripped my dick again, stroking me, but I sank my teeth into the back of her thigh and let my whiskers scrape across her skin. At the same time I spanked her ass cheek, and she yelped and giggled. "Not like that."

"Okay..." She climbed off of me and sat with legs spread, touching herself, and I got up and grabbed a condom from the nightstand.

"You're going to make me come again, right?" she said, teasing me, rubbing her clit with two fingers while I stood by the bedside.

I rolled the condom on and grabbed her hips, pulling her toward me, and she giggled and squirmed, half-heartedly struggling to get away. I pulled her to the edge and spread her legs wide. My sheathed dick pressed against her pussy, sliding through the moisture that slicked her hole.

"I'd like nothing more than to make you come three or four times every single day for the rest of my life." I bent and hooked my arms around her legs just behind the knee and pulled her harder against myself then dipped my hips and pushed my cock into her tight hole. I slid in and out of her slowly, savoring the feeling of her pussy sliding along my shaft.

"Harder," she panted. I pushed her legs back and leaned over her. My hips banged into her, and my headboard banged against the wall so hard I thought it would wake Christopher but I didn't stop. Her moans filled the room, and a steady stream of "oh God oh God oh God" filled the room.

My balls drew up, and I knew the end was near for me. I felt her pussy clamping down around me, her third climax so close too. I wanted us to come at the same time. "God, I love you, Mindy..." I moaned. "I want you to be my wife."

That was all it took. "Oh, god, I'm coming," she grunted, and her eyes rolled back in her head.

"I'm gonna come too," I growled.

"Do it, Jace. Come," she moaned, in a high-pitched voice. I came, and I came, and I came. My cock throbbed and pulsed as I filled the condom and she milked me. But long after my dick was spent, her body continued to convulse. I slid in and out of her, pleasuring her to the very last twitch before pulling out.

"Oh, holy cow," she sighed, laying her head back down. I raked a hand through my sweaty hair and then worked the condom off my dick. I was so hard I could go again, but after that performance I needed to catch my breath.

Mindy crawled up onto the bed and lay down, pulling the covers over her glistening body. I walked into the bathroom and flushed the condom, then returned to lie down next to her. She snuggled into my chest and wrapped her arm around me and I held her there while we caught our breath. The idea of having a different doctor did concern me a bit, but with Mindy by my side advising me, I believed it would still be okay.

"Feel better?" I asked her, and she nodded against my chest, kissing me. "Good." I smoothed my hand up and down her back. I knew what I had said during sex and I meant it, even though the sight of her lying on Constance's pillow did make my heart feel a bit uneasy. We'd had this bed for ten years, made love in it. How many times had I held her while she cried and mourned her own death as the sickness developed? But still, I wanted Mindy to be my wife.

"Jace?" she said, her voice timid.

"Yeah?"

"What if you don't like me?" She felt so small in my arms as she said that, like her inner child was screaming for validation. I could feel her insecurity through her skin, clinging to me for hope.

"Min, what do you mean? I really like you."

"I mean, when you get to know the real me, my demons, my secrets." I heard the emotion in her voice and wanted to run to it immediately to comfort her.

I reached for her chin and forced her to look me in the eye. "Don't you ever think that. Okay? I don't care what your darkest secret is. No matter what you've done, or where you've been, I will never stop liking you. Okay?" I concentrated my firm gaze on her eyes that sparkled with emotion. I wanted to say more, reassure her more deeply, but unless I knew exactly why she was feeling insecure, there was nothing I could do.

"Even if—"

"Dad, can I have a snack?" Christopher's voice cut Mindy off as he burst into the room. She scrambled, pulling the blanket tightly across her chest and turning to her back. "Dr. Scriber?" he asked, hand still on the doorknob. "What's going on?"

"Oh god," she mumbled, and I got the sense she wished she could melt into the mattress and vanish.

"Chris, please go to the kitchen. I'll come out in a second." I sat up, and ran a hand through my hair as he stared at her.

"Dad, why is she here? Why is she using Mom's pillow?" His voice rose in pitch and his face contorted into a painful grimace.

"Please, go wait in the kitchen," I said again.

Christopher slammed the door and retreated, and my shoulders slumped. I covered my face and mumbled, "I'm so sorry, Mindy. I have to go talk to him."

"It's okay. Go... he needs you." Mindy sat up and touched my shoulder. "Go on, it's okay." I looked into her eyes where I saw the same amount of pain, but I knew I had to go. I got dressed as quickly as I could and headed out to find him standing by the back door stewing, his little arms folded across his chest.

"Bud, I'm sorry I didn't tell you she was coming over. I wanted her to have dinner with us, but she was late and you went to bed early." I walked over to him to touch his shoulder but he moved away and shut the curtain.

"You let her use Mom's pillow? Why did you do that? Why was she on Mom's side of the bed? You had sex, didn't you?"

At twelve he wasn't stupid, but he wasn't old enough or mature enough to understand the complexity of the situation.

"Christopher, we just need to talk about this. Okay?" I gestured to the bar and he sat on a stool while I got him some chips and a cup of his juice. Mindy's cup sat there untouched. She should have drunk it. I should take it to her.

"How can you do that to Mom?" he asked as I set his snack in front of him.

"Bud, Mom is gone. She's been gone a long time. She isn't coming back. She wouldn't want us to leave this giant hole in our hearts and lives. She would want us to be happy." I tried to smooth his hair but he pushed my hand away.

"Don't," he snapped, and stared at his snack with an angry scowl. "Why are you replacing her?"

"I'm not replacing her, Top. I'm finding someone to be my life partner."

"That's just a replacement." He pushed the plate away and glared at me. "If I die, will you replace me too?"

His words were arrows slicing through my heart. "God no, Chris..." I tried to catch him but he stormed off, leaving his snack. I heard his door slam and I knew I would never calm him down tonight. I sat for a second just pondering his reaction. I had to make him understand what was going on, even if it meant family coun-seling to help with that.

My heart had never felt so torn open as I picked up Mindy's glass of juice and walked toward the bedroom. There was no questioning what I felt for her—love. And I loved my son too, but I wanted her, and maybe I was selfish, but I needed her too.

I pushed open the door; it wasn't latched. I could have sworn I latched it. The bed was empty, and my eyes turned to the adjoining bathroom, but the door was empty and the light off. "Mindy?" I called, but there was no reply. I looked around, thinking maybe she was in a dark corner or something, but when I turned the nightstand lamp on and set her glass down, I saw a note scrawled on a sticky note.

"Jace...

I'm really sorry if I messed things up between you and your son. I want you to know that I really like you too, but I don't know if this is going to work out. I just need some time to think about things. I'll work on the referral. I'm letting myself out the back.

~Mindy"

I dropped the note and dug into my pants to find my phone and call her, but after three attempts and all three of them going straight to voicemail, I sank onto the side of the bed and closed my eyes. What did "need some space" mean? And after that comment about still liking her if I knew her secrets, I wondered if she was going to hide from me.

God... Why couldn't something just be easy for once?

16

Mindy

Afraid that Jace would show up at my apartment in the middle of the night to try to convince me to come back, I went the only place I could think of. I stood outside Georgia's apartment door knocking, praying they were awake and I wouldn't bother them. It took a few seconds but the door swung open and Ben was there with a concerned expression.

"Mindy? Is everything okay?" he asked, stepping aside so I could enter. I walked in and saw Georgia seated on the couch with her legs propped on the table, two glasses on coasters there too. She looked up at me with surprise and quickly sat up and put her feet on the floor.

"I need someone to talk to," I blurted out, brushing past Ben and heading straight for my best friend's arms. Georgia pulled me in and laid my head on her shoulder. "This whole thing is so messed up, Geo."

I heard the door shut and then I felt the couch shake and knew Ben had sat down. I hoped he wasn't upset with me interrupting their time, but where else was I supposed to go?

"It's okay, babe. Just talk to me." Georgia rocked me like a sick child as I explained everything once again—my failure to tell the truth, the risk at my job that was now escalating, and then I added the bit about Jace loving me. When I was finished venting, and almost on the verge of tears, I sat up and leaned back, resting my head backward.

"I don't feel like I have to tell you what to do again, huh?" she said, patting my knee. "You want a drink?" she asked, but I shook my head. I didn't need alcohol clouding my thinking now.

"No, thank you. That's the last thing I need. I can't drown my problem; I just need help." I clamped my eyes shut and whimpered. "This is really bad, guys. I screwed up so badly. Andrews is going to fire me, or the board will, and Jace is going to hate me. Just when I finally find Mr. Right, it turns out I'm Mrs. Wrong, in every way."

"Don't say that about yourself." Georgia swatted my arm and nudged me. "You are not Mrs. Wrong. The situation is tricky, yes, and you have some fessing up to do, but if he really feels that way about you, then you two could still work it out. In the meantime, you shouldn't be leading him on anymore. No relationship that is built on a lie can survive."

I covered my face with my hands and let out a groan. "I know," I mumbled, and it came out muffled, so I dropped my hands and sat up. "I'm just so terrified of losing him."

"Christopher?" she asked.

"Jace," I said. I felt trapped, panicked, and shaky. "After what you said, I know I can get a lawyer and fight for Chris. I don't want it to come to that, but I could. Right? So I won't lose him. But I could lose Jace." I shook my head and blinked back tears. "And I could lose my job too. Not just my job, my ability to practice medicine at all. And I'm really good at my job; I love it."

"Do you want me to speak to Dr. Andrews for you?" Ben chimed in, sipping his drink. "It might not prevent a blow up, but it might bring compassion in the decision they make at least." He eyed me over the rim of the glass and I shrugged.

"I'm not sure that would help at all, but thank you." My heart wrestled and I felt hopeless. The ache in my gut only got worse as the night went on too, and I doubled over to hold my stomach and rock myself. I wanted this to be over.

"Are you okay?" Ben asked, touching my back.

"Do I look okay?" I asked, letting some tears fall.

"Babe, he's trying to help." Georgia held my hair back and tucked it round my ear. "Is it your stomach? You're having a flare up?"

I nodded and buried my face between my knees. Just acknowledging it made the dam burst. I sobbed and rocked until my gut was cramped up tighter than a miser's bank account. How had I let it get this bad?

"Alright, Geo, I'm going to the pharmacy. I'll be back shortly." The couch moved as Ben stood, and I cried as he left the house, keys in hand jingling. Georgia got me a pillow and blanket and helped me lie down, and by the time Ben got back the spasms were so bad I'd run to the bathroom three times already thinking I was going to lose it.

He offered some liquid medicine that tasted like chalk and I drank the entire container down. It was disgusting, but Ben knew what he was doing, and he knew my condition, so I trusted him.

"Try to sleep, okay, hun?" Georgia said, pulling the blanket over my shoulder. I nodded through my tears and she left a box of tissues on the coffee table within reach.

I did try to sleep, but it evaded me almost all night. Each time I dozed off I had a bad dream that Jace found out and screamed at me, or that Andrews fired me and I lost my apartment and was forced to live on the street.

Somewhere around three a.m., as noted by the clock on the cable box, Charlie, Geo's son, woke with a nightmare. I startled myself to a wide-awake state and listened intently as she spoke to him in calming tones. Her ability to soothe his heart made mine scream. I wanted that. I wanted my son, and I wanted to soothe him and be his mother. I cried again, this time really crying myself to sleep as the medicine kicked in and the pain eased. Jace had to know, but I needed him to understand. I just didn't think for a second he would, and that gave me nightmares.

17

Jace

I gave Mindy her space for a few days as she requested. The following Monday, after I submitted the digital files from Christopher's capsule test, I sat in the waiting room with the machine to return, ready to hear what the diagnosis was. I left him in school, because Mindy said there was no need for him to attend this particular appointment, but I still felt nervous about seeing her again. After the way we were interrupted during such an intimate conversation and the way she asked me to give her space, I worried she was getting cold feet about us.

"Mr. Turner? The doctor is ready for you," a nurse called from the door. I approached and she said, "Oh, I can take that for you. Go to her office in the back, the third door on the left."

I thanked the younger woman and made my way down the hall-way. My palms were sweaty, the air thick with anticipation and anxi-ety. Mindy's door was open, and I heard her talking. When I pushed the door open she looked up at me, phone receiver to her ear, and held up a finger. I paused in the doorway and she nodded and dismissed the caller, so I let myself in and shut the door, locking it behind me. The expression on her face said enough.

"What's wrong?" I asked, but before I could even sit down she was in my arms and I was baffled. "You need to talk?" I guided her to the chair and sat down and she sat on my lap and let me hold her for a moment.

"It's bad, Jace."

"How bad? Your parents? What's wrong?" I encouraged her to sit up but she remained reclined against my chest.

"My boss." She took a deep breath and let it out. "He asked to see me as soon as my appointment with you was over. I'm scared."

"Ah…" I rubbed her thigh, then let my hand rest on her hip. "Okay, well just be brave. Do you want me to go with you? I can explain that it was me. I was the pushy one."

Mindy squirmed a little then sat up and climbed off my lap and walked to the door and unlocked it. It was like she was avoiding the topic. She sat in her chair and rubbed her face for a second. "There's more to it than that."

I got the feeling she wasn't telling me something, but I didn't want to push her, not when she was already feeling down. She had enough to face; she didn't need me being nosy or pushy.

"Alright, well just try to stay positive." I sat up in the chair and really studied her. Her hair was a little messy, makeup smeared as if she'd been rubbing her eyes. She looked tired and stressed, and I could tell this was weighing on her. "How are things with your parents?"

"I haven't spoken to them." She pulled out a file and folded it open, revealing some paperwork. "Uh, if we could just do this part, I think maybe it will help me feel less guilty when I go meet my boss." Her eyes turned up to meet mine and I wished I could take away her pain. Only then did I notice the faint hint of mascara lines down her cheeks and the black droplets on her white lab coat. She'd been crying again. I opened my mouth to ask her about it when she said, "It's definitely Crohn's." She turned the file around so I could see the papers, but the words made no sense.

She scratched her head. "He has all the biomarkers and even the imaging reveals the scarred colon of someone with Crohn's disease. The good news is I don't think he needs a specialist, so I can refer him to Dr. Ben Wilks. He's a pediatrician at the hospital here and really knows his stuff."

I felt the wind get sucked out of my chest. "I guess that's the bad news too?"

Mindy bit her lip and nodded. "I'm so sorry, Jace. I will definitely be here to advise you and make sure Christopher gets the best care possible."

"I know you will." I smiled at her and reached for her hand but she pulled away, taking the file with her.

"There's something else." The grimace on her face turned to sheer terror. She froze and I watched her chest begin rising and falling faster.

"What is it? Is it Chris? Is something else wrong?" One of my greatest fears was losing my son, but Mindy put that fright to bed immediately by shaking her head.

"No, not at all. He is going to be just fine with the proper diet and exercise." She put both of her hands on her desk, palms splayed outward. "It's about you and me, and well, Chris too actually."

Here it was. She was going to tell me she didn't want to destroy my relationship with him and that she was breaking up. "No, Mindy..."

A knock on the door interrupted the tense moment and I turned to see a man walk in. He was a bit younger than me, but not by much, with a long white coat. On the coat the name "Andrews" had been embroidered. This was Mindy's boss.

"Sorry to interrupt," he said, smiling at me and extending his hand. "I'm Dr. Callum Andrews, head of internal medicine."

I rose to meet him and shook his hand and Mindy stood too, though it was sheer panic in her eyes. "Nice to meet you." When I took my hand away, he put his hand in his pocket. He was intimidating, broad shoulders and a commanding presence. I could see why Mindy was a little afraid.

"We weren't quite finished," she mumbled, wringing her hands.

"That's alright, I can wait." He folded his hands in front of himself and stood there watching. Now it was really awkward, because I wanted Mindy to come over for dinner tonight, but I hadn't gotten the chance to tell her. I just knew she was trying to unburden herself of something—something that had started when we made love and she never got to tell me. I turned to face her, thinking quickly about how I could communicate with her.

"So, the updates you wanted, from Chris's test diary, I'll email them to your office then?" She looked at me confused for a second until—my back turned to her boss so he couldn't see me—I mouthed "I'll text you."

She looked a little nervous, brow furrowed and eyes drawn, but she forced a smile and nodded. "I look forward to that, and I will send them on to Dr. Wilk's office for his staff to review them too. He should contact you in a few days to set up an appointment. In the meantime if you need anything you can call any of my nurses who'd be happy to help. It was really nice to meet you and I hope Chris recovers quickly."

Mindy reached her hand out to shake mine and I shook it, but I wanted to pull her into my arms, shelter her from whatever was next and make her heart feel calm. Her palm was sweaty despite her fingers being cold, and all I got was a polite nod as she stepped around Dr. Andrews. "I'll wait in your office, sir," she said and then she was gone.

"Mr. Turner, I hope you don't mind if we have a chat." The tall man shut the door and Mindy was gone, vanished down the hallway. He walked around her desk and my eyes followed him.

"Of course not, Dr. Andrews" I told him, sitting as he sat. "What's this about?" I knew very well what this was about. He was giving me some sort of heads up about her being removed from Chris's case due to our relationship, and I just had to endure it. I felt like telling him I already knew and he didn't have to say a word, but I figured that might anger him.

"Please, call me Callum." He tapped his fingers on the desk and smiled. "I just want to cut to the chase." His lips pursed and he looked down for a second, almost as if it pained him to say what he was about to say. "Dr. Scriber crossed some lines in this relationship and the hospital is well aware that she—"

"I know what she did, sir. I am the one who pushed her." I held my breath for a second as he looked me in the eye like he was shocked. "This isn't her fault. I am the one that initiated the entire thing."

Dr. Andrews' eyebrows rose slightly and he sighed. "Well, that changes things."

"And the sex in her office, I apologize for that too. It was a horrible choice on my part and it will never happen again. She has already referred my son to a different doctor." I watched his face contort in confusion and then resolve.

"So, you're ending an affair?"

"No, we won't be ending the relationship, but we are going to do things the right way now. I don't think her judgment was affected at all." I stood, ready to leave. I wanted to catch her before he got to his office to scold her.

"Mr. Turner, please sit for a moment."

I stopped and turned toward him, slowly lowering myself back into the chair. He scratched his head the way she had just done a moment ago. This whole thing was blown too far out of proportion. Mindy wasn't unethical, just distracted and maybe in love.

"Mr. Turner, with your son being adopted, a certain level of care is expected. Dr. Scriber didn't follow protocol, and we suspect it's because of her relationship to you and your son." He leaned his head down as if insinuating something that I didn't quite catch. "When a child doesn't have a full medical history, we run the gamut of tests to be sure we rule out everything. DNA tests aren't one of them. And Dr. Scriber only tested for a very targeted class of disorders, when in reality, Christopher should have been tested with a much broader scope. With no medical history, we have to know everything."

DNA test? What was he talking about? I didn't understand what was happening. I shook my head and licked my lips. "What are you saying?"

"I'm saying, given her relationship to you and the boy, she cut corners because she made assumptions about his heredity and could have risked his health by skipping crucial steps. Dr. Scriber is being put on suspension, and you will have to see a different doctor now. They will run the appropriate tests if you request, and we will give Christopher the best care possible."

He tapped his finger again but I still didn't understand. Mindy would never put Chris in danger. She loved him like a son. I could see it in the way she cared for him. My mind reeled over the news that she would be suspended. I pulled my phone out and shot her a text telling her to come to my house at six for dinner, and sat there staring at my hands.

"I just want to make sure there won't be any lawsuits."

My eyes rose to meet his again. "Lawsuit?" I offered a confused expression. "Why would I sue? She's a terrific doctor. She never did anything wrong."

"I'm glad we agree. Now we just have to let the ethics committee decide that too." He stood and offered his hand and I rose and shook it.

What the hell was going on? DNA test? I didn't understand. Was this what she was trying to tell me? God I needed to talk to her now.

18

Mindy

Passing Evelyn in the hallway on the way to Dr. Andrews's office, I felt my stomach lurch. She had an apologetic expression and grabbed my arm. "God, Min, I'm so sorry. I heard he's on the warpath. Look, I didn't tell him about the DNA bit, okay? I'm not sure who did."

"It's not your fault, Eve," I told her, sighing. "I made my bed and now I have to lie in it."

"I still feel guilty. I would never have told him anything, except he asked me. That lab assistant started all of this." She let her hand slide down my arm to my hand and she squeezed it. "I tried to explain that it was just a misunderstanding but he insisted on talking to you."

"Thanks." I pulled away from her and nodded with a frown on my face. "I better get in there."

Evelyn continued walking. I turned and watched her for a second, her ponytail swaying with each step, and she vanished around the corner. I knew the train had left the station and there was no getting it back now. It was better this way. At least part of the guilt would be removed from my shoulders today, even if it meant some horrible repercussions.

Dr. Andrews's office was open, so I let myself in and sat in a chair, wringing my hands in my lap. I didn't feel scared or anxious anymore. Instead, my heart felt dead. There was no point in feeling anxiety; what was done was done. I just had to wait and hear how bad it was. I assumed I would be terminated today and have to find another job while the medical board decided if I got to keep my license. My parents would love that; me being fired over this whole thing they already were pissed at me about.

I sat there for about fifteen minutes waiting before Dr. Andrews walked in. I didn't rise to meet him though I should have. My butt was firmly planted on the chair, my heavy heart weighing it down. He sat across from me and frowned—grimaced maybe? I tried not to look at his face because despite not feeling anxiety, I felt massive amounts of shame. Never in my career had I even flirted with the line of being unethical. I always kept a high standard.

Until now.

"Mindy, you and I have been somewhat close for a while now." His words only heaped on more shame. "I'd consider you a friend. Would you?"

I nodded, not looking up at him. I'd consider all of my coworkers to be on my friend list, though they weren't all the type I'd open up to or go out with. We were friendly enough to cover each other's backs, encourage and support each other, and help where needed.

"I've been in situations in the past that were quite gray ethically. This is not one of them." I watched his hands fold together on his desk and I looked up into his eyes to see compassion. "I saw the DNA results, and then the other tests. Kylie Pleiman told me a vial was missing and I looked into it. Would you like to give me your side of the story?"

I wanted to shake my head no, but it would come out either here or at an ethics review board and it would be easier here in the privacy of his office. My tongue felt like lead; I didn't know if I could even speak. I wrung my hands more, staring down at them for a few seconds while he waited, until I finally got the nerve to speak.

"So, when I was sixteen, well really fifteen, I did some experimenting with my boyfriend at the time. I got pregnant and my parents weren't very happy at all. We have a very small Jewish community here, and they are very devout. It was a shame to them, so they hid me away, homeschooled me until I gave birth, and forced me to give up the baby." My hands shook as I spoke, and I tried not to get choked up.

"When I was introduced to Mr. Turner, I knew I had seen him somewhere. He looked familiar, but I knew I could help his son. He made an appointment and in the meantime, I remembered where I'd seen him. When I signed the adoption papers, the adoption agency gave me a photo of the parents. It was twelve years ago, and he's aged a little, but I swore it was him."

"So why didn't you just tell him your suspicions and ask for a test?" His voice was calm and rational. He wasn't angry or lashing out how I thought he would be. The compassion only made me cry, and I couldn't continue for a second. He handed me tissues and spoke calming words. "I understand this must be very difficult for you; you are one of the most ethical and moral doctors I know. I was shocked to hear this; that's why I'm asking for your side of the story."

I nodded and wiped my eyes, then continued. "So I was afraid if I told him that, he would leave and I'd never see him again. You have no idea how badly I wanted to reconnect with my son, or how many times I called the adoption agency hoping for information." I sniffled, blew my nose and wadded the tissue up. "So when I saw this man who looked like the man in that picture twelve years ago, with a boy the same age as the boy I gave up, well I screwed up. The boy looked like my father. My gut told me it was my son. I accepted him as a patient with the hope that I could run a DNA test and find out if he was mine."

"And you found out he was?" Dr. Andrews head dipped and his gaze penetrated me, soothing my heart. Again, I nodded, crying harder. He had no idea what finding Christopher had meant to me, though I could see in his eyes he was trying to. "Mindy, I'm on your side, okay? But you have to understand this is a horrible breach of ethics. That man could sue the hospital."

"I know, Dr. Andrews. I just couldn't let my little boy get taken again." I reached for the tissues myself this time and blew my nose.

"Okay, so you told him and everything is worked out now. He promised not to sue."

"What?" I asked, confused.

"Well, he knows. Right? He seemed to understand what I told him, about you not testing thoroughly because of your relationship to him..." He looked at me with concern now, maybe a bit confused himself.

"No, he knows nothing." I shook my head wondering how much he knew. It was time to be one-hundred-percent honest. "Mr. Turner was attracted to me from the beginning. He asked me to meet him privately, but I protested it because of the ethics of me dating the man who was the father of my patient."

"But you were the patient's biological mother." He shook his head. "I'm not following."

"I had an affair with him." I blurted the words out like they were toxic, and his face fell.

"Oh my, I see."

"You have to understand that this entire thing got way out of control and now I'm not sure how to even make it right. I just wanted to be with my son." I wiped my eyes again, feeling the emotion passing finally. "The rest just sort of—happened."

"Thank you for telling me, Mindy. Now, you have to understand that this is not my decision. I am putting you on a two-week suspension pending the outcome of an ethics hearing." I nodded and he kept going. "The board will review everything and will probably have some questions of their own. It's a paid suspension, but it may result in termination."

"I understand."

"I'm so sorry this happened. I believe all things happen for a reason though. Maybe this will lead to your happy ending." He stood and offered his hand. I was thankful he was such a kind man.

"I'll clean out my locker for now." I shook his hand and we said our goodbyes and I did what I said. I cleaned my locker and walked to my car where I sat and cried some more. Instead of going home, though, I went to the only place I knew there was comfort without judgment.

Jace's office.

I'd never been here before, only passed by it. I knew he was likely back here working, and when I glanced at my phone to check the time, I saw he sent me a message asking me to come to his house for dinner. This was even better, because maybe in this non-intimate setting I'd have the guts to tell him everything. I jammed my phone into my pocket and walked into the office.

It was nice, laid out similar to a doctor or dentist's office with a reception and waiting area. I told the woman at the counter that I was here to see him and when she used the intercom to page him, her face contorted, eyes going wide.

"He said come right back," she told me, as if she were amazed by it.

I let myself through, hesitantly looking around. "Down on the left," she said, pointing, and I nodded my acknowledgement.

I saw the door with his name on it and knocked before entering, but Jace had a few people in his office. He stood immediately, a look of concern on his face.

"Jenny, Howard, I need a minute," he said, and the two looked up at me. They looked important, and I felt out of place.

"I'm sorry, I can come back," I told him, gesturing with my thumb over my shoulder.

"Nonsense. These two were just leaving." Jace gave them a stern expression and they both stood. The man eyed me as he passed, but the woman smiled politely. When they were gone, Jace shut the door behind them and took me into his arms. I was here, ready to confess everything, but he poured on the affection and gave me no space to even speak.

"Baby, I'm so sorry I got you in trouble. I told him this was all my fault. I told him we were going to a different doctor now. I heard you were getting suspended and I felt horrible, but you were gone by the time I left your office, and I'm just really sorry."

"Jace, I..." I tried to interrupt his rambling, but following his words came kisses, a storm of them raining on my forehead and cheeks.

"Please forgive me. I'm so sorry," he kept saying, and I felt horrible. He shouldn't have been the one apologizing. I should have been the one saying I was sorry. I tried to relax in his arms, but he held me so tightly while he tried to make me feel better that I felt suffocated, until he held me at arm's length and said, "You are really the best thing that's ever happened to me, Mindy. Please, say you forgive me."

"I—"

"Please," he pleaded.

I looked into his eyes and felt a knife go through my chest as I said, "I forgive you."

He kissed me hard, parting my lips and shoving his tongue in my mouth. I could hardly take a breath. It was like I was his salvation, easing his guilty conscience or something. God what I wouldn't have done for that feeling—relief from guilt. But knowing he wanted me this badly, that he was desperate to keep me, gave me a small comfort. I kissed him back, forgetting entirely that we were in his office.

The taste of him on my tongue was intoxicating, and I found myself pressing my body against his, wanting more of him. He responded eagerly, his hands roaming over me, igniting a fire within me that burned hotter with each passing moment. I moaned into his mouth, unable to control my body's response to his touch.

Jace broke the kiss, his breaths coming in ragged gasps. "Mindy," he whispered, his voice husky with desire. "I need you. The thought that I might lose you, I just...."

I didn't hesitate. I wanted him just as badly as he wanted me. I pushed him back onto his desk, sending papers and pens scattering to the floor. He laughed, a deep rumble that sent shivers down my spine. I climbed onto the desk, straddling him as I pulled off my blouse, exposing my breasts to his hungry gaze.

He groaned, his hands reaching up to cup them, his thumbs grazing over my nipples after he folded the cups of my bra down. I arched my back, pressing myself closer to him as he teased me, sending jolts of electricity through my body. I could feel the wetness pooling between my legs, aching for him to fill me up.

Jace leaned forward, taking one of my nipples into his mouth, sucking hard as he slid his hand down my pants. I cried out, my body writhing as he rubbed my clit, sending me spiraling into deep arousal. He worked my pussy as I rose up and unbuttoned his pants, sliding his dick out. He was mostly hard, but I stroked him until his cock finished swelling. I wanted him inside me.

Then I climbed off the desk, and I pulled off my pants, leaving only my panties on as I straddled him again, my knees on the edge of his desk. He rubbed my clit hard, his fingers moving fluidly against me. I moaned, thrusting my hips against his hand as he worked me. My body was aflame with desire, and I wanted him to make me come

"Please," I begged. "I need you."

He let go of my clit, his hand reaching around to my backside as he stood, lifting me up. I wrapped my legs around him as he turned and laid me on the desk. The way his cock stood erect, sticking out of his pants, was arousing, especially when I watched him roll a condom on, retrieved from his pants pocket. I didn't know why I could never get the words out; maybe that was fate too.

The only thing I knew was that I needed him inside me—now.

19

Jace

After feeling horribly guilty and panicked that I might lose Mindy for the past hour, seeing her walk through that door was a miracle. And seeing her splayed on my desk ready for me to take her was even better. I rolled the condom on as she shimmied out of her panties and dropped them.

"Please, Jace, I need you in me," she cooed, reaching for my hips. I massaged her pussy, smearing her moisture around as I leaned over her and kissed her, then let my kisses trail to her chest where I took a nipple in my mouth and sucked it gently.

As I did, I slid my cock into her pussy, watching her face as I entered her. I was mesmerized by her expression as I slid deeper and deeper inside her, the walls of her pussy squeezing my cock as it moved into her. I could feel her vaginal muscles milking me, massaging me with little spasms and contractions as I glided in and out of her. I was so turned on that I didn't think I'd last very long, which was fine with me because Mindy's pleasure was more important to me than my own.

"Harder! Faster!" she panted, and I obliged. I fucked her until my thighs were slapping against hers and she was moaning and gasping. My breathing was ragged and my heart was racing. I had never felt more alive than I did at that moment.

At that point, I felt her pussy clench around me, and she groaned and lifted her hips off the desk, grinding her pussy against my body. I felt her pulse around my cock and I knew she was coming. I growled and thrust into her harder. I knew I was going to come soon, and I knew I was going to come hard. I bit my lip, trying to hold back, but I was just too close.

It all happened so fast. I thrust into her one last time, and as I did, I felt my balls tighten and my cock throb. I groaned, feeling the cum shoot from my cock into the condom. Cum gushed out of me, so much that I thought it would come out of the sides of the condom. I shuddered, moaning and gasping as I emptied myself into her. I pumped into her a few more times, riding out my orgasm, until I was totally spent.

At that point, I felt so weak and dizzy I had to sit on the desk beside her. I took a few deep breaths, and felt my heartbeat slow. I was spent. My body was sweaty, and I could feel my cum starting to leak out of the condom and trickle down my shaft. But Mindy lay there across my desk with her legs spread and I couldn't help myself. With one hand I slid the full condom off my dick and tossed it into the bin at the end of my desk, and with the other, I reached up and touched her tender lips, playing with her clit lightly. She shuddered and her legs shook violently.

"God, you're so sexy..." I breathed on her pussy, cool breath making her clench, and I watched her holes constrict. As they did I slid a finger into her and she looked down at me.

"Again?" she asked, breathless, and I nodded at her.

"As many times as you can take."

She groaned and I felt my cock twitch as if to say, "yesssss." I slid my finger in and out of her, and she shuddered and moaned. I pushed another finger into her and started to thrust into her with my two fingers. As my fingers pumped into her, I slowly lowered my head and began to lick her clit. She groaned and her hips bucked against my face as I pleasured her.

She tasted amazing, like iced tea and strawberries. I licked her clit gently with my tongue, and she started to grind against me. I knew she was close to coming again. I curled my fingers up to find the rough spot inside her pussy that would drive her crazy. I stroked that spot with my fingers as I licked her clit, and she moaned loudly. Her whole body shuddered and she raised her hips off the desk, grinding against my face and hand. I felt her orgasm explode from her, and her cum rush out of her, spilling down her thighs and soaking my hand.

Mindy's pussy clamped down on my fingers, gripping me until it was difficult to push into her, but I kept thrusting, now standing and leaning over her. She looked up at me, her eyes glazed with pleasure. Though her orgasm began to fade it was obvious she wasn't done, and I wasn't done with her. I leaned on the edge of my desk between her thighs and she looked at me, her eyes looking deep into mine. She smiled and I knew what she was thinking. I raised my eyebrows and she nodded.

"Yeah?" I asked. "Again?"

"You said as many times as I could handle." Mindy shrugged and grabbed my wrist, forcing me to keep thrusting. My fingers sank into her again and again, and her g-spot stayed swollen and tender.

"So I did." I smirked at her and retreated, falling to my knees to the ground between her thighs. Her pussy was so wet, I licked both thighs and all over her lips to clean her up, then put my fingers back in and began to suck on her clit. She tasted so sweet, and her pussy was so warm and wet, I could have spent hours licking her.

"Oh wow, Jace," she moaned, clawing at my hair. "It's so good."

I felt her clench around my fingers. "Is it?" I asked as I thrust into her again. "You want another one?"

She nodded, closing her eyes. "I want it again."

"Beg for it," I said. "Beg for another orgasm." Her hands fell; she couldn't reach me when I rose up to see her face, and she panted.

"Please Jace," she gasped. "Please make me come again."

I smiled and licked her clit, then looked up at her. Mindy moaned and arched her back, reaching up to take my face in her hands as I lowered to her valley again to flick my tongue over her clit. Mindy reached down to grab my hand, forcing me to thrust my fingers deeper and faster.

When her coil snapped and she started convulsing, I felt it and knew she was having another orgasm. She pulled my fingers deeper inside her, holding her breath and moaning. "Oh my god, I love you."

I couldn't believe what I heard. Mindy confessed she loved me? I wanted to stop then and there and kiss her, lavish my love upon her, but I knew she felt so good; I couldn't stop.

I growled against her clit, gently moving my face from side to side as I sucked and she spasmed. This one seemed to be the strongest one yet, and she jerked and gasped for breath. I could tell she was trying to be quiet, and then her body began to calm.

I pulled out my fingers, spreading her lips with my thumbs, and I dipped my tongue in her juices again. Her body convulsed again; it felt like she was having another orgasm, but I knew it was the aftershocks.

My tongue slid up and down her pussy in long, slow strokes. Mindy had stopped shaking, and now she was just gasping for air. Her arms fell to the sides and she spread her legs, letting them hang as she reveled in her afterglow. I stood between her thighs and put my dick away, zipping my pants, then took her hand and helped her sit up. Her hair was fussed and her makeup streaked, but she looked calmer than when she'd come in. I felt it too.

"Wow, that was incredible," she mumbled and ran a hand through her hair. Then she took a deep breath and blew it out. I picked up her panties and slacks and handed them to her. As she took them, I kissed her and lingered closer to her face.

"I love you too, Mindy," I whispered. She tipped up her chin and brushed her lips over mine and I knew it wasn't just a slip of the tongue. She meant it. My guilt about my late wife was mostly gone. I knew moving on was the right thing, and that it was okay. I was just worried about Chris and how he'd react. His tantrum the other day had caused a stir in the house and he had mostly hidden in his room except for meals when I told him he had to come eat, but even then he remained silent.

"So Andrews gave me paid suspension, but there will be an ethics review." Mindy dressed and sat in one of my client chairs to put her shoes back on. I sat beside her and took her free hand.

"We'll get through this, okay? He can't do much. We are going to a new doctor, so the unethical bit is over now." I wanted to comfort her and reassure her but she didn't look convinced. "You look a little sad. Is it about the way Christopher responded the other day? I know that was sort of abrupt and he interrupted. Then you were just gone."

"I sort of felt like I was intruding, or that I caused a problem." She sat with her hands folded in her lap and her head down.

"Oh, babe, I promise that's not the case. He is struggling to understand how to move on. I'm going to get him back in counseling because this new step in the journey seems more difficult on him than I thought it would be." I took her hand and kissed her knuckles, elated that we were finally on the same page. I couldn't hide my cheesy grin.

"Jace, can we talk about something? It's important." Her eyes bored into mine and I knew she was serious.

"Yeah, sure," I said, lowering her hand to my lap.

"So, the day we first met, I thought I knew you from somewhere."

"Knock knock." Howard's voice interrupted and I looked over my shoulder to see him walk right in. Had he done that five minutes ago, he'd have gotten a show for sure. I scowled.

"What is it?"

"The meeting? With Threshold..." His eyebrows rose and I glanced at Mindy. This was a super important meeting. I couldn't miss it. The same time I opened my mouth to say something, her phone buzzed in her pocket.

"Min..."

She pulled it out and her shoulders dropped. "It's my Mom. I have to take this." Before I got a chance to say another word, she stood, pecked me on the lips, and brushed past Howard.

When she was gone, I stood to go with him, but I knew I had a sour look on my face. Nothing in the world would be the same now. I'd want to be home with her all the time. That made me grin. Life was changing for the better and I couldn't wait to see where it took me.

20

Mindy

My phone vibrated and I looked down to see my sister's name on the caller ID. My heart knew the only time I had to tell Jace was now, but that moment had passed yet again because of his meeting. I blurted out that I had to take the call and walked out without saying anything, just a kiss goodbye. I knew he'd be there for me if and when I was ready. I just wanted it to be over with and now wasn't the time. Not before his big meeting.

"Vi, I'm here." I held the phone to my ear to avoid any small talk as I walked through the office to the front door. It was rude to answer my phone in public but I wanted to hide.

"Min, Mom and Dad went to your apartment. They said they were going to wait for you to get home from wherever. You need to go home."

"They're what!" I barely made it to my car before freaking out. "Why would they do that?" My parents had my spare key just in case something happened and they needed to go into my apartment while I was away or at work for any reason. It was a safety measure, not an open invitation.

"Mindy, Dad found out about your suspension. Don't ask me how, but he did."

"How do you know?" I was shocked and horrified. That had happened less than two hours ago. I had only confirmed it with Jace just before. My father had connections—I knew that. But I didn't realize he was this connected.

"They told me. Look, I love you. We don't have to get into this. I'm not going to tell you 'I told you so,' but you just need to get home. Okay? Go and just try to be calm. They love you and they want what's best for you."

I was so upset I hung up on her. She didn't deserve that, but I would apologize later. For now I had to find out why my parents thought they owned me still. They had no right to stick their noses into my personal business like this. My life was mine to live, not theirs.

The car carried me across town as quickly as traffic would allow me, and when I saw their car parked in my spot, I knew Violet wasn't lying. They were up there waiting for me like an ambush predator. My body was already on edge from all the anxiety over the past few days. This was the last thing I needed. I thought I'd made it clear to them that I didn't want them meddling.

As soon as I opened the front door they started in on me. Dad paced the floor while Mom gave me a tongue lashing.

"This has gone too far, Mindy. The hospital director told your father what you did. You did a DNA test on that boy? Are you stupid?" My own mother called me stupid and she had no idea how that hurt.

"Why are you in my house?" I slammed my keys on the table and threw my purse onto the couch. "You have no right!"

"Do not speak to your mother that way, young lady." My father's angry voice and squared shoulders didn't intimidate me anymore. I had carried the pain of the past in my heart and mind for so long, nothing ever felt right. "You have dug up the ghosts of the past, and that is an unholy thing."

"No, you tore my child out of my arms and ripped my heart to shreds." I seethed, chest heaving with emotion as I pointed my finger at him and shouted. "He was mine, not yours. I carried him, birthed him and loved him. And you stole him and gave him away. I didn't get to hold him, or nurse him, or see his first steps. I went through depression but I wasn't allowed to show it. I wanted to die, but I had to put on a happy face. I was never allowed to say how much it hurt." I let them have all of the anger and pain that I'd carried. I just let it vomit out of my mouth in a fit of angry rage-induced tears, screaming and pointing.

"He was mine! And you stole him!"

My father shook his head and stormed out, leaving the door open behind him, and I expected my mother to do the same. She was every bit to blame in the situation as he was. I reeled around, ready to shout at her too, but the pain in her eyes and the tears streaming down her cheeks were new to me. She looked ashamed and apologetic, eyebrows dipping in the center.

Mom walked over to me and wrapped her arms around me, though I remained stiff in her embrace. "Mindy, I'm so sorry. I never knew you were hurting this badly. I didn't know what it did to you. We thought we were doing what was best for your future."

This was the first apology I'd ever had about this situation, and sorry wasn't good enough. Sorry would never remove the pain, or give me back my son, or heal the rift between my heart and my parents' hearts.

"Please leave," I said calmly. I didn't look her in the eye or even flinch when she walked away. I didn't see if she left; I just wanted for the door to click shut and then I burst into tears and fell onto the couch.

I fell asleep there in a heap of emotion and woke up around five thirty. After Jace's text asking me to have dinner, and what happened this afternoon, I didn't know what to think or feel. I wanted to be there, but I also wanted to get in my car and drive away and never come back. My desire to work things out with him won out, and I got up and washed my face and headed to his house.

When he opened the door for me, I could see things were already tense in the house. Christopher sat at the kitchen table with food in front of him, but he was scowling. Jace didn't say a word, but he did kiss my forehead and nod at the table. Then he shut the door behind me and we walked to the table. I sat at his right hand, with Christopher across from us. He didn't even look up.

"Topper, please say hello to Mindy." Jace rested his forearms on the edge of the table and watched Christopher spoon a few bites of soup into his mouth. It smelled delicious. I wondered if he made it or if it was takeaway. The table was even set properly; I felt bad for being late. I shouldn't have let myself sleep.

"You mean Dr. Scriber?" His tone was harsh. It surprised me. I'd never seen him like this, not even when he walked in on us after sex. Christopher finally looked up and glared at Jace. His eyes flicked to meet mine and then he looked back down into his bowl which he swished around with his spoon. "I'm not hungry. May I be excused?"

"No, you may not. You need to finish your dinner." Jace was firm but loving, just the sort of father I imagined him being.

"Christopher, I'm sorry if my being here upsets you." I reached out under the table and held Jace's hand. I needed moral support, but I got the feeling he did too.

He didn't look back at me, but he did drop his spoon and place his napkin over his bowl. "I feel sick. I want to lie down."

Jace frowned and looked at me then sighed. "Chris, I think it's important that you know that Mindy and I are dating." The boy's eyes drew up to meet his father's gaze and he shook his head, brow furrowing.

"No. You can't replace her." He looked genuinely hurt. "You promised."

"Christopher, I'm not replacing your mother. No one will ever replace your mother. I'm finding someone to be my life partner. I know you don't understand this, but I want you to try to accept it. We can go see Dr. Phillips again if you think that will help." Jace had mentioned getting Christopher some counseling, so I assumed that was the counselor's name.

"I don't need a new Mom. I don't even want one. Okay?" He stood up and his chair tipped over and slammed onto the ground. "The first one threw me away, and the other one left me here to be alone."

Christopher ran off, feet slapping on the tile floor, and Jace's head dropped. "Mindy, I have to go talk to him. I'm really sorry about this."

"Go," I told him, but inside my heart was shattered to a million pieces. Jace walked out and I let my tears fall freely.

Christopher had no idea how hurtful those words were to me, but I didn't blame him one bit. I would never have thrown him away, and the pain I felt when my parents ripped him from my arms would never begin to equal the pain I knew he was feeling. I pushed the soup away, unable to fathom eating a single bite when my son was hurting so much. What I wouldn't have done to be the one holding him right now, comforting his heart.

Part of me wanted to run, to leave and never cause him that pain again. But deep in my gut, I knew I loved Jace more than anything, and Christopher more than ever. Tonight was the night I was coming clean, and I didn't care if hell rained fire, or if the waters below rose up to drown me. I was telling Jace the truth.

21

Jace

I sat on the edge of Christopher's bed for twenty minutes trying to comfort him but he just wouldn't talk to me. I didn't feel right leaving him, so I stayed until I heard him snoring lightly. By the time I returned to the living room, Mindy had cleared the entire table and rinsed the dishes. They sat stacked in the sink, and the pot of soup sat to the side. She gestured at them.

"I didn't know where your Tupperware was and I didn't want to snoop."

I walked straight up to her and kissed her forehead, holding her by the shoulders. "You're amazing, you know that?" She smelled good, like baby powder. I missed having a woman around. They always make things smell nice.

"I don't feel amazing." Mindy pulled away and picked at her fingernails. "It's been a rough day."

I sighed, knowing she'd been through the wringer today. "I know it has. Let me put this away, and we'll talk as much as you need." I reached for the cupboard where I kept my bowls and lids and took one out. Mindy leaned against the counter and watched me. I could tell she was upset. "So you had an important call?" I thought I'd segue into the conversation easily as I put away the leftovers.

"My sister... She called to tell me my parents were in my apartment. I rushed home to a huge lecture and a big fight. They screamed at me for digging up ghosts and how I should let things in the past alone. It's so frustrating that they think they can still control my life. It makes me want to move out of town or something."

She wasn't making sense, but the fact that it had to do with her parents told me enough. She had been so upset the last time she interacted with them. I got a lid and covered the dish, then slid it into the fridge and rinsed the pan while I tried to encourage her.

"Mindy, your parents are only trying to protect you and love you. It just seems to me that they're misguided. I'm not sure about everything that's going on but I'm here." I dried my hands and tossed the towel on the counter. "Do you want me to hold you? Rub your back? Let me comfort you." I brushed a strand of chestnut hair out of her eyes and she leaned into me.

"I'd like that."

I took her hand and led her around the kitchen table, through the open concept living room to the short hall adjoining my master suite. We heard Christopher snoring loudly when we passed his door, so I felt comfortable taking her right into my room and locking the door. Mindy stepped out of her shoes and we walked with stockinged feet to bed. She bit her lip and stood there for a second, then looked up at me.

"This would be more comfortable in fewer items of clothing."

I caught a hint of a smirk and knew exactly what she wanted. "I think I agree," I said, nodding.

Both of us stripped clothing off. I kept my boxers on and Mindy left her t-shirt and panties, but she pulled her bra off without removing her shit. Her nipples were hard, showing through the thin fabric. She climbed into bed and lay down, and I curled around her. I pulled the hair off her neck and kissed her lightly on the shoulder.

"I'm sorry you're having a rough day. How can I make it better?"

Mindy turned to face me, her eyes shining in the dim light. "You already are," she said, her voice husky with desire. She leaned in and kissed me deeply, her tongue exploring my mouth. I responded eagerly, wrapping my arms around her and pulling her close. We kissed for what seemed like hours, our bodies pressed together, the heat between us building steadily. Mindy's hand found its way to my waistband, and she began to slide my boxers down my hips. I helped her, pushing them down to my knees and kicking them off.

I lifted her shirt and reached for her breasts, kneading them gently, and she moaned in response.

"Mmm, that feels good," she said, her eyes closed in pleasure.

"I love your boobs," I said, pressing my face into the cleavage and inhaling her scent.

"I love your hands on them," she said, reaching down to my crotch. She wrapped her fingers around my erection and squeezed lightly. I sucked in a deep breath as her fingers gripped my shaft, stroking and squeezing.

"I want to make you feel amazing..." I kissed her hard, propping myself on one elbow with one tit in my hand. Her nipple hardened between my fingers as I twisted and teased it.

"Gonna have to get these panties off first, I suppose," she said, grinning. Mindy slipped her panties off and tossed them on the floor. I put my knees between her legs and pressed them open. My nostrils flared as I inhaled the scent of her arousal. I slowly ran one hand up the inside of her thigh, and she shivered. I ran my fingers over her labia, teasing her, and she moaned.

She tugged her shirt over her head and lay there on the bed in front of me in all her perfection. "God you're so beautiful." My fingers slid into her moisture, rubbing and smearing it around.

"Make me feel good, Jace," she moaned before pulling me in for another kiss. Her lips were sweet and soft, and her tongue danced with mine as I stroked her clit. She began to grind against my hand, moving her hips in time with my fingers. I slipped a finger inside her and thrust slowly. She broke the kiss with a moan, her back arching and her head falling back.

I pushed a second finger inside her, thrusting them in and out in time with her movements. She began to buck her hips against my hand, her breathing heavy and ragged.

"Oh my god, Jace," she moaned. I could feel her clit swelling against my fingers, and I rubbed it with my thumb. Mindy's breathing grew more and more ragged, and she pushed her hips against my hand. "Jace, I'm going to come," she moaned. She weaved her hand into my hair and pulled my face toward hers for a passionate kiss. Her tongue danced with mine as her orgasm hit her.

She gasped into my mouth and moaned and I stroked her until the orgasm passed, and she relaxed against the bed, a satisfied smile on her face. When she pulled me down on top of her, my cock nestled against her thigh. She kissed me deeply, and I pulled her leg up so that her knee was on my shoulder. Her eyes glazed over with desire as I slid inside her. Her hips grinned against mine, and we began to move together.

"I love you, Jace," she moaned, her hands on my shoulders.

"I love you too, Mindy." Her eyes closed and her mouth fell open. "God, you feel amazing," I groaned, my voice thick with desire.

"I love you, Jace," she moaned over and over.

"Babe... I need to get a condom." I slowed my thrusts and reached for the nightstand drawer. She rolled away from me, and my cock slid out of her. "Hey... don't go too far."

"I'm not." Mindy got on her hands and knees and held my dick erect while I rolled the condom on, then climbed on top of me and straddled me. "Mmmm... just like that," Mindy moaned as she lowered herself onto me. She leaned forward and kissed my lips and I grabbed her hips, thrusting my cock deep inside her.

She began to rock on me, grinding her clit against my pubic bone. It was incredible the way she clenched her muscles around my girth. Her pussy was hot and slick; I wished I could feel her without the condom.

"Mmmm..." Mindy mewled and leaned forward. She grabbed the headboard and began to rock back and forth, her breasts bouncing as she rode me. "Oh my god, Jace... I'm going to come again..." Her hair swayed over my face, brushing lightly on my skin, and I studied that expression of pleasure. I wanted to see that every time we made love.

I reached up and grabbed her tits, squeezing them. When her pussy clamped down around me hard, and she whimpered out her enjoyment, I took over thrusting. She bounced harder, and I slid my hands down to her hips again. Her body shuddered and spasmed and she rested her hands on my chest. Her orgasm waned, but mine was still building. I flipped her over, laying her on her back, and continued my thrusts.

"Harder... Please, Jace..."

I pounded into her. Faster and faster. The warmth of our bodies wrapped around us and the scent of sex filled the room. "

You're so pretty," I whispered as I thrust into her. "I love you."

"I love you, too," she whispered, gasping for air. "I'm going to come again... I can feel it..."

I thrust harder and faster until her body shook and I felt her clench down.

"Yes, yes, yes," she moaned as her body shook and spasmed around me. "Oh, Jace..."

I thrust once more, and then I felt my orgasm hit. It was deep and intense and I had to bite down on my lip to keep from screaming out. I didn't want to wake Christopher.

"I love you," she whispered again as she kissed me and I collapsed onto her. I noticed tears streaking down her face and brushed them away.

"I love you," I whispered back. "I love you so much. Are you okay?"

"Yes, just a bit emotional. Sometimes when an orgasm is really good, or I feel a strong emotional connection I just cry." She smiled and swiped at her eyes then curled into my chest and held me.

We lay there, tangled in each other, for a while, and when I feared the condom would fall off and make a mess I extricated myself from her limbs and sat on the edge of the bed to take it off. I felt her hand on my back and smiled. I missed that sensation.

"Do you think he'll ever accept me?"

Her question was a fair one. I knew given time Christopher would adjust, though whether he would ever accept her was a different matter. "I hope so." I lay back down and wrapped my arm over her belly. "We just have to give him time and space to deal with it."

"Jace, I really screwed things up." Mindy turned her back to me and I pulled her tightly against my body. She was moist with sweat, her skin salty everywhere I kissed her.

"No, babe. You didn't. Things aren't screwed up. We are going to make it all work out." I didn't know why she thought she had screwed up, but I wasn't going to let her lie there feeling bad about herself. "Everything will be just fine."

"But what if it's not? What if it's so messy that nothing works out?" Her voice was filled with emotion. I wanted to take those heavy feelings and throw them to the bottom of the ocean.

"Things are never so messy or complicated that they can't be sorted out." I wondered if she was talking about her parents now? Or if it was still about Christopher. "He's just a little boy who lost his mother. It takes time to move on from something like that. I'm sure with just a little patience and care he will come around. In the meantime, I am helplessly in love with you and I don't think there are enough horses to drag me away from you."

"Yeah?" she asked, sounding lighter. "I've seen the Clydesdales in the Liberty Festival Parade. They're pretty strong."

"They've got nothing on me. You don't even know how strong my love can be." I kissed her arm and smiled and she looked up at me over her shoulder.

"You'll have to be very strong to love me past all my faults." Suddenly she was serious again, her eyes searching me, testing me.

I steeled myself and looked her right in the eye. "There is nothing you could say or do to make me not love you, Mindy. Nothing."

I didn't know what darkness she had lived through that she was ashamed to tell me, but I resolved in my heart that no matter what it was, I'd love her through it. She deserved that.

22

Mindy

The red glow of Jace's old radio alarm clock told me it was nearing three a.m. but I felt like we'd only been here talking for a few minutes. He was so easy to talk to, and we had more in common than either of us knew before this discussion. I was raised in a strict religious family and so was he, though they were different religions. That face gave us both an appreciation for serendipity and providence, which we both believed to be the reason we were lying in this bed together at this very moment.

Jace brushed a wisp of my hair out of my face and curled it around my ear when I yawned. It had been years since I stayed up this late. My schedule at the hospital didn't allow me to be a night owl like I was in college. And Jace looked tired too, the soft wrinkles around his eyes deepening as the minutes passed. We'd talked about Christopher and his mother, her death, his mourning, my struggle with my parents, and even our hobbies and interests. I'd been working up the courage to tell the truth all night.

"You know, I've never pulled an all-nighter with a girl." Jace grinned at me and tickled my side a little.

"Oh is that right?" I asked him, feeling so close and connected to him. The security he'd built in my heart over the past few hours was nothing short of miraculous. I'd never been so vulnerable and real with anyone. Which is maybe why I never had a successful relationship or even wanted one for that matter.

"Yeah," he said, moving closer. "What do you think men and women do this late at night in bed?" His hand slipped under the comforter and rested on my hip. He was being flirty and I sort of liked it. I hesitated only because I wanted to tell him the truth.

"Not sure..." I didn't respond to his advance, but I didn't pull away. I wanted everything to be one hundred percent calm and peaceful. I knew it would come as a shock, so maybe connecting a little physically would help him be more open to the news.

"I think it's when they experiment." He wagged his eyebrows and I chuckled.

"Experiment how?"

Jace's eyes flicked to the night stand where his beer sat collecting condensation. Around two-thirty he ran to the fridge for refreshments, and brought back two beers. He had opened his and had a sip, but mine sat on my side of the bed unopened. I had no idea what he was insinuating.

"Well, I want to try something..." He reached for his beer, took a huge gulp, and then set it back down.

"Try what?" I snickered and watched as he, with a mouth full of beer, snuck under the covers. His hand was cold from the bottle, and his lips were colder when he forced my knees apart and buried his face in my valley. "Oh wow!" I sucked in a breath and grabbed his head as he plunged his tongue into me, licking me and sucking my clit. "That's so cold." I folded the blankets back and laughed and gasped as he ate me.

The cold beer on his lips felt like ice against my hot flesh. His face was flushed and my legs were wide open, my hips lifting off the bed to meet his mouth. I couldn't help but moan and gasp. It was an exquisite feeling.

"Mmm," he moaned. When he finished he arose and kissed me.

His face was shiny from where the beer had warmed it up. He kissed me again, and I tasted myself and the beer on his lips.

"Jesus, that was hot," I said when we broke away.

"You mean cold?" he asked, smirking.

"Do it again." I narrowed my eyes at him and raised one corner of my mouth. Propped on my elbows with my legs open so he had easy access to my pussy, I watched him take another mouthful of the beer and return to my sex.

This time he licked me with the entire flat of his tongue, up and down my folds. I gasped and moaned, my hips rising off the bed to meet his mouth. I felt his tongue slip inside me and I moaned again. He was driving me wild. The contrast between his cold tongue and my hot flesh was incredible. I loved it.

"Oh, God, yes!"

He groaned and hummed with his tongue fully inside me, flicking my g-spot.

"Don't stop, don't stop, don't stop," I chanted, my thighs trembling.

I felt his fingers on my clit and I almost came. He was alternating his tongue in my pussy with his fingers on my clit, and I could feel my orgasm building. My hands slid into his hair and I pulled him into me as his tongue and fingers drove me wild. I was moaning and gasping and crying out; I was so close. He grunted and groaned, his tongue working furiously.

"Jace, I'm coming," I grunted as my orgasm broke over my body in convulsions and jerking muscles. Jace continued to lick, suck and finger me through my orgasm, his tongue and fingers still going. "Oh, God, please, please, please," I moaned, and he plunged his tongue back into my pussy. My body shuddered and my thighs trembled with the force of my orgasm. "Don't stop," I moaned, and he didn't. He continued to lick and suck me.

The moment I stopped shaking and my hips stopped jerking, he pulled away and scrambled to his knees. He kissed me and his fingers slipped between my thighs. He slid two fingers inside of me. "Like that?"

"The orgasm or the cold?" I mumbled, barely coherent. The after-glow was intense when combined with fatigue.

"Both... either..." His fingers worked my pussy good, massaging me and keeping me aroused.

"Yeah, I did." I draped my arms around his neck and pulled him into a deep kiss. His fingers worked in and out of me and made me want more. "What else do you want to try?" I smiled against his mouth and he shrugged.

"Something really bad? I mean... if you liked the cold beer on my lips, maybe you'll like something a little thicker?"

"Thicker?" I asked.

Jace reached for the beer bottle and grabbed it. Condensation dripped from it, landing on my chest. I hissed and grinned. "What are you doing?" I watched as he shook it, allowing the condensation to drip onto my boobs. It felt cold and made me shiver. I snickered.

"I'm putting cold beer on your pussy. Don't you wanna see what happens?" he asked.

"Uh..." Cold fingers and a tongue were one thing. I wasn't so certain about the entire bottle—until he swirled it around my nipple and it went immediately hard.

"God that's sexy," he groaned.

The icy bottle chilled both nipples and then he slid it across my stomach, over my mound and teased my inner thighs. "Do you want it to touch you?" he asked, using a warm thumb to press and massage my clit.

"Oh heck, yes," I begged.

He slid the bottle down my slit, and touched me. I shivered in pleasure. "Cold," he whispered, pressing a kiss to my lips. He slid it back up to my clit, and this time I felt the cool condensation dripping over my lips. I shuddered, closing my legs slightly, but he pushed them back open. "Enjoy it..."

I tried to enjoy, but my pussy ached to be filled. I looked down at what he was doing, teasing my lips and hole with the cold bottle. My juices were smeared all over the label, and his tongue darted in and out of his mouth, as if licking me off of his lips.

"I'm going to need you to make me come again now," I whispered and clenched, craving him in me.

"I will," he promised, and left the bottle on the bed. He slid a finger inside me, and brought his mouth to my frigid clit, licking and sucking it. I let out a low, primal moan and bucked my hips. I felt him smirk against my skin as he pushed a second finger inside me. HIs hot lips against my cold skin were even better than before.

"Oh, god, Jace, now..." It only took thirty seconds for me to come, and it was the most intense orgasm I'd ever had. I jolted and shook the whole bed for at least five minutes straight. His fingers hit the right spot again and again, and every time his tongue flicked my clit I jerked with involuntary spasms.

"Mmmm, seems like someone likes temperature play."

He rose up on his knees between my thighs and picked up the bottle and set it back on the table. As he did, he grabbed a condom out of the drawer and tore it open. His dick was hard, a bead of precum on his head. He stroked it a few times while I watched and swirled my fingers around my sensitive nub. Then he rolled the condom on.

"Where did you learn that little trick?" I asked him and he shook his head.

"Nowhere, I just wondered what it would feel like when I took a drink earlier." His grin was priceless.

"Put your dick in me already," I ordered, snickering and reaching for his body.

Jace took his dick in his hand and rubbed the head of it against my clit a few times before he pushed it into me. I was already wet, so it slid right in. He thrust in and out of me, his hands on my thighs as he watched his cock disappear and reappear from my hole. I gripped my breasts and toyed with my nipples and moaned.

"I love it when you moan," he said, his voice low and his eyes on mine. I whimpered and threw my head back, my eyes closed. His hand slid to my butt and he squeezed the cheek there, his thrusts faster. I opened my eyes and watched his face as he ground into me. I pushed my hips out and squeezed my pussy around him. "Oh, god," he groaned.

"You like that?" I asked.

"I love it," he breathed.

His breathing grew more ragged and his movements were frantic. I closed my eyes and let him have his way with me, his hands gripping my butt. He leaned forward and bit my neck. It was sharp and his teeth dug in, making me cry out. He pulled back, and then he thrust into me again.

"Oh god, it's so deep." I clawed at his sides. "You're so deep."

"You're so tight," he murmured in my ear.

He fucked me harder, his cock almost splitting me. I felt his fingers slide to my clit and rub it in circles. I moaned and arched my back, giving him better access to my neck, where he nibbled and sucked. His thrusts became short and fast. I felt my orgasm build and I pushed my hips out to meet his. I was so close.

"Come for me, Mindy," he begged. I felt his cock jerk inside me.

"Oh god," I cried out, and I came. I wrapped my arms and legs around him and ground against him as my body milked his dick.

"That's right. Just like that. Come for me," he coaxed.

"Oh my god," I breathed, as I rode out the waves of my orgasm.

"That's right, Mindy," he said, thrusting into me one last time. "That's my girl." I felt his dick jerk inside me, and he moaned as he came. He lay on top of me, his head nestled in my neck, breathing hard. I felt his cock pulsing as my pussy squeezed it. "That was amazing, Mindy. You're amazing," he said, pulling me closer to him, with his cock still inside me.

I kissed his shoulder and tried to catch my breath as he rolled off of me and pulled out. I didn't bother watching him stand and remove the condom. And when the bed shook, indicating he had returned, I pried my eyes open and looked up at him as he hovered over me.

"So good," I mewled, trying to smile. I felt so safe and connected to him. It was time to tell him. I had to be.

"Yes, so very good. I can't wait to try all sorts of new things with you." He took a deep breath and blew it out, then splayed his hand on my stomach. "Have you ever done that before?"

I swallowed hard. I wasn't interested in talking about my limited sexual experience with him. It was now or never.

"I've had a few sexual partners, but no. I've never done that." I bit my lip and continued before he had a chance to interrupt. We'd been at this point so many times and every time something had stopped me. Not this time though. "Jace, I need to tell you something."

"Sure, what is it?" He didn't look concerned or pull away. He was calm and staring right into my eyes. He had no idea the storm about to hit, and I silently whispered a prayer that everything would be okay.

"The day we met in the coffee house wasn't the first time I'd seen you." I watched his face carefully.

"It wasn't? You mean you really did see me around the hospital before?" He peeled a sweat-slicked strand of hair off my forehead and pushed it back out of my face.

"Not exactly. I was given a picture of you twelve years ago. The day I gave birth to a tiny, premature baby boy." I held my breath and waited, but he shook his head.

"What are you talking about?"

"Jace, I ran a DNA test on Christopher when we drew his blood for the Crohn's test." I sat up and curled in on myself. "I recognized you from the image the adoption agency gave me. You were older, but my gut said it was you. The man and woman who adopted my son were Jason and Constance. I never knew their last name, just had a photo. So when I saw you and I noticed Christopher looked a lot like my father, I ran DNA." I turned and looked into his eyes, begging him to put the pieces together so I didn't have to spell it out.

"What?" he mumbled, sitting up. He looked hurt and confused. His head moved from side to side, eyes searching my face. Then he climbed out of bed and stood there staring down at me, saying nothing. My heart hammered in my chest, panic rising.

"Say something?" I whispered, slipping off the bed on my side.

"I'm... You're..." His chest rose and fell in an accelerated breathing pattern and tears welled up in my eyes.

"I'm Christopher's biological mother." I forced the tears to stay back as he sat on the bed facing away from me. "Jace..."

His shoulders slumped and the room felt icier than the bottle of beer. I shivered and knew it was anxiety chilling me. He was upset. So upset that he couldn't speak. I had done this to him and now I felt so guilty and ashamed.

"I'm so sorry," I said, letting my tears fall. Crying, I picked up my clothes and shoes and rushed out. I dressed as quickly as I could and got my keys and phone and left. It was what I feared most. Jace was angry and hurt, and it was all my fault.

23

Jace

I sat on the edge of the bed reeling in shock. Mindy walked out and I let her; I had no idea what the right response was to that confession. I didn't even know how long I sat there in utter shock. My shoulders grew tense and began to ache; my eyes were heavy from lack of sleep. And I knew Christopher would never understand her surprising appearance in our lives. Mindy walked into our lives like a breath of fresh air and now I felt like I was suffocating. But was it her? Or was it because I processed things a lot more slowly than most people?

Raking a hand through my hair, I turned and climbed back into bed, taking the pillow she had laid her head on all night and hugging it to my chest. I didn't bother covering up; I was too numb to care if I was cold. The pillow smelled like her shampoo, and it was a shred of comfort while my mind wrestled with the emotions I was feeling.

I loved her. There was no doubt about that in my mind. There was nothing I wanted more than to just be with her and make her a part of this family. Her being Christopher's biological mother changed nothing about the way I felt about her. She hid things and lied, and now I understood what her boss meant when he spoke about the DNA. But Mindy wasn't a liar or unethical. I'd spent enough time with her listening to her broken heart about her parents and their actions when she was a child to know she never meant to hurt me.

And the way she treated Christopher this whole time—it was above and beyond what a doctor does for their patient. Now I fully understood why. She suspected him of being her son from the beginning, which meant every tiny interaction she had with him had been with that in mind. She doted on him because she loved him. The way she took interest in everything about him, even his hobbies. She was soaking up all the information as much as she could because she missed twelve years of his life. How could I not see that?

Christopher, though, he was going to have a very difficult time accepting this. There were going to be hard conversations and probably some arguments, not only between me and Mindy, but also between me and Chris, because I wasn't about to let her go. I was hurt, yes, and a little angry, but there was no other woman in the world that could fill my heart the way she did.

I fell asleep hugging that pillow and I dreamt of her all night long. Some dreams were not so great, but others were so real and comforting. I wanted to stay there, where the chaos didn't exist and we could be happy. But I woke up to Christopher asking if he could stay home for the day.

"No, bud. I have to go to the office today. I have a meeting with Howard." I pushed myself up off the bed to a seated position, keeping the sheet wrapped over my lower half.

"So you can just replace Mom whenever you want, but if I want to skip school you make me go?"

"Chris..." I sighed but he turned and stormed out. I let him go and slouched on the side of the bed for a moment. I knew he didn't understand things as they were; it was going to be even worse when we added this new layer of complexity to the mix. I reached for my phone and called Mindy. I wanted to tell her it was okay and that we just needed to talk things out, but she didn't pick up. Her phone went straight to voicemail. I checked the time. I slept well past when I was supposed to be up to take Christopher to school, so I had no time to go to her place before I dropped him off or went to work.

I showered quickly and made Chris's lunch, then we rushed out the door so I didn't miss my meeting. Christopher was sullen and moody the whole ride to school. I knew he had emotions to work out and I wanted to help him with that, but I was a bit relieved when he hopped out of the car at school because I had my own emotions to deal with. I dialed Mindy's number again as I was driving, but again it went to voicemail.

I tried twice more as I drove to the office, and once again as I rode the elevator to my floor. She had to have shut her phone off, which meant she thought I was very upset with her. I couldn't see how she'd want to end things with me after that confession. The only thing that made sense was that she was afraid of my reaction, which made perfect sense because I hadn't reacted at all last night. I just let her walk out.

"What's your problem?" Howard asked as I walked into the conference room. Jenny looked up at me and glanced at Howard, then dipped her head as if minding her own business.

"Nothing," I snapped. I looked down at my phone call history— six attempts with no answer. I wanted to talk to her so desperately.

"Something's wrong, because you're staring at your phone like you just got a call telling you your pet turtle died." Howard sat in the chair at the head of the table with one leg crossed over the other knee. He rocked the chair back and drummed his fingers on the tabletop.

"Just leave it, Howard." I sat down in my normal chair and laid the phone down in front of me. If she called I didn't want to miss it. "Let's just get started, okay?"

"Sir, the bank called. They want to know about the revenue streams today." Jenny's reminder fell on deaf ears. I only wanted to resolve this issue with Mindy. I didn't care about banks and revenue streams.

"Thanks," I mumbled and touched my phone screen. It lit up and I sighed.

"It's the girl?"

"What?" I scowled at him.

"The girl—the one you're seeing... Did she dump you or something?"

"I said leave it, Howard."

"Jace, there is something going on, and it's gonna screw up our vibe here. We've been partners for a long time. When something is bothering you, you always hide it. And then it bottles up and we end up in a mess because you can't focus on your job." Howard leaned forward and stopped drumming his fingers. "Spit it out."

I took a deep breath and sighed. "It's really complicated."

"I don't care." His eyes flicked toward Jenny. "Could you excuse us?" he asked her and she nodded and got up and left the room, shutting the door behind herself. "Now, tell me what the heck is going on."

"Yes, it's the girl." I ran a hand through my hair and realized I hadn't done my hair this morning. My tie wasn't straight and I forgot my lunch. "It's a long story."

"Try me," he said, sitting back.

"Well, it doesn't make her sound very good, but she is quite possibly the only perfect woman on this planet..." I was hesitant to really tell him everything, but I needed to get it off my chest before it ate me alive like a parasite sucking my life out of me. "She is Christopher's biological mother." Howard looked confused, but I didn't give him time to say anything.

"Mindy just bumped into me at a coffee shop. She recognized me but I'd only seen a picture of her when she was sixteen. I thought I felt like I knew her from somewhere, but I never did place it. Anyway, she ran DNA tests on him because of her suspicion and she was really afraid to tell me the truth. I, of course, pursued her because I was very attracted to her. I knew nothing about the DNA test or her real relationship with my son. We got really close. How, we fell in love." I shook my head at the absurdity of this.

"So she lied to you and practiced unethical medicine? So you're dumping her, right?"

"God no," I told him. "See, her parents forced her to give Christopher up when he was just a newborn. She was so traumatized by it that it has destroyed her relationship with her parents. I've watched her wrestle with the pain for weeks now. She never meant to hurt me, and it's not her fault I fell in love with her and pursued her in the middle of this mess. No, I'm not breaking up with her. I am in love with her."

"When did all this come out?" Howard's fingers drummed again, and I sighed.

"Late last night."

"Then why the heck are you sitting here?" He chuckled.

"What? Because we have a meeting. I have work to do."

"You don't want to go to her and talk it out?" he asked, shaking his head. "I assume you've tried calling her."

"Straight to voicemail six times."

"God, you really do know nothing about women." Howard pushed my phone toward me and it fell off the table into my lap. "Go get the girl, Jace. You're in love with her. She did some messed up things, but it sounds like she's in love with you. And you'll make her dream come true. Because any woman who will go through all of that just to find her son again is the kind of mother you want for your kid."

My heart started to palpitate. Howard was making more sense than he ever had. "You're right…" I stood slowly. "What if she won't talk to me? What if she's too afraid?"

"Knock her friggin' door down, buddy. Just get the girl."

He didn't have to tell me twice. The meeting could wait. Mindy's heart was too important. She needed to know that nothing had changed. I still wanted her.

24

Mindy

I didn't ask her to come and she didn't call, but here my mother was, sitting on my couch staring at me. I could tell she'd been restless for the past few days. I could see it in the way there were bags under her eyes that resembled the bags under my eyes.

"How did you find out then?" My chest was tight, my words tighter. After everything they'd put me through they were still meddling. I knew that all families had issues and that mine was no different than any other struggle known to mankind, but it was happening to me. I was hopeless that it would ever get better, especially now that Jace knew everything.

"Your father has connections at the hospital, Mindy. They were concerned about your career."

"Or he was snooping," I accused, shaking my head.

"You did something illegal." She frowned and folded her hands over her knees. "We care about you."

"If you cared at all, you would never have taken my son from me. I was a kid, Mom. I needed your support and love."

"We thought we were loving you the best way possible." I heard the compassion in her voice, the remorse, but it wasn't enough. Words don't fix what actions destroyed.

I looked away, too hurt and angry to respond to her again. It didn't matter how many times I explained it to her, there was never going to be any closure here. They refused to admit they did something wrong to me. Even if they did, it wouldn't undo what was done and give me back the years I lost. I just didn't know how to move forward in life with them. A therapist once told me that the good and the bad could coexist in life without clouding each other. That if I could focus on the positive aspects I'd be much happier.

But how was I supposed to do that with the past staring me in the face? And now, I had nothing. My career was probably over. Jace would probably never speak to me again. In fact, he'd probably take Chris and leave forever just to keep him away from me. I screwed up so badly. Even my friends were probably ashamed to continue our relationships. All because I let my pain from the past drive me my whole life.

So looking at my mother, I knew it would never get better until I made it better. I just had no clue how to make that better. I was just supposed to forget that it ever happened and move on with my life like a normal person?

"Mindy, you must follow Hashem in all your ways. You would never have been in that situation or this one if you had put Him first."

I knew her words were meant to be comforting, but I gave up on God and faith a long time ago. Any God that could rip my baby out of my arms because it was the right thing, didn't deserve my respect. And any person who could follow that god loyally while being the hands that perpetrated that crime against me, couldn't be trusted.

"I'd like you to leave now," I said coldly. If I had to hear one more lecture about how I ran away from my faith, I was going to scream.

"Mindy, please. Your father—"

"My father isn't speaking to me. I don't need to hear what he thinks or feels from you. If he wants to say something to me, he can say it himself." I glared at her. Things were really broken. I was really hurting. "Respectfully, Mom, I have had enough for today. I have a lot on my mind. I just want to be alone."

Mom sighed heavily and nodded. "I understand." She stood and held her purse strap on her shoulder. "Are you going to come for lunch on Saturday?"

"No, Mom. I'm not. I don't know when I'll come for lunch again." I looked down at the threadbare carpet and waited for her to walk away. She did so without saying another word to me.

When the door whined as it opened, I collapsed back against the chair and stared at the ceiling. Life was so heavy I just wanted to crawl into bed and stare at the wall. It was emotionally exhausting. I couldn't do it anymore.

"Oh, hello. Is Mindy home?" The rumbling baritone of Jace's voice filtered through the air to meet my ear and I straightened in my seat. My heart pounded instantly. What was he doing here?

"Yes, she is in a sour mood, but she is here." Mom glanced at me and stepped out the door, and Jace stepped in.

He glanced at Mom as she left then looked at me and then back at Mom. I didn't know whether to go to him or run to my bedroom and lock the door. It didn't matter what the right decision was because I was glued to the seat as he shut the door and turned to face me.

"Mom?" he asked. I nodded but said nothing. He didn't look angry or upset even. He walked toward me and I felt every muscle in my body contract. I wasn't ready for this. I had never been ready for this moment. But here it was, and my heart felt panicked. "You look like her." He sat on the end of the couch, so close to me he could reach out and lay his hand on my knee if he wanted to. And he did. "Christopher looks like her too."

I was breathing way too fast. It was a risk of hyperventilating, but I couldn't control it. All I could do was grip the arm of the chair and stare into his heavenly blue eyes, wondering how he could be so calm. He was clearly here to break up with me or something. No one receives news the likes of which I gave him last night and sticks around to see it through. I wanted to ask him what he wanted, but my tongue stuck to the roof of my mouth. I thought a silent prayer to

Hashem, that he would make right whatever it was that I had screwed up—that if there was a God, he would fix it like my mother said.

"Mindy, I don't want you to say a word until I'm finished. Okay?"

I nodded and thought how convenient that was, because there was no way I could speak right now. I had fallen so in love with him, that when he said what I knew he was about to say, I knew my heart would shatter into a million pieces and I'd never recover.

"I'm hurt." He stared into my eyes as he spoke in a mellow tone. I felt tears welling up. "You went behind my back and you lied to me too." I licked my lips and looked away from his cerulean gaze. "You should have told me this the minute we met."

"I..." I blinked and tears fell.

"Let me finish."

I looked back up at him and nodded, now letting the tears flow freely. Here it came—the death blow. My lip quivered; my body wilted. I blinked and more tears sluiced down my cheeks. I wanted to plead with him to hear me out before he ended it, but I had nothing to say. It was entirely my fault and I deserved it. I had handed him the knife to do with as he pleased, and because I cut him first, he'd take his pound of flesh now. I braced myself for his next sentence.

"I'm really hurt, and very angry about some things. But it changes nothing." He clenched his jaw and looked me in the eye. Confused, I swiped at my eyes and shook my head.

"What?"

"It changes nothing, Mindy." He reached for my hand and held it. "There is no excuse for your behavior, but I understand why you did what you did. You must have been so happy to see your boy again, then so scared and confused. It changes nothing for me. I am so in love with you, and I believe that even if you had told me the instant you recognized me what your suspicions were, that I would still have fallen in love with you."

"I don't understand." I wiped my eyes again and shook my head at him. He was making sense; I just didn't know why he'd say these things.

"I forgive you," he said, holding my gaze. "Because that's what love does. It forgives. And that forgiveness breeds a deeper trust and intimacy, because I know you never wanted to hurt me or Christopher."

"But Jace, I—"

"You were scared and confused." Jace pulled my hand and I stood and moved closer to him; then he pulled me onto his lap and wrapped his arms around me. "If you think one tiny problem like this is going to make me not want you anymore, you're wrong. I told you last night, Mindy. I am in love with you. I want you to be with me forever."

I burst into tears again, sobbing and clinging to him.

I cried for the pain I caused him. I cried for the way my heart hurt for weeks now as I kept that secret, and for how it might hurt Christopher when we told him. I cried for the anger buried in my chest over the past and how all I wanted was to feel whole again. Jace held me as I sobbed so hard my entire body shook, and he never stopped speaking comforting words into my ear.

"I'm here, pretty girl. I'm not letting you go. You are a treasure to me. You never deserved what happened to you and I know you only did what you did because you wanted your heart to feel something different. You are the best thing that has ever happened to me. I love you."

He held me until I had cried all my tears and then he held me some more. I'd never been so loved in my life and I didn't know if it was the silent prayer, or fate, or what it was, but being in Jace's arms felt right. Like this was what was meant to be, what was always supposed to happen.

"Are you okay?" he asked, kissing my temple.

I nodded and sniffled. "I can't believe you are just forgiving me."

"We'll have some difficult talks, I'm sure. But now is not the time for that. Right now we have a sick little boy who needs his mother."

Jace's words brought more tears and I wailed again. He had no idea what those words meant to me, that my boy needed his mother. My god, how long I'd needed to hear someone say that to me. The image of my boy being ripped from my arms had stained too many moments, too many memories of Chanukahs and family gatherings. It was all too much.

"You know what I think?" he asked, pushing some hair out of my eyes. I looked up at him. "I think if there is a god, he wants us together. Because I can't imagine any other woman in the world lying in bed beside me every night, or raising my son." His lips pressed against my forehead and I sniffled again. My nose was running so badly I had to blow it.

"I'll be right back," I told him, climbing off his lap. I shuffled to the bathroom and blew my nose, and when I turned to walk back into the living room, he was there.

"Kiss me," he said, pulling me against his body, so I did. A long slow passionate kiss that lingered and made my knees go weak.

"Jace, I'm so sorry."

"Shhh," he said, kissing me again. "I have already forgiven you. It's time to repair." His lips brushed over mine, and his tongue reached into my mouth as he held me. I didn't resist. I felt gross and emotional, but I couldn't imagine any other thing that would feel so right.

When he pulled away, I draped my arms around his neck. "Repair?" I asked, confused by what he said.

"When couples fight, something breaks. And if you don't repair it, the break gets worse over time. So I like to repair quickly."

"But we didn't fight." I shook my head and shrugged.

"There was a break though." He took my hand and led me into the bedroom where the only light peeked in through the gap in the drapes. "Now, let me repair that..."

25

Jace

I led Mindy into the bedroom and turned to kiss her again. She seemed hesitant, as if she didn't fully believe I would forgive her like this. I touched her gently, pushing the hair out of her eyes as I kissed her. I let my hands roam down her curves to her hips, then lifted the hem of her t-shirt. "Jace," she cooed as I raised the shirt. She lifted her arms and let me pull it over her head.

There was a timidity in her eyes I'd never seen, not even the first time we had sex on my counter. It was a vulnerability she'd never given to me, and it was healing her heart. I knew in my gut that this was exactly what she needed to know how much I truly meant it when I said I loved her.

She moaned softly as I revealed her lacy bra, cupping her breast gently, and I knew we were both lost in the moment. I slid my hands up her back and unclasped her bra, letting it fall to the floor. Mindy's eyes widened with surprise and a hint of fear, but I knew she wouldn't stop me. The moment was too intimate, our need for each other more than just sex. "I love you," I whispered, then I kissed her neck, savoring the taste of her skin as I reached for the button of her jeans. She groaned as I unzipped them and slid them down her legs.

"I don't know why..." Her hands rested on my shoulders as I crouched and helped her step out of her pants.

"You don't need to know why. You just have to believe it." I stood and unbuttoned my own jeans, letting them fall to the floor. I pulled my shirt off, then reached back to her body, resting my hands on her hips.

"I'm trying, but—"

"No buts." I slid my fingers into the elastic of her silky panties and pushed them down slowly. Mindy sat on the edge of the bed, letting me pull her panties all the way off.

"Jace..." she mewled again, but this time, I heard the desperation of her heart. She knew now too that this moment meant a union unlike the one we had before that conversation. That this meant I wanted forever, no matter how messy it was.

I slid my boxers down and stood before her, my cock at attention, begging for her soft touch. I knelt on the floor and kissed her breast as she wrapped her arms around me. Her body trembled as I kissed my way down her stomach and she gasped when I kissed the inside of her thigh.

"Jace..."

"Shhh, let me love you." I slid my hands up her thighs and pushed them apart, then I lowered my mouth and kissed her mound. I tasted her sweet juices, and Mindy moaned loudly as I slid my tongue inside her, then between her folds, lapping her juices, gently sucking her clit. Her body quaked as I slid my tongue inside her again, then out, then I sucked her clit between my lips, biting lightly. Her hands grasped my hair, holding on to the only solid object in her world as I pleasured her with my mouth.

This was where I belonged, on my knees worshiping the goddess that changed my dark world and brought light back where it was needed. I pushed a few fingers into her and thrust, massaging the rough patch just inside her body. Mindy scratched at my head as I knelt between her legs and lapped at her pussy.

"Wow... oh god, yes," she mewled and it encouraged me to do more. So I thrust faster, feeling the tension build in my groin. She came hard, convulsing and jerking, and I kept my mouth on her until the last wave had passed over her. I stood, and Mindy pulled me to her, kissing me wildly as she wrapped her legs around my waist. I slid into her wet entrance, and she arched her back, thrusting her breasts into my chest.

"Oh, Jace, more."

I kissed her neck, then her lips, and she tilted her head back, thrusting her breasts and pelvis up, demanding more. I forced her body backward across the bed as I pushed into her, and she clawed at my back, moaning. She seemed to get louder with every thrust.

"Harder, Jace. Please, harder."

I rocked my hips, pounding into her, and she kept her legs wrapped tight, her ankles locked at the small of my back.

"Yes, oh god, yes." She wrapped her arms around my neck and brought her lips to mine.

"I love you, Mindy," I grunted, rolling my hips back and forth, sliding into her.

"I love you, too, Jace." She rocked her hips back and forth with mine, meeting every thrust.

"Oh god, I'm going to..."

I felt her pussy clench, squeezing my cock and milking me. It was stronger than the first orgasm, or maybe it just felt that way because I was inside of her. But her body spasmed and I felt her juices spill over my swollen cock, coating the shaft and dribbling onto my balls. Mindy shuddered and pulled my hips against her, urging me to go deeper, so I pushed in as hard as I could.

"God you feel so amazing," I growled, biting down on her shoulder.

"Wow, I love you." Mindy kissed my chest, peppering my skin with her hot lips.

"I love you, too."

I pulled out and rolled over onto my back, bringing Mindy with me so she could lay on my chest. She re-aligned my cock so she could hold it in her hand, and I rubbed her back while she rubbed my dick.

"I want to taste you," she whispered, and I nodded.

Mindy positioned her head over my lap and slid her tongue along my shaft, licking it like a popsicle. I watched her, my eyes locked on her long, chestnut hair. She looked up, meeting my gaze, and smiled. Her tongue darted out, flicking the head, and her lips wrapped around my cock, sucking it into her mouth. I felt her tongue wiggle against my sensitive skin and I closed my eyes, a low groan rumbling from my chest. Her hand stroked me as she sucked me, her mouth tightening around my shaft.

She pulled away, leaving my cock wet and shiny, and she giggled. "You're kind of a mess."

"Am I?" I grinned. "Well does it taste good?" Her own juices moistened her lips, and she crawled up to kiss me. I could taste her on her tongue.

"It tastes like love to me."

I pushed her hip, forcing her body to straddle me and then I looked up into her eyes as her pussy slid over my dick. "I don't want to use a condom this time."

Mindy put both of her hands on my chest and stared down at me, her eyes searching me. "Okay," she said, agreeing slowly.

"Because I want a family," I told her, knowing what it might mean.

She nodded, again whispering, "Okay."

Mindy lifted her hips and I held my dick upright so she could

slide herself onto me. She moaned as she sank onto me, and I waited, letting her adjust to the feeling of me inside of her. When she began to move, I stroked her hips, guiding her on top of me. Her body slid up and down mine, her hips rolling as she thrust against me. She leaned her head back, looking at me with wide eyes, and she moaned, loud.

Mindy leaned forward, and I squeezed her hips, my fingers digging into her flesh, and I held onto her, my hands supporting her as she continued to move. She placed her hands on my chest, leaning forward, her hair falling around my face, and then she pressed her lips against mine. She kept her hips rocking against me, and as she kissed me, she groaned, her throat vibrating against me.

"I love you," I whispered against her lips.

"I love you," she moaned, her breath coming fast. I slid my hands up her back, gripping her shoulders, and I lifted my hips, thrusting into her.

"Harder," Mindy said, and I obliged her, pushing into her harder. I felt her body tense, she began to shudder, and then she moaned loudly. I watched her unravel before me, her eyes closed, her lips parted, and I felt her pussy contract around my dick. "I'm going to come," she whispered, barely able to get the words out.

I held her hips, my fingers sinking into her flesh, and I slammed into her, harder and harder. Her body was quivering against mine, her pussy contracting around my dick, her juices dripping down my shaft as she continued to come. I thrust into her hard, and then I felt my own orgasm building. I thrust into her, my dick swelling within her, and my balls churning as they pulled up tight to my body. "I'm going to come," I told her.

"Come inside of me," she whispered.

I thrust into her one last time, hard, and then I felt my cock twitching as it began to pump my release inside of her. My body tensed as I came. I groaned, my eyes closed, and then I felt Mindy's body go limp. She fell forward, her head resting against my chest, and her hips still moving against me as she came down from her own orgasm. We stayed like that for a while, our bodies pressed together, our hearts beating against one another. I loved the way she felt in my arms, and I loved the way she smelled. I loved everything about her, and I knew then that she was it for me.

She rolled off me and I turned on my side to hold her in my arms. I felt our juices on my balls and pulled her against myself. I felt like we were really one now, like her allowing me that privilege somehow sealed our fate.

"Why?"

"Why what?" I asked, kissing her forehead.

"Why do you still want me after everything? I lied and went behind your back."

"I think if fate or god or destiny, or whatever you want to call it brought us together, then we shouldn't fight it. We should at least attempt to make this work." I tangled my legs with hers and kissed her again and again on the forehead and temples.

"But I'm really messed up and my heart is really broken." Mindy sniffled again and played with a few strands of my chest hair.

"Everyone has a past, babe. I'm not afraid of yours." Brushing a few hairs back from her face, I kissed her one last time. "Look, I want you to move in with me for a few days. We'll try it out, see what Christopher thinks about having a mother figure back in the picture. What do you think?"

"Oh god, I don't know."

"You don't have to, but I really want you to. Who knows, you may never come back here." I grinned. In this moment all of our issues were gone, blocked out by a bubble of hope and love. Mindy looked up at me and a soft smile curled one side of her mouth upward.

"Okay, I'll try it..."

"I can take off work. We can just enjoy life together, really build on what we have. I don't need anything more to prove that you are the woman I want to spend the rest of my life with, but it would be nice to get a feeling for what that would be like, don't you think?"

"You think Christopher will go for that?" She looked skeptical, but I knew there was no better way of doing this than to jump in with both feet.

"You are his mother. We have to start somewhere, right?" I propped myself up on one elbow and looked down at her. "I want my family to be whole now, and more than ever you deserve a second chance."

Mindy smiled and nodded and tears filled her eyes again. She covered her mouth and nodded, but when she blinked tears cascaded across her temples. "We'll do counseling or whatever it takes, because I'm going to make this right for you."

"You're really not angry?" she asked, questioning me again.

"We don't have to talk about that right now, okay? Right now, the only thing that matters is that you are okay, and we are together." I grimaced. "And that I have a lot of sex stuff on my balls and I need a shower. So, let's go clean up. Shall we?"

She giggled and nodded again through her tears. I slid off the bed and offered her my hand, and we walked across the hallway with juices running down our thighs. This was one of many times, I hoped, that we would be this intimate and close. Life had a funny way of working things out in ways we never expected. If someone had told me I would run into my son's biological mother and fall in love with her, I'd have told them they were so wrong. But look at me now?

We showered and washed each other, talking softly about how life had changed us both. When we were finished, I helped her pack a few things into a suitcase, then I drove her home. My home. Our home. The home I wanted to turn into a brighter place, the way she turned my heart around.

26

Mindy

I sat at the bar in utter shock. I knew Christopher was having a difficult time adjusting to my presence, but his comment was hurtful and rude. I avoided eye contact, fearing I might cry and give him any sort of encouragement that his behavior was acceptable. I had no idea how to handle situations like this because Jace and I hadn't divulged to him that I was his real mother yet. Jace stood and rested a hand on my shoulder.

"Christopher, I would like you to apologize to Mindy for calling her a homewrecker. She isn't even close to that. I invited her here." He squeezed my shoulder and my heart sank a little farther.

I knew my son was just hurting. No little boy should ever have to bury his mother, and even though it was two years ago, that pain had latched onto his heart and not let him go. I couldn't blame him, though he shouldn't act like that ever. There was no excuse for it, though I did understand.

"I don't want to apologize. I want her to leave. My mom is what I want. Not another woman."

"I'll be right back," Jace whispered to me, kissing me on the cheek then following Christopher to his room. A similar scenario had played out last night too, just after dinner when Christopher asked for more ice cream and Jace told him to leave it for me since I hadn't finished my dinner yet. Christopher went off about how he never had to share before, and that he wished I was gone. Jace had to talk him down then, just like he was now.

I urged him to let me go home so we could just ease into this situation a little more slowly, but he promised me he knew his son and that Chris would adjust quickly. I wasn't so sure, but being at Jace's house was better than being locked up at my apartment just waiting for my parents to show up again unannounced. Besides the fact that they'd set a date for my ethics review, and my nerves were shot.

My phone started to vibrate so I pulled it out. It was Violet, her smiling face staring back at me from the caller ID. I sighed, not really wanting another lecture, but she loved me. I knew that. And I hadn't gotten the chance to tell her that Jace knew everything and we were together still. We had a few difficult conversations ourselves, but no arguments. I felt better about things already. So I swiped right to answer and held the phone to my ear.

"Hey, Vi, what's up?"

"Mindy, please don't hang up." The voice I heard was not the one I expected and I felt simultaneously worried and trapped.

"Mom? Why do you have Violet's phone? Is she okay?" I glanced at the hallway where Jace disappeared and knew no matter what was going on, I didn't want to be sitting here on the phone with my mother when he returned. So I stood and meandered back toward the bedroom, ready to lock myself into Jace's private bathroom if need be to have some privacy.

"Mindy, I'm so sorry to worry you. Violet is fine. She doesn't know I have her phone. She came for dinner this evening and I borrowed it." Mom sounded emotional, like maybe she'd been engaged in an argument prior to making the call.

"You mean stole it?" I hissed. I passed Christopher's room. The door was open and Jace sat on the bed talking to him. Both of them looked up at me as I passed, and I ducked into Jace's room. I pushed the door and it swung almost shut behind me, but didn't latch. I ignored it. The boys were busy talking and this wouldn't take forever.

"No, Mindy." Mom sighed. "I am not trying to anger you. I want to apologize to you."

"Mom, there is nothing left to say here. All I've ever tried to do was make you and Dad happy and proud of me. From the moment things happened when I was sixteen, I swallowed every bit of my emotion, carried it like a dagger in my heart. I over performed, earning top marks, and graduated early. I wanted you to be proud because I felt like I brought shame on the whole family. Because you convinced me I brought shame on the whole family.

"But I hadn't. I was a kid and kids make dumb choices. I needed my parents to have my back and help me learn from my mistakes and poor choices. But what you did, what Dad did, is unforgivable. I just tried so hard to forgive because family is everything to me."

"Mindy, please, your father and I feel awful."

"Do you?" I asked, angry. "Does he actually feel awful, or are you apologizing for something he doesn't feel bad about in the least?"

"Oh honey..."

"No, I don't want to hear another empty apology. If you two are really sorry, you should be supporting me now when I need it most. My job is on the line, and my entire future with my son." I didn't know why I was even expressing this again. It didn't matter how many times I explained this to them, they never got it. I was fighting a losing battle. One day they would be a part of my life, but not until I healed, because only after my heart was whole again could I be patient enough to actually forgive them.

"Please come to dinner on Saturday. Your father will apologize."

"No, Mom. I have no interest in coming to dinner. I don't want to sit across from someone who could hurt me so badly and not care. I don't really want you to be a part of my life right now. I need you to stop calling me and stop putting Violet up to pressure me into coming. She doesn't deserve that either."

"Mindy..."

"Goodbye." I hung up so frustrated I wanted to cry, and cradled the phone in my hands.

"Was that your mom?" Christopher's tiny voice reached my ears. I didn't realize he was there and I didn't know how much he heard."

I cleared my throat and said, "Yes." I scooted over and patted the bed and he came toward me.

"Dad wanted me to apologize." He glanced over his shoulder before sitting down. Jace was not there, though I suspected maybe he was listening at the door.

"He did?" I asked, feeling a little ashamed of myself for not shutting the door properly. "What do you want?"

"Well, I want my mom back." He sighed and swung his feet. "If my mom was here I'd never talk to her like that because she's my mom. You just respect your mom, you know?"

I wanted to protest and explain that he didn't understand the dynamic, but he was right. Which only made me feel even more ashamed. He had lost the only mother he'd ever known, and me treating my living parents like that must have seemed very wrong to him. He'd probably do anything to have five more minutes with his mother.

"You're right, Topper." My heart sank. It took a child—my child—to teach me that family is still family even when they hurt you. It didn't make the pain any easier to shoulder or the anger any easier to bear but it did make me think about how I could have handled things differently.

"At least you have a mom."

His little shoulders slumped and I wanted to scream at the top of my lungs that I was his mother, but I knew it wasn't the right time or place. "You're right about that too. I'm so sorry if I hurt you earlier. I'm not trying to replace your mom. I just want to be a part of your dad's life, maybe yours."

He looked up at me with his large chocolate eyes, ones that made me think of my father as a little boy. That thought made me feel guilty for holding such a grudge toward my father. At one point he was a little boy, forced to grow up into a world where all he wanted to do was protect his own child, and I couldn't imagine his emotional reaction to learning I had gotten pregnant at such a young age. Everything about this little boy was healing me and he didn't even realize it.

"I miss my mom a lot. Every single day she would make me lunch and write a little note for me. I don't get notes now. At bedtime she would tuck me in and sing me a song. No one sings to me now." I saw a tear trickle down his cheek.

"I'm sorry you don't have those things. I know it's hard when someone you love just isn't there anymore. You have to learn to do things without them, and it doesn't feel good."

"Yeah," he groaned. "Anyway, I just wanted to tell you I'm sorry for calling you names, and saying you were a homewrecker."

I reached out and touched his chin and he looked up at me. "I'm not trying to wreck your home. Your dad is hurting too. He just wants someone in his life to love again, to be his partner. I'm trying to make him happy, not take your mom's spot."

He shook his head and looked back down at his fingers curled into tight balls in his lap. "Yeah, he can date again. I just don't want a new mom. I mean, can't he just do it somewhere else?"

An idea occurred to me, one that would challenge me to my very core, but I thought maybe it would work. "How about this... You promise me to give your dad some space, let him heal his heart and find love, and I will promise you that I'll try to fix things with my parents. Because you're right, family is important."

He looked up at me with doubt in his eyes but he nodded. "I guess I can try that."

"Then we're friends?" I asked, reaching out my hand.

He shook it. "Friends, I guess."

"Now, how about you go wash your face, and we'll finish dinner."

Christopher headed off to his bathroom and I trekked out to the kitchen where Jace had just sat down. I knew he was eavesdropping on the conversation. "You're literally incredible, you know?"

"What do you mean?" I asked, sitting on his lap and wrapping my arms around his shoulders.

"You did in a five minute conversation what I've been trying for weeks to accomplish. You have a gift." He kissed me, nipping at my lower lip.

"I don't know about that. I just know I love my son and I want his little heart to be okay." I kissed him back, deepening the kiss until we heard Christopher clear his throat.

"Get a room," he said. We looked up at him and he stuck his finger in his mouth and fake gagged, and I chuckled.

"Let's finish dinner now," I told him and we all took our places at the table. Maybe this wasn't going to be so bad after all.

27

Jace

I stood outside the door leading to the offices where Mindy's father worked. My palms were a bit sweaty and my hands shook a little. I'd had to do a little digging to figure out what he did for a living and where his office was, but I managed to uncover the fact that he was a very wealthy banker who had his fingers in a whole lot of pies. It made me a bit more nervous to know that, but nothing would deter me from seeking his blessing.

The door creaked open and I entered. The offices were on the top floor of the only high-rise in the city, the best view of the Hudson River Valley anyone could get. His receptionist looked up from her place behind her tall counter and smiled at me. "Can I help you?" She was a middle-aged woman with blonde hair and fine lines around her eyes. Pretty, but she couldn't begin to compare to Mindy.

"I need to see Mr. Joseph Scriber please." I strolled up to the counter and rested a hand on it while she clicked away at her keyboard. She smelled like she took a bath on perfume; it was a pleasant scent, just overpowering. Her floral top was nice too; it just screamed "cat lady."

"He is occupied right now, and I don't see your name on his calendar." She looked up at me through narrowed eyes. "Why do you need to see him?"

"How can you say you don't see my name? I haven't told you my name." I chuckled at the absurdity but I understood. These were the same sort of excuses that Jenny would have given to anyone at my office who didn't have an appointment with me.

"I'm sorry, Mr...."

"Turner. My name is Jason Turner." I leaned on the counter. "I don't have an appointment. I just need to speak with him about his daughter."

I watched her type into her keyboard more, but from my position leaning over the counter I could see she was typing into a messaging app, not his calendar search bar. Figured—she was giving me the runaround. It's what wealthy types did when they had no interest in being bothered. I felt like if Mindy's father knew I was here and what I wanted, he would want to speak to me.

"Could you page him?"

She glanced up at me and shook her head. "We don't use pagers. That's outdated technology."

"Then can you use the intercom?"

"What did you say your name was?" she asked, fingers hovering over the keyboard, and I realized she was directly messaging him through the app on her computer.

"Jace Turner... Is he in the building?" I leaned across the counter farther and she turned her monitor so I couldn't see her anymore.

"Mr. Turner, I'm going to have to ask you to leave now."

"Why? I just need a quick word with the man. I haven't done anything wrong." I straightened and glanced down the hallway. "He's down here?" I asked, pointing. I started moving that direction before she even answered. Of course he was this way; there was no other place he could even be. I read the signs on the doors as I passed, and the woman scurried along behind me protesting.

"Look, you can't come back here. Mr. Scriber is a very busy man he—"

I stopped in front of the door with his name on it and opened it, thus cutting her off.

"I'm so sorry, sir," she blubbered apologetically. "He didn't listen." She shook her head and sighed and Mindy's father looked up from where he sat at his desk.

He scowled and slowly rose, tucking his tie into his jacket and buttoning it. "You may go, Linda."

I walked deeper into his lush office. The furniture was all leather; both his desk and the table across the room for meetings were constructed of solid marble. Gold inlays on the furniture glistened as if he polished them every day. He had a state-of-the art computer on his desk, fountain pen perched waiting to be used, and a flatscreen TV hung on the far wall.

"What can I do for you, Mr. Turner." He didn't look happy to see me. There was no hand outstretched for a handshake, no smile on his face. His calculated stare iced me to my core, but I didn't back down.

"Mr. Scriber, I want to introduce myself to you."

"We met once before, when the boy was born. I know who you are."

I took a deep breath and blew it out, realizing I was going to have to fight for every inch in this relationship. The man was shrewd, just the way I'd expect a businessman to be. And his posture would have been intimidating if I didn't already know in my heart that Mindy was truly mine.

"Then you know how much I love your daughter and grandson." I took another step closer and his brow furrowed so I stopped mid-stride.

"I do not consider the boy my grandchild." Mr. Scriber strolled around the end of his desk and folded his hands in front of his waist. "Mr. Turner, my daughter made very shameful choices when she was a child. We helped bring hope to you and your wife by offering the fruit of those poor choices so that Mindy could move forward in her life and not be hindered by the added burden of a child."

"My son is not a burden, Mr. Scriber, and neither is he a poor choice or a mistake. Mindy loves her son very much."

"Yes," he drawled, "enough to break the law and lose her career." His nostrils flared and he pursed his lips in agitation. I watched his chest rise and fall in rapid succession. "I am not interested in pursuing a greater relationship between your family and ours. I would like you to leave my office and stay away from my family, especially my daughter."

I shook my head and almost laughed at the idiocy of this whole thing. Mindy was an adult living on her own, supporting herself, creating a life of her own. She could make her own choices and did not have to okay anything through this man. In fact, I didn't need his blessing to propose to Mindy the way I wanted to; I was merely here out of respect, knowing her family was deeply religious and held very high standards for her.

"I am afraid, I can't do what you're asking, sir." I squared my shoulders, ready to take on a fight if need be. "You see, I am deeply in love with your daughter. After my wife passed away, there was a hole in my heart I never thought I'd fill again. Mindy is the woman I want to spend the rest of my life with, and it seems to be fate that—"

"Enough!" His eyes bugged out of his head and his dark skin flushed pink. "I have spoken my piece. I do not give you my blessing. Now, please leave at once."

Sighing yet again, I turned and let myself out of the room, walking past Linda, who also scowled at me. Like a mother hen, she had done her best to prevent Mindy's father from being upset, but I was just the type of man to rock the boat a little. It wasn't how I saw that conversation going, either, which only made my sluggish retreat more unpalatable.

I made my way home, angry and disappointed that Mindy's parents were just as frustrating as she described them to be. It must have been horrible for her every day of her life to live with that suffocating influence. It only gave me more compassion for her the more I thought about it. I could tell, however, that they truly loved her and wanted what was best. It seemed, perhaps, their true failure was not allowing her to make her own choices for fear that she'd make mistakes. I almost stopped by her parents' house to see what her mother would say, but thought better of it and went straight home.

When I opened the door the heavenly scent of food cooking hit my nostrils and made my mouth water instantly. I dropped my keys on the stand by the door and scanned the large open room. Christopher wasn't visible, but Mindy was, standing with her back to me at the kitchen counter working on something.

"It smells wonderful in here," I crooned, forcing a smile. Fake it 'til you make it, and God was I having to really fake it for the moment. I was too upset over the way her father acted to provide a genuine smile. I just wanted to talk some sense into him, but there was no point trying.

"Thanks, I'm making homemade lasagna. It should be done soon." Mindy hunched over something. Her curly chestnut hair was braided down her back, the tips of the long strands just brushing the belt of her apron. She wore a loose white skirt that fell just above the knee, and her bare feet made me smile. She looked at home in my kitchen.

I came up behind her, wrapping my arms around her waist and burying my face in her hair to drag in a deep breath of her scent.

"Hey," she giggled, swatting at my arms. "I'm trying to grate the parmesan cheese."

I looked down over her shoulder at the block of cheese in one hand and the cheese grater perched precariously on the rim of a glass bowl. "But you smell so good." I kissed her neck, nibbling a little.

"You sure that's not the food cooking?" She was playful, placing the cheese and grater into the bowl and pushing it to the side. Then she turned in my arms and locked her fingers behind my neck.

"No, it's definitely you. Did you put perfume on today?" I swayed my hips against hers and kissed her forehead.

"Nope, just my shampoo. I stopped home earlier to get a few more things I wanted. Your men's shampoo is yucky. I like floral scents."

God just being with her made me feel so much better. It was like the weight of a thousand cargo ships drained out my feet and left me feeling lighter than air. I didn't care that her father wouldn't bless our union. I was still going to marry this woman. I probably wouldn't even give her the choice. She was mine, through and through.

"How long until it's done?"

"Oh..." she hummed, glancing at the clock on the wall. "I think about twenty minutes or so. Maybe a bit longer."

I kissed her, sucking her lip into my mouth and nipping at it. "Take your panties off," I grumbled, grinding into her.

"Jace, I have to grate the cheese," she tittered, but she kissed me back, parting her lips so I could push my tongue into her mouth.

"I'll help you do it in a minute. Now take your panties off. I'm hungry..."

Mindy smiled wickedly, her eyes darkening with lust. She hiked up her skirt and apron and slipped her fingers into the waistband of her panties then slowly lowered them, teasing me as she did so. I groaned, my desire for her growing stronger by the second. As soon as her panties were off, I lifted her up to the kitchen counter. I pushed aside the bowl of cheese and pinned her down on the smooth surface, trailing kisses down her neck and chest. I felt the rise of her breast beneath the thin cotton of her blouse and bit down, leaving a small damp mark.

"Hungry, huh?" she asked, resting a hand on my shoulder. "I'm making a feast, and you want what? Tacos?"

Sliding my hands up her skirt, I nodded and met her gaze. "Tacos for an appetizer... Lasagna for the main course... Tacos for dessert..." I smirked at her and her tongue shot out, drawing over her bottom lip.

"Jace, I..."

"I know," I replied, reaching up and pressing my thumb against her clit. "My Mindy doesn't want to wait... she wants it now..."

She bit her lip again and nodded, and I slid my fingers inside her. I ground into her, my cock aching with need for her. I wanted to feel her, bare and wet, around me. She let her head loll backward and moaned, and I looked at her, my eyes full of lust and desire. Her pussy was hot, squeezing my fingers, and I worked her clit too, rubbing as I thrust. With my other hand I squeezed a tit, kneading it gently.

"You know, this is the sort of thing a man fantasizes about. Coming home to his woman making dinner only to spread her out and eat her first, then work up an appetite." I continued working her pussy as I lowered my mouth and scraped my teeth along her neck. This was just what I needed after that horrible interaction.

"Yeah?" she moaned, adding a slight gasp as her body twitched under my touch.

"Yeah." I nodded, biting her neck again. "I just want you... And I want you now."

"You do?" she whispered, her hands on my shoulders. "What about dinner?"

"Dinner can wait," I groaned in her ear. "I want you."

She nodded. "You want me? Then take me.." she whispered.

My fingers worked faster, thrusting and massaging her clit. Moisture puddled between my palm and her pussy. Her panting and moaning grew more intense by the second, until she was a quivering mess, clawing at my shoulders and grinding against me. I pumped my fingers in and out of her; she was getting close.

"Do you want to come?" I asked, my voice low and husky. "Do you want to come on my fingers?"

She nodded, her eyes closed. Her breath quickened and she moaned with every breath. "Oh, Jace... Oh, God, that feels so good..."

I stroked her clit again, a light but firm pressure, and she let out a loud groan. Her pussy clamped down on my fingers; she was coming. Her body shook as the orgasm rippled through her. She let out a breathy cry as she trembled on the counter. I slowed my strokes, letting her ride out the orgasm. Her breathing slowed and her body relaxed. She opened her eyes. "That was amazing," she whispered.

"You're amazing." I pulled my fingers from her pussy and licked them clean.

Her eyes widened. "Oh my..." she breathed. "That was hot."

I smiled. "You want to return the favor?"

She nodded, her face flushing. "Can I?"

"Anything you want."

With a seductive grin, Mindy spread her legs wider, resting one foot on the counter and nodding at my arm. I smirked and snickered and held her leg. With her skirt hiked to her waist, her pussy was on full display. "You know, Topper is at the park for another fifteen minutes... And I really liked it when you came inside of me the other day..." She looked down at herself and touched her clit lightly. "It might be kinda hot to watch your cum dribble out of me."

God she was turning me on so badly. I used my free hand to undo my pants and push the front down. "What about getting pregnant?" It was a topic we hadn't discussed. We'd just always used condoms to be safe. Now I was confused.

"I have an IUD. I did it years ago because building my career was the only thing I had time for." Her fingers slowly circled her clit, her eyes mesmerizing me. When she let me come inside her finally, it really was a union. She was telling me she trusted me to protect her and not give her anything, and to me it had been the same, and so much more.

"God, I want you so bad," I told her, stroking myself.

"Then come get me, and make it good. Because I've been on my feet in this kitchen for hours and I deserve it." Mindy winked at me and grabbed my tie, pulling me in.

I slid into her slowly, filling her up inch by inch.

She was so wet, and her pussy felt amazing. We made out while I thrust into her, and I could tell my cock was hitting her g-spot.

"I want to come inside you," I growled against her mouth.

"You can," she promised, her fingers digging into my hips.

I thrust harder and harder into her, loving the way she felt. The way she looked. I loved everything about her, and I wanted to spend the rest of my life showing her that.

"And someday I want to put babies inside you," I whispered, nipping at her ear as I held her leg up and thrust my cock deep into her pussy.

"Oh god, Jace," she moaned. "That's so hot."

Her pussy tightened around me as she came, and I loved watching her scream my name. I loved seeing my cum dribble out of her while I thrust my cock into her a few more times, until I could feel my orgasm rising. Her body jerked and shook as powerful contractions coursed through her. Her pussy tightened and she arched her head back again, eyes closed.

I was close too. I felt it start low in my balls, pressure building. She was so tight around my cock, and I could feel every inch of her. My heart was pounding in my chest and I knew I was going to come.

"I'm going to come," I groaned, my balls tightening up.

"Do it," she begged, her nails digging into my backside. "I want to feel you cum inside me." I thrust into her again and she cried out, and I watched her face as I slid my hand between us, stroking her clit. "Oh god, Jace," she moaned, her body starting to shake again. "Oh god... I'm going to..."

The space between us was hot with our sex. Between her juices and mine, we made a mess, but I reveled in it. Feeling her milk me dry was the greatest feeling in the world, next to holding her in my arms. I felt my orgasm burst out of me, coming deep inside her. Our moans echoed off the walls while I shot my seed inside her. I watched her face as she came again, squeezing my cock with her pussy as she finished.

I pulled out of her slowly, watching as cum dribbled out of her and onto the counter. I leaned down and kissed her, pressing my forehead against hers. We both tried to catch our breath, and I lowered her leg, helping her slide off the counter. The mess smeared on the inside of her skirt and she grimaced.

"God, it's running down my thighs." The oven timer started chiming and I chuckled and grabbed a hand towel.

"Here," I said, reaching under her skirt. I seductively held her gaze as I wiped her pussy clean and then kissed her again.

"But I'm going to drip all through dinner," she whined, grimacing.

"Hey, no pouting." I used the towel to wipe the counter then bent and picked up her panties. "This will help," I told her, once again reaching beneath her skirt. I used my fingers to push the panties up inside her slowly. She wriggled and squirmed, moaning and whimpering as I forced them inside. She acted like she was going to come again, but the timer was a bit of a distraction.

"Now, let me wash my hands and put my package away, and I can help finish dinner." I winked at her. "Because I want dessert later, and we can't have dessert without dinner first."

Mindy swatted at me again and straightened her skirt and apron. She tended to the food in the oven while I washed my hands and the counter. If this was what I got to come home to every night, I couldn't wait to put a ring on her finger.

We just had to convince Christopher this was a good thing.

28

Mindy

I sat with my legs shaking, waiting for my mother and sister to arrive. True to my word, I was trying to work on the relationship with my parents. Christopher had given me a chance to help make Jace happy and for the past week now, I hadn't extended the same olive branch to my family. So Georgia sat beside me, squeezing my hand, as Charlie and Cristopher played on the playground equipment.

"It's going to be fine, Mindy. You'll see."

I nodded, but I didn't see it. I had strictly warned my mother and sister not to say a word about my relationship with Christopher in front of him. He didn't know yet, and I didn't want that to be the way he found out. They both promised to not breathe a word of it, so a playdate in the park was set. Now, however, I was regretting it.

"She's never going to change, Geo. They still don't consider him part of their family. They never will, not even if I marry Jace." I dropped my head. This wasn't just about making amends either. A woman needs her mother in her life when she, herself, becomes a mother. How was I supposed to raise a child when I had no clue how to be a mother?

"Well, if she doesn't change, she doesn't change. There is nothing you can do about that. What you can do is try to make peace, forgive, and love your son. Sometimes there is nothing you can do to fix what got broken. You just limp forward and hope it doesn't always hurt." Georgia squeezed my hand and nodded across the park. "Looks like they're here."

Georgia had never met my mother, but Violet looked just like me, curly chestnut hair, hazel eyes, and a thick curvy figure that drove men wild. Back in the day people thought we were twins. And we both looked a lot like Mom, more fair complected than our father.

Mom smiled as they walked up and I rose to greet her. She offered a kiss on each cheek and I stepped back and gestured at Georgia. "Mom, this is my best friend Georgia Lane-Wilks. Maybe you've heard her name before. She's on Broadway."

Her eyes turned toward Georgia and she nodded. "I don't really follow Broadway much, but it's so very nice to meet you. A friend of Mindy's is a friend of mine."

"I've heard that name," Violet said, thrusting out her hand. "You're going to be in the remake of Guys and Dolls, aren't you?" Violet was always a huge theater buff, far more into the arts than I was. My focus was math and science—all I ever wanted was to be a doctor and help people so they didn't feel the way I felt growing up with Crohn's.

"Yes! I'm super excited about it. It's coming out in the fall." Georgia shook Violet's hand and I looked up at Mom, who was scanning the playground. Nervously, I took her hand and pointed at my boy.

"He's there, Mom." His mop of dark hair and the broad grin on his face resembled Dad so much there was no mistaking it. I watched Mom's eyes light up and she covered her mouth. Then she blinked away the emotion and nodded at me before sitting on the other side of the picnic table.

"It's such a nice day," Violet said, starting the awkward conversation.

"Yeah, great day for playing at the park." A weird silence fell over us. There was so much we should be talking about, but how to start that discussion escaped me. I looked down at my hands and let my shoulders droop. I didn't know why I invited them to come other than a promise I made. This was never going to work. I knew nothing would change with my mother, so there was no point in bringing up the real matter at hand—my family accepting my child. Violet would accept him; I knew that much. But when it came to my parents, there was no word in the world that would make a difference.

"So, Mrs. Scriber," Georgia started, "you're a mom. I have a question for you."

I raised my eyes to meet the gaze of my best friend who was clearly trying to save the day. She smiled at me in earnest and then turned to my mother.

"Yes, of course." Mom sat with her arm draped over the table, purse tucked under her other arm, and a placid expression on her face.

"Well, Charlie only wants to eat chicken nuggets and macaroni and cheese. How do you get your kid to eat a well-balanced diet? This struggle is real."

I held my breath. This could go one of two ways. My mom was always eager to teach and instruct other women. It was part of her DNA to want to help. But she could also be very rude or judgmental at times if she felt she was being challenged. I shifted nervously and found myself picking my own fingernails.

"Well you can't force them, dear. You'll find they go through phases in life." Mom relaxed a little, setting her purse on the bench between her and Violet. Vi smiled at me and turned to watch the kids on the playground playing. I knew she had my back, but she didn't have any idea how to fix the situation more than I did.

"Did Mindy or Violet ever do that with you?" Georgia pressed more, and I wanted to elbow her. The last thing we needed was to bring up my failures as a child. It would open the can of worms I didn't want crawling around this table.

"Oh heavens, yes." Mom actually smiled. A genuine, heart-warming, happy grin. "Mindy once went four whole days eating nothing but strawberries. She ate so many of them her fingers were stained for weeks. "I only let nature take its course. She got a belly ache and had to stay in bed for a few days. When I explained that's why she needs other food, she listened to me." Mom turned to me with the same smile. "Remember that, dear?"

I nodded. I did remember. I still loved strawberries to this day, but it was definitely a learning experience. As was this conversation, learning my mom remembered tidbits about my life I thought were ancient history. "How do you get a kid to heal and move on after losing someone they love?" The question hung in the air like a hummingbird, despite the cool breeze weaving between us. Mom nodded and sighed.

"He is struggling with losing his mother?" Mom's eyes narrowed at me and I bit my lip. I needed parenting advice and there weren't any mom groups around to help me with these issues.

"He is..."

Georgia nudged Violet and her eyes flicked to the playground. "We're going to go check on the boys, okay?"

Mom kept her eyes fixed on me, but I glanced at Georgia and mouthed, "Thank you." Then I turned back to my mom. "Mom, I am in way over my head with this parenting thing. Most mothers get to start easy, when it's just changing diapers and warming bottles. I have a pre-teen with a major trauma. And he doesn't even know I'm his real mother yet." I wanted to cry. All of this just came spilling out of my heart and I couldn't contain it.

Georgia and Violet walked away leaving me there with my mother. It had been such a long time since I sat and took advice from her, years even. This wasn't supposed to have been a moment of neediness on my part. I was supposed to be showing my mom how strong and capable I was as a mother, but I realized in that moment how uncertain I really was. How much I actually needed her even though I was still angry and hurt by her.

"Can I tell you something?" she asked, turning her eyes downward. I watched her fold her hands on the table and focus her eyes on them. The purple surrey she wore looked elegant on her, and the chunky necklace was one of my favorites. I loved when she wore it because it reminded me of Jackie O.

"Of course." I felt my wall lowering—the one I'd built against intrusion, specifically because being vulnerable around my very own mother usually meant being chastised, rebuked, or belittled. There wasn't a conversation where I wasn't corrected or "educated" as a means to help me improve my life. I just couldn't keep holding the wall up anymore. I was tired. I wanted my mom, and I needed encouragement and support.

"Just because no one finds out about it, doesn't mean it never happened."

I thought about what she said and was entirely confused. I said nothing for a moment, trying to decide what I should even say. She looked thoughtful, staring at her fingers. She stretched them out and pinched her diamond anniversary band between her thumb and finger but didn't offer an explanation until I spoke.

"What do you mean?"

Mom's eyes trailed up to look into mine. "I know the pain you are feeling, the pain you felt for so many years." She reached out toward me so I slid my hand across the table and let her hold it. There was so much emotion in her eyes that I couldn't read.

"What? How?" I scooted closer so I could hold her hand tighter.

"I mean..." Her lip trembled and she looked out over the playground. Georgia was introducing Christopher to Violet. They all had smiles on their faces. I looked back at Mom who now had tears in her eyes. "I, too, gave up a child."

When she turned to face me, I saw her pain. It was my pain. It was the same.

"What?"

"Your father and I made a choice when I was seventeen years old,

before our Ketubah was signed..." Her eyes implored me to understand but I shook my head, refusing to believe it. She would have to
spell it out for me or I wouldn't believe it. "We snuck away after the
Seder dinner and we... Well we..."

"I get it." I didn't need to hear details.

"Two months later, I learned I was pregnant. My father did not
believe in abortion, so I carried my daughter to term. I was hidden
away in a private manner, so I didn't bring shame to my family. Your
father was not allowed to see me until after my purification rights
following birth. He never got to see her." Tears rolled down her
cheeks and she swiped them away. "They gave her away, and I never
saw her again."

It all made so much sense now. They were so strict because they
knew the pain of what was happening. They tried to control my life
so I wouldn't make the same choices they made and thus I could
avoid the pain they had endured. "But Dad..."

"Your father can only exhibit the sort of love that has been
demonstrated to him by others." Her head dipped and she looked at
me through her lashes. "He doesn't understand, Mindy. And I didn't
either until you explained how badly you were hurting. It broke my
heart because in all of our attempts to prevent that pain, all we did
was make it worse."

I stared into the eyes of a very broken woman. A woman who was
admitting her wrongs and remorseful. The pain would never go away,
the truth about what was done, but for the first time in my life, I felt
hopeful that it would heal.

"I'm so sorry that happened to you." I squeezed her hand,
wondering where my sister was in this world, if they knew about her
too. Now was not the time to ask, however, so I kept my lips pressed
into a firm line.

"I'm so sorry we did this to you, Mindy. You are the highest joy in
our lives. There isn't anything we wouldn't do for you."

We sat there crying together for a moment before Christopher
came racing up. His cheeks were pink and he was out of breath. He
looked at me as I wiped my eyes and smiled broadly. "Mindy, is that

your mom?" He pointed and then wiped his face with the back of his hand.

"Yeah, bud. That's my mom." I tried to smile, but the heaviness of the conversation was too much for me. Mom, however, offered a huge golden smile.

"It's so nice to meet you, Christopher. Mindy has told me a little about you."

He thrust his chubby hand out to shake hers and she shook it. "I'm glad you're getting along now. Did Mindy tell you my mom died?"

"She did. I'm so sorry to hear that." Mom held his hand in hers longer than necessary and it made me cry more tears seeing them bonding even a little.

"It's okay. Dad says death is part of life and that everyone dies. We just have to learn how to say goodbye the right way." He shrugged and turned to me. "Mindy, can I have a dollar for the vending machine? I want a soda."

"Of course, baby," I told him, reaching into my pocket, but Mom pulled out a few crisp dollar bills from her purse before I got to my cash.

"Here. Get yourself a snack too, and one for your friend."

Christopher's eyes went wide. "No way! Thank you!" He raced off and took my heart with him. I shook my head and burst into tears, burying my face in my hands. I felt the table shake, and then I felt Mom sit next to me. She pulled me against herself and I laid my head on her shoulder as she rubbed my back.

Her head rested on mine as she hummed an old tune for a moment. Then she said, "We're going to fix this, okay? Everything is going to be alright. You'll see. I love you more than you will ever know, and I will not let my baby continue to hurt. And now you have such an incredible responsibility on your shoulders to parent this young man who needs you more than ever. He's going to go through a lot of confusion and doubt, and you're going to have to be strong. Stronger than you ever imagined."

"Mom..." I sobbed. I didn't know what to say.

"I'm here, Mindy. And I love you, and I'm not going anywhere."

A decade's worth of pain washed out of my system through those tears. Healing started deep in my soul, making me believe that perhaps there really was a god, and if there was, that maybe he was watching out for me after all. Maybe he had just been waiting for me to call out to him the way I did when I whispered that prayer.

"I love you," I mumbled, and Mom kissed the top of my head.

"It's going to be okay. You'll see."

29

Jace

"Yeah, and after that, Mindy's mom gave me a few dollars and I bought a soda for me and Charlie and we got some candy too."

I don't think I'd seen my son smile this much since before his mother got sick. My heart felt so full. When Mindy offered to take him to the park for a play date with her friend Georgia and her son Charlie, I was hesitant, but Chris really wanted to go along.

Mindy grinned at me and pointed her fork at Christopher. "This kid can run too. Let me tell you. He and Charlie had a foot race, and the boy smoked his competition." She nodded at Christopher who went on to tell the tale of challenging his "new best friend" to a race to impress Mindy's mother, and afterward they all went for ice cream.

"It sounds like you had a great day then." I took a bite of green beans. While they were at the park I made dinner of lamb chops and vegetables. I didn't feel so bad that there was no dessert after hearing Christopher had already drunk a soda and eaten candy this afternoon.

"Yeah, it was great." He put his fork down on his empty plate but didn't ask to be excused. Since Mindy had started staying here, he always rushed off as soon as his plate was empty. It was nice to see them getting along well enough that he wanted to stay until we were finished too.

I looked at her, so radiant with that smile on her face. My family was more whole than it had been in a long time, and I felt like tonight was the right night to tell Chris exactly how whole it really was. Mindy and I hadn't even broached the subject yet. I assumed she was just leaving it up to me since I was the only parent Jace had ever known. Connie would have wanted this though, for Christopher to meet Mindy one day. I had been against it at first, but meeting Mindy, I knew Connie was right.

"What's wrong with you?" Christopher asked, giggling. "You look constipated."

Mindy laughed heartily but she scolded him lightly. "Be nice, Topper. It looks like your dad has something to say."

"Oh god, you're not going to ask her to marry you right here are you?" He rolled his eyes at his father. "How lame. If you're going to do that, at least take her to a restaurant."

This time it was my turn to burst out laughing. "No, Top, I'm not proposing, at least not tonight." At least not at this table...

"So what then? Can we get a puppy?" Christopher reached into the bowl of green beans and plucked one out and popped it in his mouth.

"Not with your hands," Mindy chided but he shrugged at her. I was just happy he was eating and Dr. Wilks had gotten his flare ups under control.

"No, bud, it's more important than that." I looked Mindy in the eye and she met my gaze with a look of apprehension. "Is it okay if I tell him?" I asked her and she bit her lip.

"You're having a baby?" Chris was so full of prying questions if we didn't just spit it out I thought he'd implode.

"No bud, it's not that." I glanced at him but I wouldn't tell him if Mindy didn't consent. She blinked several times and looked around the table at him then me. Her shoulders fell and she nodded, chewing her lip like it was beef jerky. She did that when she was nervous, so I took her hand for reassurance.

"What?" Christopher's eyes bounced back and forth between me and Mindy and his eyebrows rose like he was waiting.

"So, you've been to reproductive health studies at school..."

"Yeah... You said she's not pregnant." He furrowed his brow in confusion.

"You are the baby I'm talking about." I reached out and wiggled my fingers at him and he put his hand in mine. My arms lay stretched across the table holding both of their hands. I needed that strength as much as they did at that moment. "Christopher, you remember how a few years ago, before Mom died, you asked if you could meet your real mom someday?"

"Yeah," he said, acting confused.

I looked at Mindy whose eyes brimmed with tears. "Well, when we met Mindy, she thought maybe you looked like her father a little. When she was much younger, only a few years older than you really, she made a choice to have sex with her boyfriend at the time. And she got pregnant."

Christopher's eyes narrowed then widened. He was catching on faster than I could explain, so I talked faster. "Her parents made her give that baby away for adoption, and she never wanted to. So when she met me and I showed her a picture of you, she believed maybe you were her son, the one she was forced to give away."

He stared at her. His eyes were bright, but his face was drawn in pain and confusion. He didn't say a word as I continued. "When we ran tests for your belly aches, she ran a test to see if your blood matched hers. It was a DNA test."

"You're my mom?" he asked. His voice was tiny and weak. I barely understood him. His fingers went weak inside my grasp but I didn't let his hand go.

"Yes," she said, and when she blinked tears cascaded down her cheeks. "I didn't know how to tell you, and it's okay if you have hurt feelings or don't know what to feel."

He looked thoughtful for a moment and then stared down at his empty plate. The mood was dampened by the confession. Mindy and I exchanged glances again and she squeezed my hand as if prompting me to say something.

"What do you think?" I asked, passing the squeeze on to his fingers. I knew it was a lot to process, and his little mind had been through so much already.

"Why did you give me away?" His honest, heart wrenching question caught Mindy off guard. "Because that's the one question I always wanted to ask you." He looked her square in the eye, not a hint of malice in his expression.

"I didn't have a choice, bud. I was only a child myself, and my parents took you away from me and signed the papers in my name. I always wanted to find you. I never wanted to give you away." Mindy let the tears fall freely. It was probably the best thing she could do— show her true heart to him. He was a smart kid. I knew he would get it. I just didn't realize how smart and compassionate he was until he spoke his next sentence.

"That's why you were so angry with your mom?"

Mindy pulled her hand back and covered her face with both of them. Her sobs wracked her body and tore my heart out. I wanted to stand and wrap her in my arms, but Christopher beat me to it. His short arms barely wrapped all the way around her shoulders but he held her so tightly it made my heart so proud to be his father. And just like Connie would have done, he spoke softly to her in comforting words.

"Hey, it's okay. It wasn't your fault." He patted her back and stepped away, and I handed Mindy my napkin. She wiped her eyes and blew her nose, and Christopher said, "I'm glad you're here."

"I'm glad I'm here too, bud." Her bright red, puffy nose had never looked cuter when she smiled.

"I don't think I can call you mom right now."

"That's okay. Mindy is good enough." She took his hand and held it.

"Is that why you love my dad, because of me?" More honesty and more tears sprang out of her eyes.

"Oh, heavens no. I love your dad because he is just about the most amazing man I've ever met. I am so happy that you got to grow up with him as your dad. And I think based on what I know about her, your mom was a pretty incredible woman too. I only hope I'm able to love you the way she would have."

"I'm gonna go lay down, okay?" He looked a little sad as he said the words, but I nodded.

"Yeah, bud, that's okay" I watched him walk away knowing it was only the beginning of the questions and adjustments. When he was shut into his room, I stood and pulled Mindy to her feet, wrapping her in my arms.

"You were so brave." I kissed the top of her head and she buried her face in my chest and said nothing. "I'll clean up after a bit. Let's go get you into a hot bath or something." I knew she was full of emotions after the long day, and I just wanted to help her relax.

She nodded and took my hand and followed me into the bedroom. She shut the door and locked it and crawled into bed fully clothed. When she curled up into a ball, I couldn't help but want to curl around her, so I did. I kissed her cheek and tucked her hair behind her ear.

"Are you alright?"

"I kinda just want to feel close to you."

"Like this?" I asked her, pulling her so close there was no space between our spooning bodies.

"Closer," she said timidly. I knew what she meant.

"Okay, baby, whatever you want."

I ran my hand down her side and felt her shiver with anticipation. She scooted back against me and I moved my hand across her stomach, feeling the smoothness of her skin. She let out a soft sigh as I moved my hand up to cup her breast. I squeezed gently, feeling her nipple harden beneath my touch. I leaned down and kissed her neck, nipping lightly at the skin there.

She moaned softly and lifted her hips, pressing her backside into my growing erection. I couldn't help but groan at the feeling of her against me. I reached down and pulled her shirt up, smoothing my hand over her bra. Mindy turned to her back and looked up at me. "Jace..."

"I know, baby." I kissed her and pulled the shirt completely off of her then unhooked her bra and pulled it off too. I ran my hand over her breasts, cupping them and teasing her nipples with my fingers. "I just want to make you feel good. I love you so much." I leaned down and flicked her nipple with my tongue. "Tell me if you're uncomfortable." Mindy nodded and moaned again. I did it again and she arched her back. "Good?"

I moved my mouth to her other nipple and she moaned, "Mmh-mm." I smoothed my hand down her body and unbuttoned her jeans and slid my hand into her panties. I pushed my fingers down her slit, finding her clit and stroking it gently. She moaned and her hips rocked forward. I snuck one finger inside of her, then a second and she moaned louder. I started thrusting, watching her face as I made love to her with my hand. My fingers rubbed her opening and thrust inside of her. She cried out softly, so I did it again and she rocked her hips into my hand, meeting my thrusts.

"Just take them off," she whispered, but when I pulled my hand out of her jeans to do just that, she whined. She was so perfect, even with a face puffy from crying. Her pants and panties came off as easily as her top and bra, then I stripped my clothing off too and lay back down next to her.

"Mindy, I want so badly to spend the rest of my life with you." I returned my hand to her mound and continued to rub her clit. "I want to marry you. I want to be your husband. I want to take care of you for as long as I live. I love you."

Mindy was panting, thrusting her hips into my hand. "I love you, Jace. I want that, too." She moaned. "I want that so badly."

"Do you trust me?" I asked.

"Yes, Jace. With everything." She was moving faster and faster, and I knew she was close. I slid my hand down and she gasped and moaned, her hips grinding against my movements. Her hands gripped my wrist, pulling my hand deeper and I leaned down and kissed her. When she came, her eyes opened wide and she let out a surprised gasp and her back arched. Her body trembled and her toes flexed and curled. It was beautiful to watch. She was so amazing. Her skin was pink and vibrant, her breasts rising in rhythm to her rapid breathing. She was sweaty, her hair strewn across the pillow, her face red with exertion.

The sweet smell of Mindy filled my nostrils, her perfume mixed with her wet passion and was quite intoxicating. Mindy's lips grazed mine and I tasted something tangy and sweet, like an exotic fruit, I wanted more. She moaned and sighed and gasped, her body moving in time with my hand and my lips. Her breath was quick and hard, the rasping of her throat a gentle counterpoint to the sound of the sheets moving against her body.

"God... yes," she grunted, clawing at my wrist, until her orgasm started to pass.

I kissed her and moved over her, sliding my cock inside of her. She gasped and moaned and her hands gripped my biceps. I thrust slowly into her. I didn't want to hurt her. I wanted it to be everything she expected it to be. So I penetrated her inch by inch. "I love you, you know that?" My voice was gravelly and low. Her eyes fluttered open again to take me in.

"And I love you too, Jace."

Our bodies moved together, rhythmically, and I felt the sauce of her arousal on my cock. She arched her back, pushing her breasts against my chest, and I kissed her softly. Mindy's fingers weaved into my hair, and I heard her whispering my name as her body began to shudder again. My thrusting grew harder and faster, and I nearly lost control. I felt her fingers tighten in my hair and she cried out my name, louder and louder, her body heaving against mine.

"Shhh, Christopher will hear," I cautioned, covering her mouth with mine as the second wave of orgasm hit her. Her pussy clenched around me tightly and her fingernails drew blood on my sides. I swallowed her moans and slowed my thrusts as I felt my balls pulse.

When her orgasm passed, I whispered, "I want you to have my babies, Mindy. Lots of them. I want to raise children with you and build a home."

"Oh god," she said, starting to cry again. "Jace, I want so badly to have your babies too." My heart felt full, and it was enough to make me want to never leave this safe space inside of her. I thrust again more quickly, filling her and pulling back. It was exquisite the way her strong walls wrapped around me, her juices slicking her entrance.

"I want to make you happy."

"You do make me happy. You make me so happy, Jace."

I moved faster, and my cock felt like it was going to burst outward. The sensation of Mindy's pussy was too much, and I knew it wouldn't be long before I came. I felt the tension in my balls build and I thrust faster and harder. My head was spinning, and my heart was pounding. I could feel the warmth of her pussy as it pulsed around my cock. I knew she was close too, and that was enough.

"I'm gonna come, Mindy..."

"Me too! Oh god, Jace, me too!" She let out a muffled cry as my orgasm hit me. We came together in a beautiful explosion of ecstasy, my cock buried deep inside of her. The heat flooded in around me, filling her with my seed. Her guttural gasps turned into a wail, as her pussy pulsed and gripped my cock tightly. My body tensed and I buried my face in her neck, kissing her and inhaling her sweet scent. She whimpered and cooed, and I felt her hands glide up my back and stay there.

Our bodies went slack, and I felt my cock slip out of her. The warmth of the room mixed with the heat of our bodies as we lay together on the bed. I pulled her close to me and she cuddled into my chest, kissing me on the neck.

"Jace?"

"Yes, my love?"

"I don't want to leave this bed."

"Then don't."

"I don't want to let you go."

I pulled her into another hug and kissed the top of her head. "I'll never let you go, Mindy. I love you." She squeezed me and buried her face into my chest, fresh tears escaping her eyes as I rolled to the side to hold her.

We stayed like that for a long time, wrapped up in each other's arms. I could feel her heartbeat as it slowed down to a normal pace. It was the most peaceful I'd felt in a long time. I lay there with her in my arms as I made a plan for how I wanted to ask her to marry me. She fell asleep, but my mind stayed very active. And when I slipped out to put away the leftovers and clean up, she didn't even stir.

30

Mindy

As if the drive across town to meet with the ethics committee wasn't nerve wracking enough, they had us sitting outside in the hall for almost forty minutes waiting for their deliberation. Georgia and Ben sat to my right, and Jace to my left. They were all here to support me, and Ben had volunteered to speak on my behalf if necessary. Dr. Andrews didn't know whether they would let anyone into the meeting with me, but he told me to bring them along just in case.

I sat with my elbows on my knees and my face buried while Georgia smoothed large circles on my back with her hand. Ben and Jace talked quietly about Charlie and Christopher having a sleepover at some point but I could only obsess about my future. Everything was riding on this meeting and the review board's decision.

I had graduated early from high school and college and finished my residency on time. I was one of the youngest doctors in this hospital, with the highest marks and best success rate. That had to mean something to them, or maybe that only proved to them that I was too immature to do this job. The self-doubt and fear crippled me to the point I couldn't talk. But Georgia was there, whispering in my ear encouraging words. What I wouldn't have done for it to be my mother, but I didn't think she could be that for me in this instance. Our relationship was healing, but we just weren't there yet.

"It's going to be fine, Mindy. You'll see." Her hand was comforting, and I started to relax.

"Hey," Jace said, leaning down to speak to me. He put his arm over my back, thus effectively stopping Georgia's swirling motion with her hand.

"I really screwed up, Jace. I just know they're going to fire me." I shook my head. I knew I had made this bed and that I had to lie in it, but it felt like a bed of nails and I had no clue what I was doing when I created it.

"You did, but I'm here. And that means something." He took my hand and held it, but I stayed hunched over with my face partly covered by one hand. "They aren't pressing legal charges on you. Okay? Because I am not going to sue the hospital. We are going to explain that it was just a misunderstanding and that we are in love."

"I'm here too, Min." Ben's warm baritone rumbled my chest. I saw his knees below my face as he crouched in front of me. "I'm head of pediatrics at this hospital. My word means something." He rested a hand on my empty knee and squeezed it. "We are all here to support you. And even if the worst thing happens, and they take your license to practice, I know you will make a comeback."

"You have your dream come true, Mindy." Georgia's voice entered the mix again, and I sat up and looked into her eyes. "Your baby boy is here with you now. You get to be the mother you always wanted to be, so remember that if everything else fades away or is taken, it was a sacrifice so you could have him."

"None of this would have happened if I'd just had the guts to be honest from the beginning." I ran a hand through my hair and found it tangled, so I fidgeted with it, trying to rake out the mess. Jace pried my hands away from it and placed them gently in my lap, then carefully untangled my hair and tucked it around my ear.

"You're overthinking this, hun," he cooed as he worked.

"Jace is right, babe." Ben wasn't even my friend; he was just Georgia's husband. Still, here he was going to bat for me. "These things aren't as bad as you think, and you have Jace on your side."

"I literally stole a blood sample and ran DNA on it without his consent. Even if he doesn't file charges—which I know he isn't—it's still highly unethical. They aren't just going to look the other way." Nothing they could say would ease the ache in my chest. I knew what I was up against, so when the door swung open and Dr. Andrews walked out with a stern expression, I jolted to my feet.

"They're ready for you, and your friends can come in too."

"What did they say?" I asked hastily. As my direct supervisor I worried that he, too, would come under review for letting this happen on his shift.

"I'm not going to lie, Mindy. What you did was really bad, but I think everyone involved understands what you were going through." He nodded his head and offered a look of compassion. Everyone always said he was too strict, but to me, Dr. Andrews was a kind and compassionate man. "Come with me, okay?"

I nodded and clutched Jace's hand, who was now standing beside me. Georgia and Ben trailed behind me as we walked into the room. It felt more like a courtroom than an ethics review board. The ethics committee wasn't in the room at all, but there was a high table with six chairs behind it, all facing the door. Dr. Andrews sat in a chair on this side of the table, about five paces away from where the committee members would sit. I chose the seat next to him, and Jace and the others sat too.

We waited in silence for a few minutes until the door behind the table opened and one by one the committee members filed in. First two older females entered, followed by an elderly male, a younger woman, a much younger man, probably Ben's age, and to my utter shock, my father entered the room and shut the door.

I looked at Jace with surprise and he cocked his head. Ben and Georgia stared at the members as they took their seats, completely oblivious to the fact that my father was one of them. I had no clue he was on the board; I didn't know he had any affiliation with this hospital other than a few friendships with the higher ups because of his golf club membership. He stared at me sternly and I squirmed under his gaze. It felt like high school all over again when I admitted I was pregnant.

"Dr. Scriber, could you please stand before the committee?" The oldest woman at the table tapped a stack of papers into alignment and looked at me above the rim of her glasses. Her gray hair was swept up into a bun, but a few stray hairs wisped around her temples.

Trembling, I stood and took a deep calming breath. Dr. Andrews had warned me that they would want to know the whole story, hear it from my point of view, but I hadn't prepared at all, except to brace myself for the cold hard truth. The committee members stared at me, and my hand stayed firmly gripped in Jace's. I drew every ounce of strength I could from that touch.

"Dr. Scriber," the woman said. She must have been the chairman or something, because none of the other members had much to say. "What you have done is atrocious and an egregious misuse of power. You mishandled private patient information, blood samples, and test results. You went behind your patient's back and did not disclose your actions to his guardians. And you willingly and knowingly entered into a physical and romantic relationship with the guardian of one of your patients which is both unethical and illegal. In fact, you broke more than one law."

"Ma'am," Jace said, standing up next to me.

The woman lowered her glasses and scowled at him. "Mr. Turner I assume?"

"Yes, ma'am."

"Please sit and wait until the committee has spoken." She pushed her glasses back onto her nose and huffed out a sigh, and Jace sat down, but he kissed the back of my hand in solidarity. I was ready now. I knew he had my back and no matter what happened, I had my son. That was the entire reason for doing all of this. Georgia was right. Christopher was the only thing that mattered now.

"Dr. Scriber, your father, Mr. Joseph Scriber, a very esteemed member of this board, has spoken on your behalf." She pursed her lips and stared down her nose at me as if she hated what she was about to say. "We have come to a decision based on his words. He has spoken extremely highly of you. So while your actions merit very strong consequences, your reputation and his are on the line here. It is our decision to place you on six months of probation. We have decided that your stellar reputation and the phenomenal way you have carried yourself up to this point far outweighs the ethical mishaps of this current situation."

I breathed a sigh of relief and felt tears welling up. My father spoke on my behalf? My lower lip trembled and Jace gripped my hand so tight he was cutting off circulation. I didn't know how to react or what to say so I stood there dumbstruck and speechless with tears ready to pour out of my eyes.

"You are dismissed." She looked at me sternly but I didn't move until Dr. Andrews took me by the elbow and walked me to the door. "Mr. Turner, we'd like a word with you."

The hair on the back of my neck stood on end as Andrews put a hand in the small of my back and led me out. Georgia and Ben waited with me while they spoke to Jace, and I was on pins and needles wondering what they wanted with him. When he came out the door I wrapped my arms around him and breathed him in.

He smiled at me and cupped my cheeks, kissing my forehead. "What did they want?" I asked, still panicked.

"Oh, they just wanted me to sign a statement saying I wouldn't sue. No big deal. Let's go home."

We said our goodbyes and thank yous to Ben and Georgia, and Jace drove me straight to his house. Wave after wave of relief washed over me as we talked about what it meant for my career. By the time we walked through the front door I was walking on the clouds. The entire thing turned out better than I ever expected and I felt so in love with Jace I couldn't contain myself. I turned on him and wrapped my arms around his neck playfully.

"We're alone for at least two hours. Get all your clothes off and get into that bed right now," I snickered, already working on the buttons to my shirt.

"Oh yeah? You're going to dominate me?" he asked, following behind me as I walked backward toward the bedroom.

"Oh yes. I am."

As soon as we entered the bedroom, I pushed Jace down on the bed and straddled him. He looked up at me with a mix of excitement and apprehension in his eyes, and I couldn't help but smile at him. I leaned down and kissed him deeply, running my hands through his hair and pulling him closer to me.

"God, you're so sexy," he moaned, his hands roaming over my body.

I smirked at him and sat up, reaching behind me to unclasp my bra. I threw it aside and watched as Jace's eyes widened at the sight of my bare breasts. I could feel myself growing

wetter as I watched his eyes trace over my body, and his erection growing harder under me. "Why, Mr. Turner, you like what you see?"

He groaned and pulled me down to him, his lips crashing into mine. He tugged at my pants, and I sat up to let him pull them off. As soon as they were off, I sat back down on him and began grinding against him. "God, Mindy," he moaned, reaching up to squeeze my breasts. He kissed up my stomach, and I arched my back, pressing my breasts against his face.

"You like that?" I asked, letting out a low moan as he began to suck on a nipple.

"Mmm," he mumbled. "You like that?"

"Oh, yeah," I moaned, rocking my hips back and forth. I was so wet that I could feel my juices smearing all over my inner thighs. "You need your pants off now."

"Oh, god, Mindy," he moaned, twisting his fingers in my hair and pulling me down for a deep kiss. Then he sat up and pulled off his shirt, and I stood up on the bed and dropped my panties. I grabbed his pants and boxers and pulled them off of him, and I could see his throbbing erection.

I nearly dropped to my knees in front of it, but Jace grabbed me and lifted me up, settling me on his lap. I pressed my hips down on his erection, and I could feel the head right at my entrance. I slowly lowered myself onto him, letting him fill me up.

"God, Mindy," Jace moaned. "You feel so good."

"So do you," I said, grinding my hips back and forth. Jace's hands came up and crushed my breasts together, and he began to suck on one nipple while he pinched and pulled on the other. I moaned and ground my hips faster against him, feeling his erection throb inside me.

I could feel the pressure building up in my core, and I reached down to stroke my clitoris. It was sensitive, and as soon as I touched it, I could feel that I was going to cum. I let out a long sigh and moaned Jace's name as I came. I could feel my whole body shuddering, and I gripped Jace's shoulders as tightly as I could. "Woah, oh god..."

He thrust up into me pumping his dick deeper and deeper and I clenched around him as my body shook. He kneaded my tits as my orgasm pulsed through me and I shuddered. He kissed me and then quickly rolled us over. He slid his dick out of me and positioned himself, pushing back into me. I moaned in pleasure and wrapped my legs around him, rocking with him. He hardly gave me time to recover from the first orgasm before his thrusting brought me right back to the edge.

"I'm so close! Harder!" I cried out, grateful to have the house to ourselves so I could be as loud as I wanted. "Oh god! Oh god!" I moaned, my orgasm rocking through me. I was panting, and I could feel Jace's erection throbbing deep inside of me. When my body began to calm, Jace kissed me hard, nipping at my lip.

"God I want more," I panted, pushing his shoulders until he got the idea. His lips trailed across my stomach leaving a path of moisture in their wake until his tongue touched my clit. I moaned and clutched at his hair as he sucked and licked my clit. His hands gripped my thighs pushing them farther apart and his tongue explored my folds, teasing my clit with his tongue. He slid a finger inside of me, and I could feel my wetness dripping down my thighs.

"You're so wet for me," he murmured, sucking my clit into his mouth. I moaned and pushed my hips down against his face.

I could feel my orgasm building again, and I gripped my tits as I felt my body shuddering. He slid a second finger inside of me, and I moaned out, "God, Jace..." My body was already so sensitive from my other orgasms, I knew I would come again, and harder this time.

He sucked me hard, putting a third finger in my pussy and that was it. My body shuddered and clenched around him in a third wave of orgasm.

"Oh wow," I moaned, as my body exploded in ecstasy. He reached up and rubbed my clit as my pussy clenched and pulsed around his fingers. He licked me through my orgasm, and I moaned loudly, my body still rocking with the aftershocks as he pulled his fingers out of me. I was ready to melt into a puddle on the bed, but he hovered between my legs stroking himself.

"Want to have some fun?"

"Like the ice cubes?" I asked, grinning lazily.

"Like get on your hands and knees." Jace smirked at me as I rolled over to my hands and knees.

He stroked himself as he trailed a hand down my ass. He smacked me hard on the ass and I squealed, and Jace chuckled. His fingers trailed down my back, and he gently slid a finger into my tight hole. I moaned and pushed back against him as he slid his fingers in and out of me. I was so wet from coming so many times, his finger slipped inside of me easily. I pushed back against him and felt his cock against my entrance.

"You ready for me?" he asked, rubbing his cock against the tight ring of muscles he just stretched.

"Yes, I want to feel you," I moaned. "I want you to fill me up."

He slid his cock inside of me. I gasped as his thickness stretched my tight hot hole. I felt every inch of him as he slid in, and I moaned loudly as he bottomed out inside of me. His hands gripped my hips as he pulled back and slammed back into me. He hit a spot inside of me that made me moan in pleasure.

Jace guided my hand to my clit, where I rubbed furiously as he pounded me. His fingers dug into my hips as he thrust into me again and again.

"Oh god, Jace!" I moaned, "Harder!"

My fingers were drenched in my juices as I rubbed my clit furiously. "Oh my god!" I groaned.

I could feel the orgasm building inside of me, and I knew it was going to be a big one. The sensations were incredible.

"Oh god, I'm going to come," I moaned.

Then Jace's cock swelled up and he groaned loudly as he shot his load deep inside of me. He grunted as he pumped his warm seed into me and I grunted as the orgasm washed over me and my body shook with pleasure. Each movement of his girth stretching my body made me whimper and squirm in enjoyment. Then Jace slowly pulled out of me, and I collapsed onto the bed. He slid in beside me and pulled me into his arms. I sighed happily and pressed my lips against his.

"I love you," he said, kissing my back.

"Mmmm, I love you too. I'm so glad this is all over."

"Me too, love." His arms never felt better wrapped around my body. I could fall asleep here and never wake up knowing my life felt so complete.

31

Jace

I led Mindy through the set of double doors into the restaurant. It cost me nearly twelve hundred dollars to rent out the full dining room just for us, but it was worth it. With my hands on her shoulders, a blindfold tied across her eyes, and the entire room so silent I could hear a pin drop, I guided her right to the center beneath the chandelier. Smiling faces surrounded us, Ben and Georgia, Charlie and Christopher, a few work colleagues Mindy had mentioned like Evelyn and a woman named Harper.

Mindy's parents and sister stood amongst the crowd. Following the ethics review nearly one month ago now, Mindy's father approached me. I did sign that statement saying I wouldn't sue, but I hid the fact that Joseph spoke to me from Mindy this whole time. He'd taken a moment to think about our interaction at his office and admitted he'd been wrong in his snap judgment. We spoke briefly about my desire to marry Mindy, and there in that ethics review room, he gave me his blessing. This night was the culmination of weeks of planning to make everything just right.

"What are we doing? It's so quiet."

"Shhh," I told her, walking around to stand in front of her.

So far everything was perfect. The tables were set with the finest silver flatware. Bottles of wine were chilling at every one of them. Red velvet curtains hung in front of the windows and puddled near the floor. Everyone wore some fanciful gown or a suit, even the boys. When I proposed to Constance it had been a simple, "Will you marry me?" in the bed of her father's pickup truck at the drive in. She never let me forget how I had no ring, no plan, just a heart that loved her.

I always felt like I'd failed. And I wasn't about to fail Mindy.

I lowered myself to one knee and as I did soft music started to play—some concerto or something that Violet picked out. She was the artistic one and I leaned on her heavily for advice on how to make Mindy's evening spectacular. I nodded at Christopher and he walked forward, carrying the ring. He knelt next to me, his tiny little frame so much smaller than mine, but when I planned this I knew he was the part she would cherish the most. We'd talked about it at length, and I was so excited to see her reaction.

"Jace, you're freaking me out. What's going on.?" She reached for her blind fold but I clicked my tongue at her and nodded at Georgia.

"Not yet," I hummed, and Georgia floated across the room to stand behind her. She'd wait on my signal to remove the blind fold. Ben came to stand behind us holding a bouquet of two dozen roses, one from me, and one from Christopher. It was time.

Took a deep cleansing breath and Christopher put his hand on my knee. I looked him in the eye as I started talking.

"Mindy, you came into my life in the craziest way. I never in my entire life expected to fall in love with anyone the way I have you. You and I have something Constance and I never had." I saw Christopher's eyes grow a bit sad, but he looked up at Mindy and kept a smile on his face, hand extended with the ring box open. I looked up at her too, continuing: "Your heart and your love are incredibly special to me. So I have a question for you."

"Jace..." she whispered but Christopher took over, interrupting her.

"Mindy, I have this big hole inside my heart because someone important to me isn't here anymore." Tears burst out of her eyes and she covered her mouth. It drew tears from my eyes too, but I smiled as they ran down my cheeks. "She was a really important lady and she was really great at baking and crafts and making me smile. She also made me take baths, but I guess that's okay." I chuckled and so did Mindy, bawling her eyes out. "So I have a question for you too."

I nodded at Georgia and she removed the blind fold. Mindy looked down at me, literally laughing and sobbing. She glanced around the room and shook her head as she swiped at her teary face.

"Mindy, I want you to do me the honor of being my wife." I nodded at Christopher.

"Mindy, I want you to be my mom, forever, and make me take baths." Chris held out the ring farther. I could see tears in his eyes too. My heart was so full; I didn't think I'd ever feel normal again, or maybe I would just feel like this forever, and it would be my new normal.

"Oh my god, yes," she cried. Mindy fell to her knees and wrapped Christopher in her arms, ignoring the ring. I knew this moment was special to her, and I had no way of knowing in her heart what she felt, but I felt just a smidge of it, and I was overwhelmed.

"I love you, Mom," Chris whispered but I heard it. I waited until she finished hugging her son as the entire room erupted into clapping and cheers. And when she pulled away, we all stood and embraced, leaving room for even Christopher to join our family hug.

"Oh wow," she cried, "I'm so overwhelmed."

I brushed a tear from her eyes and nodded. "Me too," I told her as Christopher pulled away.

"Can we eat cake now?" he asked, grinning, and Mindy laughed, throwing her head back.

"Yes!" Before the word left her lips he was off, finding Charlie and racing for the cake. Our family and friends surrounded us, offering congratulations and hugs. Mindy's father hung back, stoic as usual. She was so preoccupied with all the attention, she didn't notice at first, but as the party goers fanned out to enjoy cake and wine, I nudged her toward him. I knew he was a very prideful man and may not approach her on his own. She looked at me hesitantly and I reassured her.

"I asked him for your hand in marriage, and he blessed our union. I think he has some things he wants to say to you, but he's not sure how to bring them up. It's time to heal, Mindy." With my hand in the small of her back, I walked with her over to the table where her father sat with a slice of cake and a glass of wine. He looked up at us as we stopped in front of him.

"This is kosher right?" he asked, probably something he would have said at home and Mindy nodded, smiling. She bent at the waist and kissed his forehead.

"Thank you, Daddy."

He looked down, frowning as he put a bite of cake in his mouth. As a father and a man with an ego, I understood how he must be feeling. Admitting you've hurt someone is difficult, but admitting to this level of hurt is ego crippling and humbling. I listened to the conversation as Mindy sat next to him and took his hand.

"Thank you for talking to the review board. Thank you for giving Jace your blessing. We will sign a ketubah just like you and Momma did." She paused. I wanted to see her expression but I refused to look. They needed privacy. It was enough that I was hearing what they said, but I knew Mindy wouldn't have the courage to have this conversation if I weren't here.

"You are welcome."

"Daddy, I'm sorry for the way I treated you and Momma. I didn't know you gave up a child too."

The words were news to me, but I kept a straight face.

"It's true," he said curtly. I heard his fork clink on his plate. "It was very difficult. I tried to save you from that pain and I only made it worse."

Mindy reached for my hand and I held hers and squeezed it. "I know you tried your hardest. I have Jace now, and he will protect me."

"And you have a very smart, very handsome young son."

My heart swelled as he said the words. For her father to say such a thing was bordering on the miraculous.

"Hashem has truly blessed our family in you, Mindy. The pains of yesterday are redeemed and life has come full circle."

I looked down to see Mindy smiling and a tear on her cheek again. "Yes, he has. And I can't wait for you to meet my boy. You are going to love him, Daddy. He's just like you, smart and strong and brave. And I can't wait to give you a whole house full of grandbabies." She threw her arms around her father in a huge hug, knocking his cake off the plate to the floor. He laughed and hugged her back.

"It's not kosher anymore," he snickered and kissed her cheek. "I need more cake now, young lady, and bring that boy to me so I can meet him properly." He released her and she kissed his cheek before standing.

The entire night was perfect, just like I planned. Better than I even planned. We danced and laughed until close to midnight, and when Ben and Georgia asked if Chris could sleep over with Charlie, we agreed. It was late and we were tired, but it was worth it. It seemed everything was falling into place just as it should be.

When we finally traipsed into the house around one a.m. I was ready to take my soon-to-be bride to bed and crash, but Mindy had other plans. She hooked her pinky around mine and walked me to the kitchen.

You know this is where you first kissed me." She played with my tie, loosening it and pulling it away from my neck.

"Yeah?" I said, resting my hands on her hips.

"And since that first kiss turned to something really incredible, I say we commemorate the event by reenacting it." Her playful smirk and the way she started unbuttoning my shirt got my juices flowing.

"Oh yeah?" I rubbed my pelvis against her and swayed my hips. "How should we do that?"

"Well, I could go put on the same outfit I had on that day, but I think maybe it would be more fun if it was more of a loose interpretation of the reenactment." She had my shirt fully unbuttoned before I even kissed her once. Her hands splayed across my chest, pushing the shirt open.

"I think that sounds fun... Plus, we have an ice maker here." I grinned madly at her, gesturing at the freezer door. She snickered.

"Temperature play again? I kinda liked that."

"Oh, temperature play, some naughty kinky things..."

"Like what?" her fingers dexterously worked my fly while I unzipped the back of her sequined gown.

"Mmmm, well I have a French bulb whisk... It might be fun to stuff in your pussy and then pour a bottle of champagne into you and drink it out with a straw." I yanked the dress down so quickly she gasped in surprise and giggled.

"I think you're taking it a bit too far." Her eyes sparkled as she stepped out of the dress and I drank in the sight of her beautiful tits on full display. No bra tonight—incredible.

"Okay, so nothing too kinky, but definitely ice." I winked at her as I slid my shirt off and pushed my pants down.

Mindy put her palms on the counter behind her and pushed herself right up there, spreading her legs. She planted her hands between them, blocking my view of her sexy black panties, and the black stilettos she wore with her dress still remained on her feet. My god was she hot. My dick got so hard before I even had my boxers off I thought I'd nut right there.

"Mmmm, you like this?" Mindy licked her lips and slid her hands down to rub her pussy. The wetness seeping through her panties made me groan. "I got wet thinking about that ice and champagne idea."

"I want to see you in action." I kissed her, pushing my tongue into her mouth. Her lips tasted sweet.

"You're so sexy." I groaned, taking her hand off her pussy and placing it on my dick. She stroked me a few times.

"You like my hand on your dick?" She glanced up into my eyes, "You like when I do this?" I leaned in to kiss her again but she turned her head. "I want to see you in action."

"You first," I told her and pushed her hand away from my dick and slid it down her tummy to the top of her black lacy panties.

Mindy snickered and slipped her fingers into her panties and touched herself. They danced under the thin fabric of her panties, smearing the moisture. "Ooh," I moaned, "I like that." Her fingers looked so hot moving back and forth. I wanted her hand on my dick again but didn't want to ruin the show with a request. I took a step back, leaning against the fridge.

She pushed her fingers up herself, and I stroked myself at the sight of her fingers disappearing into the wetness.

"This would be easier without these on..." She leaned back and pulled her hand from her panties, closed her legs, and slipped them off without removing her shoes. As they dropped to the floor, she smirked and asked, "Get me a piece of ice?"

"What?"

"A piece of ice." She pointed at the freezer. "Get me a piece of ice."

"Uhh..." I turned and pressed the dispenser on the front of the fridge, collecting a few ice cubes. "Here." I dropped them into her hand and grinned. I loved this adventurous side of her. She squeezed the ice in her hand and rubbed it all over her soft lips. It began to melt, making a mess of her and the counter under her, which began to form a puddle. She shivered and hissed and I stroked myself a little harder.

"Oh wow," I groaned. "That looks so hot."

"Yeah?" She grinned, "Watch this." She slid it in, and I groaned and stepped closer to her.

"Oh, you're so sexy," I whispered.

Mindy bit her lip and moaned softly as she slid it in and out, and I growled a little louder. She grinned and I stepped closer to her, still stroking myself. The melting ice made her dripping wet, as she slid it almost all the way in then out.

"Okay," she moaned, "I need to cum so bad."

"Oh, yeah," I moaned. "Cum for me."

"You want me to cum?"

"God yes."

"Okay," she moaned. "Get down here." Mindy reached out and pushed on my shoulders, and I dropped to my knees between her legs. She sat on the counter with her legs spread, massaging her clit and I spread her thighs with delight.

"Oh," she moaned, as I leaned over her, and kissed her inner thigh. I leaned in and kissed her hand softly as she fingered herself. The ice was gone, a cold water trail in its wake. I stared at her, watching her fingers slide in and out of her wet pussy and groaned. I wanted to fuck her so bad. "I wanted you to cum on my face," I whispered. I pulled her hand away and licked her clit, and she moaned and arched her head back.

Mindy was delicious, salty and sweet. I sucked her soft folds, then flicked my tongue over her sensitive nub.

"Jace," she panted, hands laced through my hair. I couldn't respond. My tongue was buried deep inside her recess, drinking her juices. She moaned louder, "Jace..." I felt her clenching around my tongue, grinding against my face. "Oh god, Jace," she wailed, and I looked up and watched her come, her body arching on the counter. I drank every drop of her as she shuddered and writhed in pleasure.

"Jace... oh wow!"

"Mmmm," I growled against her skin as she clawed at my head. Her juices during orgasm were thick and sweet. I couldn't get enough of them, but when she pulled my hair, forcing me upward, I obeyed.

"In me, now," she said, her eyes flaming with lust. She kissed me, her tongue and mine dancing, and she reached down and stroked me. I groaned and thrust into her hands, and she kissed me deeper. I bit her lip and she returned the pleasure. Her hands were magic on my cock, but I wanted inside of her.

"God..." I grunted and grabbed her wrists. "You're going to make me come, woman." I grinned and held her wrists at her sides.

"That's the point," she said, smirking.

Mindy's pussy was still cold when I slid into her. It chilled my cock and sent my heart racing.

She bucked against me and I bit her neck hard, sucking and licking at the tender skin. Mindy's moans were like music, high-pitched and sweet. I tried my best to hold her close but her writhing hips wouldn't allow it. "Mindy," I groaned into her flesh. I was finding it hard to hold back. I wanted to fill her so badly, but I was trying to make it last longer. "Mindy," I breathed, trying to hold myself back. It was no use. She was so hot. I gripped her hips and thrust into her harder. Her back hit the cupboard behind her and she moaned again.

"Jace, I'm going to come. I'm so close." Her hands wrestled out of my grasp and roamed my body, clawing at my skin.

"Me too..."

"Come with me," she whispered.

"I will," I growled.

Then she bit my ear and I groaned. I wasn't going to last much longer at all now. Even her teeth grazing my ear had me ready to burst.

"I'm going to fill you," I moaned, and I thrust into her harder, faster. Her moans had become screams, and I was nearing my own.

Mindy's hands gripped my back and she held on, her nails digging into my flesh. "Yes, now... yes," she gurgled and sank her teeth into my shoulder. My cock pulsed inside her as her thick walls locked around it. She milked me, her body shuddering against mine. We both came together, her pussy squirting all over my cock and her mouth burying itself in my shoulder. I groaned as I shot my load into her. It felt like the world had gone still.

Mindy's pussy pulsed around my cock, squeezing it so hard I could barely move. Her nails and teeth were still digging into me, and the pain was incredible. But it was a good pain, a pain I felt like I'd been waiting for.

When my cock had finished pumping into her, Mindy slumped against my chest, and I was left standing, still inside her, struggling to breathe. My arms wrapped around her, holding her to me, her pussy still contracting around me.

"I love you," I whispered, and I kissed her head.

"I love you too, Jace." She looked up at me and smiled, kissing my chin. Her tongue traced over my jaw, then my lips.

"I'm not going to be able to sleep tonight if you keep doing that," I groaned as she licked my chin. She giggled and her pebble-hard nipples brushed against my chest.

"You're right, I do taste good."

"Now, now, future Mrs. Turner. I think we need to sleep. We'll have a young man full of energy to care for tomorrow." I chided her playfully and she sighed.

"Take me to bed, Mr. Turner." She slid off the counter and as she did one of her heels dropped to the floor. She bent and took the other one off and left them laying there.

This mess was a tomorrow thing. Tonight I wanted nothing more than to hold my beautiful fiancé in my arms and fall asleep. We had a wedding to plan and I couldn't wait to get started. But first... Sleep.

EPILOGUE

Mindy

I stood at the back of the crowded courtyard, reserved for our wedding day. Soft music played, and Mom hovered close to me. I was certain it wasn't exactly the ceremony she and Dad had envisioned when they helped me decide what day to host our wedding, but the combination between Jace's very traditional American upbringing and my Jewish culture was a good balance. He stood beneath the chuppah in his tuxedo, my father next to him wearing his traditional suit with his kippah pinned on his head as usual. They both looked so handsome.

And I was so honored that Christopher wanted to be like his grandfather, wearing a kippah that matched. It brought tears to my eyes, like everything else today. I was so emotionally overwhelmed I felt like I cried more today than I did for months while worrying and trying to cover up my little secret.

"It's okay, Mindy. You're going to be fantastic." Mom's encouraging words made me smile. She dabbed a handkerchief across my cheeks so as not to smudge my makeup and then kissed me once. "I'll go sit, then you follow."

Mom walked down the aisle and took her seat, then Violet headed down, just as we planned. I lingered just out of sight behind the row of trees that blocked our guests from view. Violet's lavender gown was gorgeous. Georgia helped us pick it out. I thought there was no better tribute to my best friend than to get her involved in this. She grinned at me from the back row where she had her camera ready.

I chewed the inside of my cheek and when Rabbi Benjamin nodded at me, the music changed. I stepped out carrying my bouquet of fresh freesia and greenery. Everyone stood in American tradition and faced me as I walked myself down the aisle. Each step took me closer to my future with Jace, and my stomach rolled with butterflies. He smiled at me so brightly I started to cry again, which made him cry. I noticed Mom was crying too, and even Dad had a tear in his eye.

Rabbi Benjamin nodded at me as I stood in front of Jace and Dad joined our hands before sitting down next to Mom. It was awkward, probably not what Dad wanted, but a blended family meant compromise.

The rabbi prayed and blessed our union, and Jace reached into his jacket pocket and pulled out the ketubah—our signed marriage contract and license. I grinned and accepted it from him with a nod. Benjamin stepped backward so I could circle Jace seven times, which was tradition. It symbolized my acknowledgement that my life would revolve around him now. While I didn't need this act to demonstrate that, I honored my father's wishes. He never looked more proud of me as he watched me.

When I stood in front of Jace, my seven circles done, I took his hands. "You may now exchange your vows," the rabbi said.

Jace sighed and started his first. "Mindy, from the moment I met you, I knew that you were the one. You captivated me with your beauty, your intelligence, and your wit. You challenged me to be a better man, and you have always been my rock. I promise to love and cherish you for all eternity, to be faithful to you in heart and in body, to support you in all your dreams and aspirations, and to be your partner in every aspect of life. I vow to be your best friend, your confidante, and your lover, and to always be there for you through thick and thin. I love you more than words could ever express, and I am honored to be your husband."

With tears in my eyes, I took a deep breath and began my own vows. "Jace, you are my everything. You have shown me what it means to love and be loved. You make me laugh when I want to cry, and you hold me tight when the world feels like it's falling apart. You are my safe harbor, my constant, my home. I vow to love and cherish you for all eternity, to be faithful to you in heart and in body, to support you in all your dreams and aspirations, and to be your partner in every aspect of life. I vow to be your best friend, your confidante, and your lover, and to always be there for you through thick and thin. I promise to grow with you, to challenge you, and to share in all the joys and sorrows that life may bring. I love you more than anything in this world, and I am honored to be your wife."

As we exchanged rings, I felt a wave of happiness wash over me. Jace was my everything, and I knew that we were meant to be together forever. Our wedding was the start of a new chapter in our lives, one filled with love, laughter, and adventure.

"I am proud to announce to you for the first time, Mr. and Mrs. Jason Turner," said the rabbi. "Please seal your union with a holy kiss."

Jace pulled me against his body with a fierce love I had craved my whole life. His kiss was deep and passionate. Everyone snickered and clapped, and the moment I tore my lips away from his, Rabbi Benjamin handed him a napkin-wrapped glass.

Jace laughed and laid the glass on the ground. He took my hand as he drove his heel downward and shouted, "Mazal tov!"

Everyone around us joined the shout, raising their voices together, and Jace pulled me in for another kiss. "As this glass breaks, may your marriage never shatter." The rabbi's blessing was complete and I was a married woman.

Before we could react, my parents and Violet, along with a few family friends and Jace's partner Howard had us on two chairs hoisted in the air as loud music began and they carried us around.

The hora dance was one tradition even I didn't want to miss out on. Christopher giggled and followed the crowd around as they paraded us through the courtyard, and Jace and I held hands. When they finally set us down and we had a moment to ourselves, I held him to me, staring into his eyes.

"You made me the happiest man alive, you know?"

"I did?" I asked, lavishing kisses on him.

"You really did. And now I want to make you the happiest woman alive." His arms squeezed me tight.

"You already did, Jace. I don't think I could ever be happier than this." And it was true. My family was whole again, and my heart was whole. It didn't matter what came my way. I knew with Jace by my side, life could only get better.

EXTENDED EPILOGUE

Callum

Dr. Scriber was positively glowing as she told me the exciting news about her pregnancy. I slid the paperwork across the desk in her direction—her release from probation. After the mess she got herself into, she handled the board-ordered probation like a champ and today was her first day with autonomy again.

"It's hard to believe it's been six months." She sighed happily as she took the paperwork and clutched it to her chest. If I were a weaker man I'd have made a comment about how her already large tits were growing, but she was a married woman now, for three full months. And a pregnant mother at that.

"I don't believe it either. I'm so glad to have you back at full capacity though. Some of that paperwork was a nightmare." I sat back in my chair and thought of how her punishment had brought double duty for me as well, but now it was water under the bridge. "Is Jason pleased that you're cookin' another little bun?" Her husband and I had gotten to know each other a bit better, though I wouldn't have called him a friend or anything.

"Yes, he's actually ecstatic." Mindy seemed thrilled too, though I couldn't imagine starting a family at his age—any age for that matter. The entirety of my career I'd been focused on money and promotions. At fifty, time for a family had passed. I had a few moments in life where I thought about it, but I wasn't ever one for commitment. There had only ever been one woman I would have taken the plunge with, and she was off limits. Besides she got married to a real douche who ended up breaking her pretty badly.

"Good, good… Well, it will be great to have you back around the office daily now." I stood and reached my hand out. "I have a meeting with Dr. Peters now, so if you don't mind?"

Mindy rose and shook my hand. "Thanks for having my back this whole time, Dr. Andrews. I won't let you down." She excused herself and I dawdled a bit. Peters was a close friend of mine, even after some tension years ago involving his daughter. Being my boss, however, had never challenged our relationship. We worked well together, golfed and had poker nights too. This meeting, though, was about the new trauma wing we were building for the hospital and the budgetary concerns. I wasn't really a part of the team—the head of internal medicine had very little say over what needs a trauma surgeon may have—but he valued my input. So I agreed to listen to his concerns and offer my advice.

I locked up my office and made my way down to the third floor where I expected him to be waiting. My plan after the meeting was to hit up the gym and maybe hit the town with a buddy. My social life was pretty much zero anymore. In my thirties I'd have been out on a Friday night with my single friends picking up women. Things slowed in my forties, most women already married with children. I found dating apps helpful, but women my age just wanted marriage and commitment.

It wasn't that I had a fear of commitment. I just had no need for it. I was more than happy to be single and focus on my career. Besides, as I said, the one woman who I ever thought met my standards was off limits, even to this day.

I turned down the hallway and noticed the light in his office was on, the door cracked, so I didn't even knock. I just walked right in and got a complete shock. There, bent over in front of me, were the thick curves of a woman's backside as she bent over adjusting her shoe. I said nothing at first, watching her hips squirm as she scraped what looked like gum off the sole of her heel. Her red skirt was short—short enough to reveal the black satin panties beneath it, just a hint of dark pink flesh poking out the side of the lace trim. A dot of moisture where her entrance should be turned me on, and I couldn't help myself.

"Christ.." I muttered, not even caring if she heard me. My cock was swelling and my mouth watering all at once.

The woman gasped and straightened, her long dark hair falling down her back as she straightened her skirt and turned to face me.

"Callum?" She sucked in a breath and so did I.

"Ellen?"

My god, my heart almost stopped beating. I glanced down the hallway, thinking this had to be a setup. Her father would walk in any second and see my dick at attention beneath my pants making a tent and he'd fire me on the spot.

"I thought I'd see you while I was in town, but I didn't realize I'd see you the day I got here."

Ellen Peters-Davies hosted a retreat fundraiser every year before the holidays to raise money for the hospital. I knew she was in town each year, and every event we ended up brushing elbows as she raked in the funds, but I always kept my distance. Mainly because this tent situation in my pants always happened and I never did figure out how to stop it.

She was the one. She was the reason I never got married. And here she was in her father's office looking like filet mignon on a platter ready for me to slice into.

"Uh, I have a meeting with your father."

Ellen grinned at me and fluffed her hair. She wasn't a flirt by any means, but I knew she liked me. Maybe she never got the memo that I was off limits, or maybe she didn't care. Her attraction to me might well have been yet another reason I kept my distance. I liked my neck in one piece, not hacked to bits by her father's torrid glares.

"I was just waiting here to tell him I'm home. I have all the plans set for the event next weekend. You're coming right?" She moved closer, reaching out to straighten my tie.

Normally the event—a three-day thing—was hosted in the hospital, but I had it on good authority that this year's event would be held at the Peters family ski lodge in the mountains north of here. It sounded like a very dangerous place for Ellen and I to be found together. I hadn't decided if I would attend or not.

"Because this year I'm doing a casino theme. Gambling, whiskey, and maybe some strippers too." She winked and splayed her hand on my chest. "It would be a shame if you missed that. I know how you like your women."

My reputation for getting around was mostly true—fifteen years ago. But not now. Now I was content to just work and workout. Women still flirted with me, calling me Dr. Hot Pants or something. It was flattering, but I'd grown out of the playboy act for the most part.

"Ellen, I'm not sure if it's a good idea..." Her fingers smoothed over my shirt, then my shoulder. She stepped closer and I could smell her perfume. I nearly forgot why I was even in this office. She slipped her hand down my arm and took my hand and placed it on her hip, just above the curve where I'd grab her if I was going to—God what was I thinking?

"Callum, it's about time for you to man up. Don't you think?" Her eyelashes batted and she leaned against me, her entire body from tits to knees pressing into mine. "It has been obvious to both of us for years now that we want each other. We could bang one out right here, see what happens?" Her knee drew up against my groin and she smirked. "See?"

"God, Ellen," I said, chuckling. "We do this thing every year. You flirt with me; I deny you because your father is my boss and my friend."

"And you're a grown man with a will and a mind of his own." She walked two fingers up my tie to my chin and pinched it between her fingers. "I've been single for five years now. I've started dating again. Plenty of guys want to see what I can do for them. I'm just waiting for the one I want to decide he wants me finally."

I cleared my throat and tensed as her lips brushed over mine. My dick throbbed, aching to feel her hand slide into my pants and grip me. God she had no clue how badly I wanted her, but a man is only as good as his word. Her lips parted and her tongue slipped into my mouth. I instinctively cupped her cheek and kissed her back, pulling her body tighter against mine. When she pulled away and wiped a smudge of lipstick off my lip, I heard a noise down the hall.

"Just say you'll come. I'll reserve a room in your name, right next to mine. Maybe you'll get lucky and there will be an adjoining room with one of those little doors that locks on both sides so you don't even have to go into the hallway to sneak into my bed." She winked and took a step back seconds before her father walked in. My cock tent was so obvious I had had to clasp my hands together in front of it to hide it.

"Well, Callum, I see you're ready for our meeting. And Ellen, honey, I didn't know you were back already."

Ellen smirked at me and rose up on her tiptoes to kiss her father on the cheek. "Yes, I'm ready to get to work making you some money. I was just telling Callum how much fun this year's event is going to be. Are you and Mom coming?"

"Ah, sorry, honey. Mom has another round of chemo to do, and she always feels so ill. I want to be with her. I'm sure Callum will help you run things down. Won't you?" He looked at me with eyes that said "I know what you're hiding and if you lay a hand on her I'll kill you."

"Uh, yes, sir. I'd be happy to help out."

What the heck was I getting myself into? I had just volunteered to walk right into the lion's den wearing a meat suit. Ellen wagged her eyebrows in a knowing manner and patted her father's shoulder. "I'll be off then. See you next weekend Dr. Andrews. Bye Dad."

I watched her walk out of the office and felt like she had just signed my death warrant. Because there was no way I was going to make it a whole weekend in a ski lodge gambling and drinking and not take what I had wanted for so many years. It was like Peters was setting me up for an ambush. Either way, I knew I was getting laid and probably killed immediately after. I hoped the sex was worth it.

While you wait for Callum's story, *binge read the entire series* **here.**

MY EX BOYFRIEND'S DAD (PREVIEW)

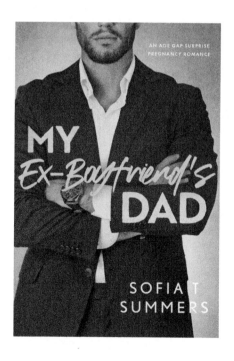

DESCRIPTION

"You're two months pregnant."
My doctor's words shock me to my core.
But he has no idea it's *his* baby.

One trip to the ER and my life is ruined. Those words said by my doctor will destroy me. And it's only a matter of time before *everyone* finds out.

I broke up with my ex because he drank too much. One hookup later and I'm pregnant? Just my luck . . .

My doctor in the hospital just happens to be the chief surgeon, Owen Thorpe—my ex's super-hot, super-off-limits father.

The one person I shouldn't have gone near.

But I did . . . and now it's too late to fix it. This baby is here to stay.

PROLOGUE

Harper

My head hurt so badly that I winced and pressed my hand to it. My arm hurt too, so much that I had to drop it to my side and not move it. Something was wrong. I could smell the stench of hospital cleaner and hear the din of machines whirring and beeping. It was hard to keep my eyes open, but I tried, blinking rapidly and wincing as my vision slowly adjusted to the bright light. I tasted blood on my tongue and knew it was mine.

Slowly, I became aware of a figure hovering over me. I squinted, trying to make out the face. It was a woman wearing a crisp white coat. She had graying hair and kind eyes. She smiled at me.

"Hold still, honey," said a female voice. I tried, but I was in so much pain. My arm hurt, my chest. All I remembered was the sound of smashing glass. I looked up and saw Becky, a charge nurse in the ER. My thoughts moved so slowly, I wasn't able to comprehend why Becky was here and what she was doing.

"Where am I?" I asked, my stomach churning. The incessant beeping sounded like it was inside my head. I moaned, and tears welled up. Every cell in my body felt on fire, like I was being boiled alive.

"You're at Hudson, baby. You've been in a car accident." Becky worked on an IV, untangling the lines and trying to hook up a drip line. I'd seen it a million times and knew what she was doing, though my head was thinking much too slowly to process things. I tried to see the monitors, but my vision was blurred. When I craned my neck, I felt like I was going to pass out. I wondered if she knew me, if she'd seen me around like I'd seen her around.

"Lily," I moaned, whimpering. A sudden moment of clarity made my heart rate increase. I heard the machine beep faster and clenched my eyes shut. It hurt to think, and now that's all I could do. Mom needed me home. She had plans. I was supposed to be there. I opened my eyes and looked down at my body, covered with a hospital gown and blanket. My pants lay on the floor, covered in blood. My arms were caked in it too, probably my own, though I couldn't tell what was cut.

"Who's Lily?"

"My little girl. I'm supposed to be home. Mom is babysitting." I tried to move my other arm, but it felt like a lead weight. I wanted to touch myself, see where I was bleeding from, what had happened. It felt like shards of glass were stuck in my hand, and I turned my palm toward my face to see, but my eyes wouldn't focus.

"Okay, we'll call Mom and let her know. Is her number in your emergency contacts?" she asked, but I had a hard time processing what she said. I let my eyes fall shut, then blinked them back open. She was there, shining a light into my eyes. "Pupils are fixed and dilated, not a good sign. She's coherent enough, talking about her daughter." The light hurt. I tried to blink, but she held my eyelids open while she did her exam.

My head throbbed, and I felt like I might throw up. How did this happen? I strained to remember, but I was foggy, unable to recall anything. When I blinked my eyes open again, I saw Owen, or at least I thought I did. He could have been a hallucination, except he spoke to me. He looked sad and hurt. His eyes locked on my face. I wanted to lean into him, feel him hold me, but I found it painful to even breathe. Why was he here? How badly was I hurt? Owen was a surgeon, not an ER doc.

"Owen, what's going on?" I almost started crying right then. Emotion bubbled up inside me. After seeing him last week, I'd been pining again, wishing I hadn't broken up with him. This had to have been some strange dream. No way was he actually here.

"You were in an accident. We need to do some imaging, Harper. You might have broken bones and a head injury." He shifted from one foot to the other. "Did you know you're pregnant?" He reached for my hand.

"I'm what?" I asked, confused. I tried hard to focus on what he was saying, but my body was about to explode. I felt bile rising up the back of my throat.

Did he say I was pregnant? I couldn't be. That wasn't possible. I had PCOS. The doctors told me Lily was a miracle, not to mention I was on birth control anyway. While my stomach felt like turning itself inside out was not the time to discuss a pregnancy. I wasn't even sure whether this was real or just a horrible dream. I wanted the bad parts to be a dream, but the Owen part . . . God, I wanted it so badly. I wanted him to be real, to be here, to want me.

"Harper, you're pregnant. Is it mine?" he asked, staring at me intently. I looked up at him as my chest tightened. Surely, I hadn't heard him right. I felt as if the air around me had suddenly become thick and heavy. I looked into Owen's eyes, standing before me, trying to discern some meaning from his words, hoping to find something that would make sense of the confusing situation.

"Owen, I'm . . ." My body convulsed, and I lurched over the side of the bed so I didn't vomit on myself. I sobbed hard, letting the emotion drain out of me. He had said I was pregnant. It wasn't a hallucination. It was real. The man I loved more than anything in this world stood right next to me while I threw up, and I had no words.

Then the nurse was by my side again, speaking, but I didn't hear a word she said. I lay back on the gurney and cried. As they wheeled me out of the room, I saw Owen. He stared at me with a hurt expression. I'd never hurt him, but there he was thinking I was a monster. I cried harder as they pushed my gurney down the hall. "Oh, God, my head," I mumbled, realizing it was as much my broken heart as it was my head hurting.

If what Owen said was true, then I had a lot of thinking to do. Just not until my head stopped throbbing like this.

1

Owen

I stood outside room 301, chart in hand. Chelsea, a fifth-year resident under me, stood next to me, waiting as I reviewed the chart on my tablet. It should be Chelsea doing this surgery, but the parents—quite worried about their nine-year-old son—asked for the absolute best surgeon Hudson had to offer, so I stepped up to the plate. I took on very few surgeries, but I had time in my schedule to handle this, and having a son myself, I knew exactly how those parents felt.

"You ready for this?" she asked. Though I had shadowed Chelsea on several surgeries, she hadn't seen me do one myself. Part of the fifth year was to be fully hands on, letting the student overtake the master, so to speak.

"Ready as ever." I nodded and opened the door, and she followed me in. I expected a couple of nervous parents and a rambunctious child, antsy and frustrated. What I didn't expect when I walked into that room was to see quite possibly the most gorgeous woman I'd ever laid eyes on.

All eyes in the room pointed in my direction as I strolled in, but I was oblivious to any but the hazel gaze coming from the nurse's direction. Her smile took my breath away. "Hey, Doctor Thorpe," she said, diverting her attention back to the boy. She was drawing blood, and he was being a good sport about it. That was the bad part about being Chief of Surgery here at Hudson. Everyone knew who I was, but I knew almost zero of the nursing staff. My name and face were plastered everywhere, but I rarely interacted with any nurses or doctors who were not directly reporting to me, and this goddess had evaded me, though I didn't know for how long.

"Good afternoon." I tore my eyes away from her to see the anxious gaze of a frazzled mother. "Mrs. Hallsworthy." I reached out my hand and looked to her right. "Mr. Hallsworthy." Each of them shook my hand in turn but didn't rise. They sat on the edges of their seats, wringing their hands as they waited for me to speak. "I'm Dr. Thorpe, head of surgery here at Hudson. When Dr. Nickels indicated that you wanted only the best surgeon for your son's surgery, I volunteered." I clasped the tablet in front of me but let my arms hang.

My mind should have been fixed on the questions I was supposed to be asking, but I couldn't help but steal another glance at the nurse. She was talking quietly with the boy, who snickered and sucked on a large sucker. Her playful banter tugged at my heartstrings. She was very good with the boy, who obviously enjoyed the attention.

"I'm really worried, Dr. Thorpe. I've heard there can be brain damage if you do this." Mrs. Hallsworthy's voice quavered as she spoke. No doubt, there was reason to be cautious, but her fears were unfounded. I grabbed the rolling stool and pulled it up, and before moving on and answering her concerns, I introduced Chelsea.

"This is Doctor Chelsea Marshal. She is a fifth-year resident here at Hudson. She will be with me in the operating theater to observe the procedure." I gestured at her, and the unhappy mother nodded abruptly, frowning at me. Chelsea pulled up a chair and sat next to me. I handed her the tablet, and she took it carefully. I sat in such a way that I could watch the gorgeous nurse working and let Chelsea explain. "If you don't mind, though I will be doing the surgery, I'd like Dr. Marshal to walk you through the pre-op instructions. She will get more practice this way, and I am here to answer any questions."

Both parents nodded as Chelsea took off in her pre-op speech. I'd heard her give it a million times. Yes, there are risks. No, we're not perfect. I tuned it out, watching the nurse, whose name I didn't catch, tickle the boy's side as he giggled.

She had such a radiant smile, I found it hard to look anywhere else but there. Her presence in the room was intoxicating. I found it hard to stay serious or burdened about the stress I was under with work simply because she was here.

While I kept one ear tuned in for any questions, I allowed myself to ponder the nurse's station in life. She was an RN, caring for a pediatric patient. She likely had at least one specialty, and by the looks of it, she either had younger siblings or maybe even children of her own.

No woman was that amazing with children without having been around them a lot, and that was one way straight to my heart. After Nancy did me the way she did, I determined that if I were to date again, it would be with someone who loved kids.

Maybe that was just my ill-fitted, preconceived notion of life and women, but I didn't believe for a second that you could be a sadistic narcissist if you loved children.

"Alright, Dr. Thorpe will walk you through the actual procedure now. Remember, because this is considered major surgery. Jake will have to stay for several days afterward. That doesn't mean anything is wrong. It is absolutely normal." Chelsea smiled at me and nodded.

Again, I was forced to pull my eyes away from the magnetic nurse as I focused on the parents. "Now, the surgery will remove a portion of his cerebral cortex to hopefully stop the seizures he's experiencing. We'd like to have him at less than one per day, down from the twelve to fifteen a day he's experiencing. The medicines, as you know, have been unsuccessful at treating this, but when we are finished, he'll be much happier and safer."

As I walked them through step-by-step what I'd be doing, I noticed the nurse packing up her cart and leaving the room. My chest immediately swelled and ached, then fell, as if there were so many words caught in my throat that I couldn't say.

I'd never been so enamored of a woman so quickly, never clicked so instantly without even speaking to someone. That nurse, however, had done something to my mind, cast a spell on me the likes of which I knew would torment me for weeks.

When the pre-op appointment was over, I excused myself and Dr. Marshal, and she followed me into the hallway where we recapped the conversation. I was distracted, thinking about that nurse, and she called me on it.

"Where's your head at?" Chelsea asked, handing me the tablet. I chuckled, caught red-handed in my reverie.

"Well, if I'm honest with you, I think I am very attracted to that nurse who was in there caring for the boy." If I were less of a man, my cheeks would be burning, but I found it easier to own my truth than to wear a mask. And over the past six months, Chelsea and I had gotten on well. I'd consider her a work friend at the very least. And her husband, Cameron, was head of surgery at Mercy in Yellow Springs. I'd known him for a long time, so Chelsea was almost like family.

She snickered at me. "But you're not really dating anymore," she said coyly, raising her eyebrows. It was true. She had tried to set me up a few times, but I drew the line. My career took all of my time, and I was really busy. I had used that line on her a number of times to dissuade her from trying to shove women in my direction.

She insisted that I needed a woman to take care of me and that she and Cameron were very happy despite being in the same situation. He had sworn off women for more than a decade after his wife died, but Chelsea caught his eye.

I just got hurt bad enough that I believed no woman would ever treat me well enough to merit a second glance. Who knew . . . Maybe that nurse was just as horrible as my ex-wife, but wow, was she fantastic eye candy.

"Yes, well, you're right. I did say that." I fumbled with my words, feeling like I was digging a hole she would bury me in.

Chelsea snickered again and patted my arm. "I can find out her name if you'd like?"

"No . . ." I shook my head firmly. "I don't need the distraction. I really don't have time for a relationship."

In my head, that reply made sense because it was what I had been telling her for months. But something in my heart felt weak, even hurt, that my brain would make that snap judgment and disallow me the chance to fantasize. It was for the best. I didn't need drama or more heartbreak.

"Alright, well, don't say I didn't offer. Look, I have to run. Cam will be here with the kids to get me soon. I'll see you bright and early for the surgery." She walked away, and while I wanted to linger there, watching for the nurse to return, I decided I should move on.

As I strolled toward the elevator, my phone rang, so I answered it. With only a few more tasks left today, I would be heading home myself. Tomorrow's surgery would go off without a hitch, and I would be set to leave for Barbados and a week-long vacation this Saturday. Dr. Fischer would cover my rounds for post-surgery, and I would come back refreshed and that nurse would no longer be on my mind.

"Yeah?" I said, holding my phone to my ear. It was Wyatt, probably with questions about the trip.

"Hey, Dad . . . Just checking whether you have some extra board shorts. I don't have any. I'm not much of a beach person, and I don't want to buy something I'm not going to wear." His words were slurred, an indication that he had been drinking again. I had told him too many times that he needed to get sober, but a child has to learn the hard way. Even if the hard way is thrice through rehab, only to relapse again.

"Yeah, bud. I have a few pairs. I'll pack them with my things. Listen, is Harper coming? Her daughter? The pilot needs a final head count." I had paid for a private plane to fly us to Miami where we would catch the commercial flight. Even the last-minute tickets—as expensive as they were—were on my dime. Wyatt just needed to get his act together long enough to let me know what was going on. It was ridiculous at times, but he was my son and I loved him. Maybe a little too much.

"Yeah, she said yes. I think Lily is coming too. Just buy the tickets, and I'll pay you back if they cancel." He hiccupped, and I rolled my eyes.

"Alright. I'll let everything lined up. Seven a.m. Saturday is when we leave."

"Yeah, I got it. Seven a.m. I gotta go. I'll see you Saturday." Wyatt hung up, so I locked my phone and slid it in my pocket.

He had been dating this Harper woman for almost six months now, and whoever she was, she hadn't gotten him to change either.

I didn't fault her.

Wyatt was the sort of person who would only learn by experience —even if that experience was very painful and came with horrible consequences. And it didn't surprise me that he wanted to borrow shorts. He barely made a living being a public defender, though I'm glad he hadn't just flunked out of law school.

I pressed the call button for the elevator and took a deep breath. Only one hour left and I would be set to head home and pack, then just one surgery and a day of rounds, and it was vacation time. Nothing better than that.

End of preview. **Get the entire story here.**

OTHER BOOKS BY SOFIA T SUMMERS

Forbidden Doctors Series (this series)

Doctor's Surprise Twins | Written in the Charts | Rendezvous with My Resident | The Doctor's Twin Secrets | My Ex Boyfriend's Dad | Secret Baby for Dr. Dreamy | The Doctor's Secret

Forbidden Temptations Series

Daddy's Best Friend | My Best Friend's Daddy | Daddy's Business Partner | Doctor Daddy | Secret Baby with Daddy's Best Friend | Knocked Up by Daddy's Best Friend | Pretend Wife to Daddy's Best Friend | SEAL Daddy | Fake Married to My Best Friend's Daddy | Accidental Daddy |The Grump's Girl Friday | The Vegas Accident | My Beastly Boss | My Millionaire Marine | The Wedding Dare | The Summer Getaway | The Love Edit | The Husband Lottery | Christmas in the Cabin | A Very Naughty Christmas | Make Me Whole | Take a Chance

Forbidden Fantasies (Reverse Harem Series)

My Irish Billionaires | Toy for the Teachers | Three Grumpy
Bosses | Feasting on Her Curves | 4 SEAL Daddies

Forbidden Promises

Maid Without Honour | The Wedding Witness | Honeymoon Hoax

WANT MORE FORBIDDEN ROMANCES?

Great News! My box sets are FREE to read in Kindle Unlimited, and priced at 99cents only. (And they are super forbidden)

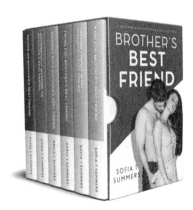

CONNECT WITH SOFIE

Want to receive extended epilogues, sexy deleted scenes, freebies, and new release alerts?

For all things Sofia, join her VIP Hangout here.

Printed in Great Britain
by Amazon

39647450R00139